PRAISE FOR TEMPORARY PEOPLE

"Guest workers of the United Arab Emirates embody multiple worlds and identities and long for home in a fantastical debut work of fiction, winner of the inaugural Restless Books Prize for New Immigrant Writing.... The author's crisp, imaginative prose packs a punch, and his whimsical depiction of characters who oscillate between two lands on either side of the Arabian Sea unspools the kind of immigrant narratives that are rarely told. An enchanting, unparalleled anthem of displacement and repatriation."

—*KIRKUS REVIEWS*, STARRED REVIEW

"Inventive, vigorously empathetic, and brimming with a sparkling, mordant humor, Deepak Unnikrishnan has written a book of Ovidian metamorphoses for our precarious time. These absurdist fables, fluent in the language of exile, immigration, and bureaucracy, will remind you of the raw pleasure of storytelling and the unsettling nearness of the future."

—ALEXANDRA KLEEMAN, AUTHOR OF *YOU TOO CAN HAVE A BODY LIKE MINE*

"Inaugural winner of the Restless Books Prize for New Immigrant Writing, this debut novel employs its own brand of magical realism to propel readers into an understanding and appreciation of the experience of foreign workers in the Arab Gulf States (and beyond). Through a series of almost thirty loosely linked sections, grouped into three parts, we are thrust into a narrative alternating between visceral realism and fantastic satire.... The alternation between satirical fantasy, depicting such things as intelligent cockroaches and evil elevators, and poignant realism, with regards to necessarily illicit sexuality, forms a contrast that gives rise to a broad critique of the plight of those known euphemistically as 'guest workers.' VERDICT: This first novel challenges readers with a singular inventiveness expressed through a lyrical use of language and a laser-like focus that is at once charming and terrifying. Highly recommended."

—HENRY BANKHEAD, *LIBRARY JOURNAL*, STARRED REVIEW

"Unnikrishnan's debut novel shines a light on a little known world with compassion and keen insight. The Temporary People are invisible people—but Unnikrishnan brings them to us with compassion, intelligence, and heart. This is why novels matter."

—SUSAN HANS O'CONNOR, PENGUIN BOOKSHOP (SEWICKLEY, PA)

"Deepak Unnikrishnan uses linguistic pyrotechnics to tell the story of forced transience in the Arabian Peninsula, where citizenship can never be earned no matter the commitment of blood, sweat, years of life, or brains. The accoutrements of migration—languages, body parts, passports, losses, wounds, communities of strangers—are packed and carried along with ordinary luggage, blurring the real and the unreal with exquisite skill. Unnikrishnan sets before us a feast of absurdity that captures the cruel realities around the borders we cross either by choice or by force. In doing so he has found what most writers miss: the sweet spot between simmering rage at a set of circumstances, and the circumstances themselves."

—RU FREEMAN, AUTHOR OF *ON SAL MAL LANE*

"Unafraid to experiment with literary form, Unnikrishnan writes stories that examine the experience of immigration, emigration, identity and exile in the Gulf and India from a uniquely South Asian perspective. Born in Kerala, he was brought to Abu Dhabi as an infant and lived here until 2001, when he moved to study in the US.... His surreal and hallucinatory style, which also defines his other short stories such as 'Water' and 'How "Sharjah" Mohan Took the Men,' have drawn comparisons with the magical realism of Salman Rushdie and the satirical humor of George Saunders, but as the title of 'Gulf Return suggests,' Unnikrishnan's work reflects on issues that are simultaneously global and specific to the experience of NRI's, long-term non-resident Indians, not just in the UAE but throughout the wider Gulf.... In Unnikrishnan's fiction, as in his life, the experience of migration is one that is both heightened and illusionary, and the sense of 'home' he illuminates—so very different from the mythic, Homeric model—can never really be returned to or relied upon to offer any sense of consolation. As such his work represents a literary response to the issues discussed in Neha Vohra's sociological study *Impossible Citizens: Dubai's Indian Diaspora*, while belonging to a new but growing genre of Khaleeji literature, including Saud Alsanousi's *The Bamboo Stalk* and Mia Alvar's *In the Country*, that Unnikrishnan hopes will provide a more nuanced picture of migrant life in the Gulf."

—NICK LEECH, *THE NATIONAL* (UAE)

"Deepak writes brilliant stories with a fresh, passionate energy. Every page feels as if it must have been written, as if the author had no choice. He writes about exile, immigration, deportation, security checks, rage, patience, about the homelessness of living in a foreign land, about historical events so strange that, under his hand, the events become tales, and he writes tales so precisely that they read like history. Important work. Work of the future. This man will not be stopped."

—DEB OLIN UNFERTH, AUTHOR OF *REVOLUTION*

"From the strange Kafkaesque scenarios to the wholly original language, this book is amazing on so many different levels. Unlike anything I've ever read, *Temporary People* is a powerful work of short stories about foreign nationals who populate the new economy in the United Arab Emirates. With inventive language and darkly satirical plot lines, Unnikrishnan provides an important view of the relentless nature of a global economy and its brutal consequences for human lives. Prepare to be wowed by the immensely talented new voice."

—HILARY GUSTAFSON, LITERATI BOOKSTORE (ANN ARBOR, MI)

"Absolutely preposterous! As a debut, author Unnikrishnan shares stories of laborers, brought to the United Arab Emirates to do menial and everyday jobs. These people have no rights, no fallback if they have problems or health issues in that land. The laborers in *Temporary People* are sewn back together when they fall, are abandoned in the desert if they become inconvenient, and are even grown from seeds. As a collection of short stories, this is fantastical, imaginative, funny, and, even more so, scary, powerful, and ferocious."

—BECKY MILNER, VINTAGE BOOKS (VANCOUVER, WA)

"There is much to admire in Unnikrishnan's fanciful and fervent debut, a collection of stories about the lives of guest workers in the United Arab Emirates.... Unnikrishnan explores the depredations, sorrows, and longings of these foreign laborers, who are often treated as disposable, with a dark whimsy.... Interspersed throughout are briefer pieces, from one paragraph to several pages in length, concise meditations that offer up the book's best expressions of what it means to be an outsider in a land far from home."

—*PUBLISHERS WEEKLY*

"Unnikrishnan tells [his] stories in experimental prose that moves from vignettes that read like mythical texts to transcribed interviews. The most compelling writing renders the characters' plights in the abstraction of magical realism.... A careful, patient reader will love Unnikrishnan's inventive and caring connected tales."

"Please, if you care for my opinion, read this writing of Deepak Unnikrishnan and support him. He is a magnificent fellow with an intricate and beautiful mind; this work he does now, already wonderful, is but the smallest part of what he will do in time."

"This is a fascinating, difficult, and chaotic read, but I couldn't put it down. Its linked stories, myths, or allegories examine the condition of the guest-worker subclass (but they are a silent majority) in the Gulf states, where nary an Arab worker is to be found. It gets an A+ for language play and for illuminating a sore point of social injustice that any visitor to the United Arab Emirates would have seen, if not understood."

Deepak Unnikrishnan

TEMPORARY PEOPLE

RESTLESS BOOKS
Brooklyn, New York

First Restless Books paperback edition March 2017

Paperback ISBN: 978-1-63206-142-3
Library of Congres Control Number: 2017934293

Cover design by Rodrigo Corral and Haelee You

Printed in the United States of America

1 3 5 7 9 8 6 4 2

Restless Books, Inc.
232 3rd Street, Suite A111
Brooklyn, NY 11215

www.restlessbooks.com
publisher@restlessbooks.com

Prof. (Ted) Chesler, the book's been written. Return for a day. In your basement office in Robison Hall, smoke and tell me stories. My teacher, my much-missed friend, thank you.

For Acchan & Amma, battle-scarred parents.

For Meenu & Raya, women I love, why I've remained alive.

For Milo the animal, because he was family.

For anyone who left, then remained in the Gulf for family's sake, only to leave again.

For Gulf kids raised without mothers/fathers/countries/confidence.

For us, inventors of realms/identities, manglers of language(s).

And finally, for my city, for what it did to/for me.

CONTENTS

The Names

BOOK

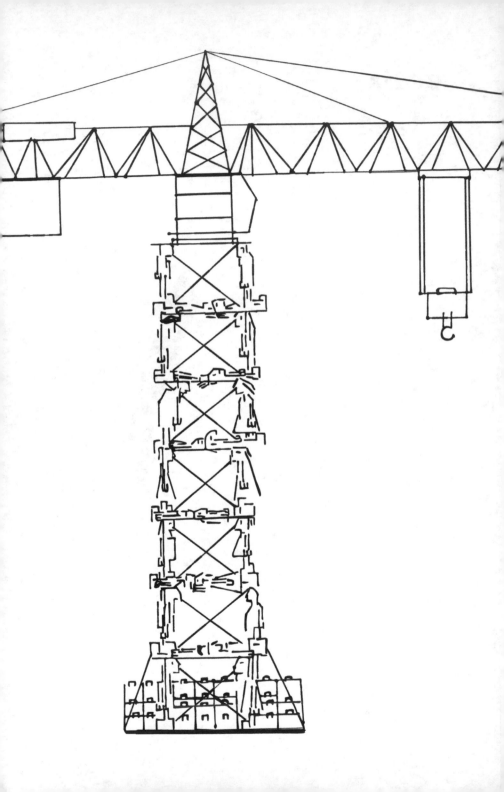

LIMBS

There exists this city built by labor, mostly men, who disappear after their respective buildings are made. Once the last brick is laid, the glass spotless, the elevators functional, the plumbing operational, the laborers, every single one of them, begin to fade, before disappearing completely. Some believe the men become ghosts, haunting the facades they helped build. When visiting, take note. If you are outside, and there are buildings nearby, ghosts may already be falling, may even have landed on your person.

—NAME WITHHELD BY REQUEST

IN A LABOR CAMP, somewhere in the Persian Gulf, a laborer swallowed his passport and turned into a passport. His roommate swallowed a suitcase and turned into a little suitcase. When the third roommate, privy and vital to the master plan, ran away the next morning with the new suitcase and passport, he made it past the guard on night duty, onto the morning bus to the airport, past the bored ticket agent at check-in, past security, past pat down and a rummage through his suitcase, past using the bathroom once, twice, thrice, to pee, to shit, to sit, past Duty Free, where he stared at chocolates and booze and magazines and currencies, past families eating fast food in track suits or designer wear, past men and women sleeping on the floor, past his past, past his present, past the gold in the souks, the cranes in the sky, petrol in the air, dreams in his head, past God and the devil, the smell of mess halls, past humidity and hot air, past it all, until he found an empty chair in the departures lounge, where he sat and held his future in his hands. It was then the little suitcase sprouted legs and ears, and the passport developed palms and long fingers as well as a nose and a mustache, and soon after the boarding call, at the very moment the stewardess checked his documents, the third laborer was asked to wait.

The stewardess needed time to figure out what protocol she should follow or what precedent there was for the man and his possessions. The man preferred not to wait and ran as fast as he could through the door to boarding, past passengers who had already gone through and formed a line inside the tube with the little windows, waiting like blood in a syringe, now followed at an animal's pace by the little suitcase on legs, ridden like a horse by the passport with the long fingers, a sight that both fascinated and terrified and caused personnel, propelled by some odd sense of duty, to stand in the way of the trio and block their path, to protect the plane and its pilots and cabin crew from what they couldn't define. It didn't matter what they did, it wouldn't have mattered what they did, because the man leading the charge, in an act of despair, opened his mouth wide to ask them all to get away get away, wide wide wider, until he swallowed the first person in his path, then the next, and the next, refusing to stop running, as the little suitcase did the same, opening and closing itself, running into people, sucking people in like a sinkhole, aided by the passport jockey, who assisted by stuffing in those who fought desperately to escape. It happened so quickly, the running, the swallowing, the stuffing, the madness, that when the three of them reached the aircraft doors, they seemed at first surprised rather than jubilant, then relieved as the pilots and cabin crew stared from the other end of the tube, where everyone, including the remaining passengers, had now run to watch them like cats watching dogs.

The little suitcase, the little passport, and the man caught their breath, inhaling and exhaling raggedly, as though nails filled the air, while in the distance, with the sound of a million horses, well-meaning men with guns and gas rushed the gate where the stewardess had screamed and then fainted. The trio realized it was now or never, abhi ya nahi, do or die, so they rushed into the empty plane, locked its door, and the little suitcase and the little passport found seats in First Class and put on their seat belts, while the man ran to the back of the plane and began swallowing everything in sight, starting with the two lavatories, the trolleys with the veg and non-veg options, the apple juice and the Bloody Mary mixes, the seats and the magazines, the tray tables and the blinking lights, the blankets and the overhead bins, the socks and the TV monitors, the cabin air, with its lingering halitosis and mint candy smell, swallowing everything in sight, moving expertly from Economy to Business to First, swallowing even the little suitcase and the little passport, swallowing the carpets, the emergency exits, the airplane controls and smudged windows and the odor of pilots, slipping down the aircraft's nose and continuing to swallow as he moved from the aircraft's beak towards its base, swallowing wings, wheels, luggage, fuel, skin, presence, until the man was not recognizable anymore and had turned into an enormous jumbo, observed from the cordoned-off terminal by dumbstruck passengers and the men armed with guns and gas, whose leader wondered on his walkie-talkie what sort of protocol ought to be followed here, but he needn't have bothered. The plane had begun taxiing down the runaway, past other waiting aircrafts, ignoring pleas from the control tower to desist, to wait a minute, to let's talk this through, to whadabout the hostages, but the plane didn't care, it went on its merry way, picking up speed, lifting its beak, tucking in its mighty wheels, returning its cargo.

CHABTER TWO

BIRDS

ANNA VARGHESE WORKED IN Abu Dhabi. She taped people. Specifically, she taped construction workers who fell from incomplete buildings.

Anna, working the night shift, found these injured men, then put them back together with duct tape or some good glue, or if stitches were required, patched them up with a needle and horse hair, before sending them on their way. The work, rarely advertised, was nocturnal.

Anna belonged to a crew of ten, led by Khalid, a burly man from Nablus. Khalid's team covered Hamdan Street, Electra, Salaam, and Khalifa. They used bicycles; they biked quickly.

Anna had been doing this for a long time, thirty years, and many of her peers had retired—replaced, according to Khalid, by a less dependable crew. Seniority counted, and so Khalid allowed her to pick her route.

Anna knew Hamdan as intimately as her body. In the seventies, when she first arrived, the buildings were smaller. Nevertheless, she would, could, and did glue plus tape scores of men a day, correcting and reattaching limbs, putting back organs or eyeballs—and sometimes, if the case was hopeless, praying until the man breathed his last. But deaths were rare. Few workers died at work sites; it was as though labor could not die there. As a lark, some veterans began calling building sites death-proof. At lunchtime, to prove their point, some of them hurled themselves off the top floor in full view of new arrivals. The jumps didn't kill. But if the jumpers weren't athletic and didn't know how to fall, their bodies cracked, which meant the jumpers lay there until nighttime, waiting for the men and women who would bicycle past, looking for the fallen in order to fix, shape, and glue the damaged parts back into place, like perfect cake makers repiping smudged frosting.

When Anna interviewed for the position, Khalid asked if she possessed reasonable handyman skills. "No," she admitted. No problem, he assured her, she could learn those skills on the job.

"What about blood, make you faint?" She pondered the question, then said no again.

"OK, start tomorrow," said Khalid. Doing what, she wondered, by now irritated with Cousin Thracy for talking her into seeking her fortune in a foreign place, for signing up for a job with an Arab at the helm, and one who clearly didn't care whether she knew anything or not. "Taping," Khalid replied. "The men call us Stick People, Stickers for short. It's a terrible name, but that's OK—they've accepted us."

Construction was young back then. Oil had just begun to dictate terms. And Anna was young, too. Back in her hometown, she assumed if she ever went to the Gulf she would be responsible for someone's child or would put her nursing skills to use at the hospital, but the middlemen pimping work visas wanted money—money she didn't have, but borrowed. Cousin Thracy pawned her gold earrings. "I expect gains from this investment," she told Anna at the airport.

When Anna arrived, flying Air India, Khalid was waiting. "Is it a big hospital?" she asked him as he drove his beat-up pickup.

"Hospital?" he repeated. Over lunch, he gently broke it to her that she had been lied to.

"No job?" she wept. There is a job, Khalid assured her, but he urged her to eat first. Then he needed to ask her a few questions.

"Insha'Allah," he told her, "the job's yours, if you want it."

Anna built a reputation among the working class; hers was a name they grew to trust.

When workers fell, severing limbs, the pain was acute, but

borne. Yet what truly stung was the loneliness and anxiety of falling that weighed on their minds.

Pedestrians mostly ignored those who fell outside the construction site, walking around them, some pointing or staring. The affluent rushed home, returning with cameras and film. Drivers of heavy-duty vehicles or family sedans took care to avoid running over them. But it didn't matter where labor fell. The public remained indifferent. In the city center, what unnerved most witnesses was that when the men fell, they not only lost their limbs or had cracks that looked like fissures, but they lost their voices, too. They would just look at you, frantically moving what could still move. But most of the time, especially in areas just being developed, the fallen simply waited. Sometimes, the men fell onto things or under things where few people cared to look. Or they weren't reported missing. These were the two ways, Anna would share with anyone who asked, that laborers could die on-site.

Then there were those who would never be found. A combination of factors contributed to this: bad luck, ineptitude, a heavy workload. A fallen worker might last a week without being discovered, but after a week, deterioration set in. Eventually, death.

Anna had a superb track record for finding fallen men. The woman must have been part-bloodhound. She found every sign of them including teeth, bits of skin. She roamed her territory with tenacity, pointing her flashlight in places the devil did not know or construction lights could not brighten. Before her shift ended in the morning, she returned to the sites, checking with the supervisor or the men disembarking Ashok Leyland buses to be certain no one was still missing, and that the men she had fixed, then ordered to wait at the gates for inspection, included everybody on the supervisor's roster. The men were grateful to be fussed over like this.

Anna wasn't beautiful, but in a city where women were scarce, she was prized. She also possessed other skills. The fallen shared that when Anna reattached body parts, she spoke to them in her tongue, sometimes stroking their hair or chin. She would wax and wane about her life, saying that she missed her kids or the fish near her river, or would instead ask about their lives, what they left, what they dreamt at night, even though they couldn't answer. If she made a connection with the man or if she simply liked him, she flirted. "You *must* be married," she liked to tease. If she didn't speak his language, she sang, poorly, but from the heart. But even Anna lost people.

"Sometimes a man will die no matter what you do," Khalid told her. "Only Allah knows why."

Once, for four hours Anna sat with a man who held in place with his right arm his head, which had almost torn itself loose from the fall. A week prior, Anna had a similar case and patched the man up in under two hours. But in this case, probably her last before retirement, nothing worked. Sutures did not hold. Glue refused to bind. Stranger still was that the man could speak. In her many years of doing this, none of the fallen had been able to say a word. "Not working?" he asked. Anna pursed her lips and just held him. There was no point calling an ambulance. No point finding a doctor.

"Remove the fallen from the work site," Khalid had warned her, "and they die." It was simply something everyone knew. Outside work sites, men couldn't survive these kinds of falls. If the men couldn't be fixed at the sites, they didn't stand a chance anywhere else.

The dying man's name was Iqbal. He was probably in his mid-thirties and would become the first man to die under her watch in over five years. In her long career, she had lost thirty-seven people, an exceptional record. She asked about his home.

"Home's shit," he said. His village suffocated its young. "So small you could squeeze all of its people and farmland inside a plump cow." The only major enterprise was a factory that made coir doormats. "Know when a village turns bitter? If the young are bored—" Iqbal trailed off.

He'd left because he wanted to see a bit of the world. Besides, everyone he knew yearned to be a Gulf boy. Recruiters turned up every six months in loud shirts and trousers and a hired taxi, and they hired anyone. "When I went, they told me the only requirement was to be able to withstand heat," Iqbal said. Then there was the money, which had seduced Anna, too. "Tax-free!" he bellowed. They told him if he played his cards right, he could line his pockets with gold.

Before making up his mind, Iqbal had visited the resident fortune-teller—a man whose parrot picked out a card that confirmed the Gulf would transform Iqbal's life. He packed that night, visited Good-Time Philomena, the neighborhood hooker, for a fuck that lasted so long "a she-wolf knocked on the door and begged us to stop." Then he sneaked back into his house and stole his old man's savings to pay for the visa and the trip.

"Uppa was paralyzed—a factory incident. Basically watched me take his cash," Iqbal said. Anna frowned. "I wouldn't worry," Iqbal reassured her. "My brother took good care of him."

"And how is he now?" Anna inquired.

"Died in my brother's lap," he replied. "I couldn't go see him."

As Anna continued to hold Iqbal's head, he told her he expected to have made his fortune in ten years. By then, he'd have handpicked his wife, had those kids, built that house. His father, if he'd lived, would've forgiven him. Former teachers who scorned him by calling him Farm Boy or Day Dreamer would invite him to dine at their place. But then he fell, didn't he? Slipped like a bungling monkey. He was doing something else— what, he seemed embarrassed to share.

"What were you up to?" Anna urged. "Go on, I won't tell a soul."

Iqbal smiled. "I was masturbating on the roof. The edge," he confessed. He had done this many times before. "It's super fun," he giggled. "But then a pigeon landed on my pecker...." The bird startled him. He lost his balance.

"You didn't!" Anna laughed.

"Try it, there's nothing like it. It's like impregnating the sky." Or, he added, "in your case, welcoming it."

"Behave," Anna said. "I could easily be your mother's age. Or older sister's."

"The heat," he said softly. "The heat felled me."

"Not the bird?"

Iqbal broke into a grin. "I came on a bird once. It acted like I'd shot it."

Like Anna, Iqbal had known heat ever since he was a child. He knew how to handle it, even when the steam in the air had the potential to boil a man's mind. But the Gulf's heat baked a man differently. First it cooked a man's shirt and then the man's skin. On-site, Iqbal trusted his instincts. Water, sometimes buttermilk, was always on hand, but frequent breaks meant a reduced output, and Iqbal knew his progress was being monitored. He had trained as a tailor, as his Uppa was a tailor; he knew learning a new trade took time. So he followed one rule: when his skin felt like parchment paper, he stopped working and quenched his thirst, sometimes drinking water so quickly it hurt. The sun never conquered him. His body was strong. But what he couldn't control, he told Anna, were the reactions of people he passed in the street, especially if he volunteered to go to one of those little kadas to buy water or cold drinks for his mates in the afternoon.

"How so?" Anna wondered.

"In the summer," Iqbal continued, "you burn, the clothes burn. You smell like an old stove." Then he asked her, "Don't you burn?"

"Everyone burns here," she replied quietly. "But you fell today? What was different?"

"It seemed like the perfect day," Iqbal said dryly. "What do the others tell you?"

"The others?"

"Those who fall." Iqbal didn't wait for an answer. "Outside, whether you believe it or not, heat's easier to handle. For me, anyway." On building tops, he insisted, most men shrivel into raisins. "Men don't burn up there; they decay."

"But it's cooler up there, no?" Anna asked.

"Fully clothed, in hard hats? No," said Iqbal. "I once saw a man shrink to the size of a child. At lunchtime, he drank a tub of water and grew back to his original size." Still, the open air allowed the body to breathe. "You have wind." Indoors, in the camps, in closed quarters, packed into bunk beds, not enough ACs, bodies baked, sweat burned eyes, salt escaped, fever and dehydration built. Bodies reeled from simply that. Anna nodded. There was a time Anna patched up a man with skin so dry, she needed to rub the man's entire body with olive oil after she pieced him together.

Even though they were all immune to death by free fall, there was nothing they could do about the heat. At lunch break, getting to the shade under tractor beds and crane rumps became more important than food. With shirts as pillows and newspapers as blankets, the men rested.

Iqbal asked Anna if she would mind scratching his hair. "You're new," he teased. "You look new, like a bride."

Anna smiled. "I have grandkids now." She dug her nails into his scalp.

"They told you to fear the sun, didn't they?" said Iqbal.

"Who?"

"Recruiters," said Iqbal.

"No," she replied.

"Well, no one mentions the nighttime," Iqbal sighed. "They should." At night, heat attacked differently, became wet. "I knew a man," Iqbal continued, "who collected sweat. He would go door to door with a trolley full of buckets. After a week's worth, this man— Badran was his name—dug a pit near the buildings we lived in. It would take him a long time to pour the buckets of sweat into that pit. The first couple of times, I watched. Then I began to help. Soon we had a pool—a salty pool. It was good fun. We floated for hours."

"Didn't Badran get into trouble?" Anna asked.

"Badran was a smart fellow," said Iqbal. "He resold some of that pool water to this shady driver of a water tanker. The driver would get to the camp at around three a.m., take as much water as truck could carry. Everyone knew. The important people all got a cut."

"Where did he take the water?"

"I asked Badran many times," said Iqbal. "He never said."

"Badran must be doing well for himself," said Anna.

"He was, I suppose," said Iqbal. "He died a few months ago."

"How?"

"Accident," replied Iqbal. "Was his time."

"Where?"

"We were returning home in a pickup. Near Mussafah the driver hit something. Badran fell. . . the wheel. . ." Iqbal paused.

Anna didn't push him. She knew what he meant. Every night, Anna told Iqbal, she had dinner at this little cafeteria owned by a man from her town who served her leftovers that weren't on the menu. She ate for free while Abdu, the cafeteria owner, gossiped. Abdu made a good living. Where his place was, every night, trucks and buses ferrying labor would stop. Badran and Iqbal may have stopped, too, sitting by the windows, worn out.

"Maybe," said Iqbal. "Once I sat next to a man who was so hot he evaporated before my eyes. I took his pants; someone took his shoes; his shirt was ugly, so no one wanted that."

Anna laughed. Iqbal's speech was slowing. She continued massaging his scalp.

"I once knew a man who wanted to die," said Iqbal. "He'd realized pretty early it was hard to die in the workplace or in the camps. He wasn't unhappy. He just wanted to die."

"So, did he?" asked Anna.

Iqbal grinned. "You see, that's how this story gets complicated. Charley knew what he wanted, but he was also fair. He had a wife and kids back home he wanted to make sure were provided for. He'd figured the best way to do that would be to die performing some work-related task. That way they would be compensated."

"Did he succeed?"

Iqbal thought about the question. "I am not sure," he finally said.

"What happened?"

"Well, he asked me to help. I liked him, you know. I said yes. He said it would take some time, a year or two, but it could work. So Charley tells me that every couple of months he would give himself an accident. He'd start with small ones. Fall off the first floor, lose a few toes. Then he would build up: third floor, sixth floor. Thing is, he'd tell me beforehand. A note, some secret code indicating when he planned to do this, and where. So I'd wait for the deed, and before anyone found out I'd go to him, remove one piece of him—don't know, a finger or something—then throw that into the trash bin. Stick People would fix him up at night, but there would be a part missing. He promised himself four accidents a year. If he played his cards right, in three years, he'd be properly broken, just not fixable, and the company would be bound to inform his family. So that's what we did for a while."

"His family wouldn't have gotten a cent," Anna confided.

"Let me finish," said Iqbal. "We'd done enough for me to administer the hammer blow in a few months; it had taken longer than we had anticipated—six years. One night, Charley sought me out. 'I want to live,' he said. I didn't know what to say. I had removed a few fingers, toes, a kidney, his penis. His legs were half the size they'd been when he arrived, and now he wanted to live."

"What did you do?" Anna asked.

"He's very happy now," smiled Iqbal. "Sometimes he asks me if he can watch me jack off since he can't anymore."

"Was he there today?"

"No, not today." Iqbal's breath grew increasingly labored. "Soon," is what he said. Anna nodded, gently touching his face. Iqbal turned towards her. "Do you know the prayer for the dead?" She shook her head.

"There's this dream I've been having. . ." Iqbal began.

"Listening," said Anna.

"A man I knew, Nandan, kept a bird, a pigeon in a cage, that he brought to work every day." As Nandan worked, Iqbal shared, he never let this bird out of his sight.

"Never?"

"Not for a second," Iqbal confirmed. "The bird could fly, but he weighted it down with an iron lock around its neck. It weighed enough to make the bird stoop all the time." Iqbal felt bad for the bird, trapped in that cage, so he made up his mind to set it free when Nandan wasn't looking. "I almost succeeded," he said. He was on the roof, picking the lock, about to set the bird free, when Nandan cornered him. Someone had seen Iqbal headed for the roof with the birdcage. Nandan demanded Iqbal give back his bird. "I wouldn't, of course," said Iqbal. In a fit of rage, Nandan lunged for the bird. Iqbal slipped, losing his grip on the bird; it fell to the ground a few feet away from both men, not far from the edge of the roof, eighteen stories up. The bird, in a panic, or perhaps, hope, began hopping toward the edge and jumped. "But I hadn't had time to remove the lock," said Iqbal.

"That's terrible," said Anna.

"In a way," said Iqbal. "After the incident, I began having these dreams."

"Dreams?"

"Promise not to laugh," said Iqbal.

"I promise," said Anna. Weeks after the pigeon fell to its death, Iqbal began having dreams in which he stood atop the roof of some building he helped construct. "My family's with me; we all have wings. The sun's cold. You following me? Cold! We fly." And as they fly, he shared, he notices that their feet possess talons, with which they can grip the top of the building, and they pull, and they fly, and they pull, and they fly, or try to fly, until they rip the building off its foundations, taking it with them, towards the gelid sun." It was Iqbal's final tale. Before dawn, he was gone.

Anna stayed with him for a few minutes, wondering if she ought to wait until morning, but she decided against it, filling out a note she attached to his chest. *Deceased*, it said, listing Khalid's company's name and address and a point of contact. Then she got back on her cycle.

*

Hamdan, Anna's haunt, her hood, was growing, from a tiny city center to a mutating worm that refused to tire. The streets grew streets, parked next to slabs of steel and glass towering over trees planted to grow in exactly the same way. Roads were widened and swept regularly to keep them spotless and black. Imported planners erected tall, stringy American-style street lights. If you paid attention, you could hear mercenary architects barking instructions to create the perfect city: *Move. This. There. That.* They never slept, shouting orders into the night, into the wee hours of the morning, never resting. The city was a board game and labor its pieces , there to make buildings bigger, streets longer, the economy richer. Then to leave. After.

Hamdan had once been little, with a runt-like city center, unsure and uncertain, but was now coached in ambition to exact maximum mileage from death-proof labor as they constructed its buildings. Anna had trouble keeping up with the pace. More workers than ever were falling.

Once, after Iqbal, a man she helped patch up, Kuriakose, sought her out, stood outside her door, begged her to come with him to his boss to demand unpaid wages. He just wanted to return home. She could fix this, he was sure. She went along. The boss had called the cops. Before arresting her, an officer asked her what she did. When he heard she worked for Khalid, he let her go with a warning. Khalid had been furious. "There's a system in place here; we obey," he said.

"What happened to him?" she wanted to know.

Kuriakose was sent home. His roommates collected some money for him, but he had to go.

"The lies are there to see," Khalid liked to say. "It falls like slime. It falls off people like slime." The man had a point. There were no lies at the gates as ships docked, people pinned like barnacles, as planes landed spitting out new arrivals, as smugglers chucked live cargo miles away from port or land. Everyone came to secure their futures.

The city flirted with these people, making all give and give up. The air was spiked; everyone wanted a taste. Anna, too, she admitted. She had thought about bringing her family over, but she didn't want her children turning into in-betweens. Children she saw everywhere, those with cultivated accents, kids fattened by cable and imported chocolate, coddled by Japanese electronics and American telly. No, her kids would respect her land; they would know it. "Know the land, not the mother," Khalid had warned her. They'd been walking near the corniche.

"You see that," Anna said, pointing at a dark man fixing the sprinklers, as dark as the tiny nanny pushing a baby stroller past them, less dark than the men in the buildings nearby, nutting and bolting, even falling quietly when they slipped, falling quickly. "I've been lucky; my kids don't understand."

"Tell them," Khalid replied, "before they stop caring." Then he held her hand. But Khalid had been right. Her husband, then her children faded from her life. "What to say?" she asked Khalid. He said nothing. He couldn't understand; he had sent for his wife as soon as she was pregnant with their first child. With little to say, the two of them watched the barricaded sea. There was some tide, spittle, chewing-gum wrappers, fizz cans, little fishes licking ice-cream cups, and matches floating like little rafts, hitting the stone walls, where algae clung. Not far away, a thin man roasted peanuts in a wok of salt. The night was damp and the sky was flecked with gray.

Anna cycled slowly. "It's like impregnating the sky," she said out loud. Iqbal's words. I ought to try it at least once, she thought, deciding to take a shortcut by the corniche, which was now under construction. Months ago, on her morning walk, she had noticed Caterpillar scoopers and tractors parked near the date palms. She heard dredgers in the water. There was smoke everywhere. The sea was being kicked farther out. More fountains were being built. Anna didn't understand why, but she sat on a bench and wept. The construction was part of a larger plan. Anything with an old soul was being taken apart. It was what they did with the old souk, with its markets: tore it down, moving the merchants to a more modern building.

"They put us in a room!" Kareem Ikka, her grocer, scoffed, offering Anna piping-hot chai. The toy sellers were put in rooms, too. Her son and daughter had visited twice. The first time, she took them to the souk on a Friday, where they had to make their way past wayward tanks, robot monkeys, rotating princesses, woofing dogs. They bumped into people, she made them smell attar. She bought them cotton candy and a falooda each. The only mall she'd taken them to was in Hamdan Center. If they visited now, she wouldn't know where to take them. She didn't know the new malls as well. Or her children. But those thoughts would need to wait. She had arrived at her destination.

Watchman Babu greeted her with a smile. They were old friends. "Best job in the world," he told her once. The man who owned the empty building, a big shot named Majid, refused to sell. He was biding his time, waiting for its property value to soar. When he died unexpectedly, his son Rashid, who had been very close to his father, couldn't part with the building, and kept it, even though his brothers wanted him to sell. There was now an on-going property dispute. The case was being heard in the courts. Babu had been there from the beginning. He lived on the first floor, where he hosted parties for his bachelor friends. One such party, many years ago, led him to the roof. It wasn't a tall building, only six floors, but when his friends found his crumpled body, they had no hope, until Anna happened to cycle past. She saved his life, but he lost use of his right leg and an eye. Over time, they became firm friends, and sometimes Babu allowed Anna to sleep on the roof, which she did when she wanted to think. Tonight, she wanted to think. She fell asleep on the cot Babu laid out for her. She was soon dreaming.

She was standing on the roof of a very tall building, near the edge. Below, the city looked like drops of paint. The wind was strong. Iqbal was there; he gave her a friendly nod. There were many other faces she didn't recognize, men and women. There were hundreds of them. It was a hot day. The sun was brutal. It was then that she noticed that she had on the most magnificent wax wings—perfectly detailed. The others did, too, testing them by flapping them up and down to see if they worked. Anna wanted to try her new wings immediately, but sensed everyone was waiting for a signal. Then she heard the door to the roof open. She turned around and watched as hundreds of red-eyed pigeons, the size of schoolchildren, with their wings clipped, bells on their feet, iron lockets on their necks, walked towards them, extremely disciplined. Each bird stood behind a wax-winged man or woman. The one behind her stood so close Anna could smell its scent, hear it cooing. Anna's legs trembled. Before she had a chance to ask what now, the bird gave her a firm push. As she fell, she recalled asking Iqbal what the birdman Nandan had named his pigeon. As she tried flapping her giant wings, doing it all wrong, having trouble catching drift, she remembered Iqbal laughing. "Take a guess," he had said. She was falling with her back to the ground, peering upwards. The glint of the sun made it difficult to see. She sensed people falling past her, falling with her, dropping like rocks, trying to steady themselves, putting those wings to work. As she flapped harder, she thought she faintly caught sight of many bird heads peering down at her. Their beaks were moving. "Fly," they seemed to be mouthing. "Fly!"

CHAPTER THREE

Expat. Worker.
Guest. Worker.
Guest Worker. Worker.
Foreigner. Worker.
Non-resident. Worker.
Non-citizens. Workers.
Workers. Visa.
People. Visas.
Workers. Worker.
A million. More.
Homeless. Visiting.
Residing. Born.
Brought. Arrived.
Acclimatizing. Homesick.
Lovelorn. Giddy.
Worker. Workers.
Tailor. Solderer.
Chauffeur. Maid.
Oil Man. Nurse.
Typist. Historian.
Shopkeeper. Truck driver.
Watchman. Gardener.
Secretary. Pilot.
Smuggler. Hooker.
Tea boy. Mistress.
Temporary. People.

Illegal. People.
Ephemeral. People.
Gone. People.
Deported. Left.
More. Arriving.

CHABTER FOUR

FONE

NEAR JAWAZAT ROAD, THERE used to be an ordinary looking ka-dakaran who owned a little kada. In the back, where he kept the surplus Basmati rice, the colas, the cooking oil, and the hardcore porn, was what some customers sought him out for, a fone. The device resembled a rotary phone, but it wasn't a phone; it was a *fone*. The fone did the one thing you would expect a phone to do: it could make calls. However, it couldn't receive any. The fone's main purpose was teleportation. A man could use the fone to talk to his wife, and as his wife cried softly into the neighbor's phone, her husband would hover over her, like a giant bee, seeing his wife cry like that, feeling satisfied that his wife could cry like that, content that he could see her cry like that, even though she wouldn't be able to see him, or even know that he was there, so close he could see the dirt on the back of her neck. And he was so happy he could see her cry like that. Or a woman could be speaking to her daughter, a daughter who hasn't learned to form words yet, but is instead biting the phone, like it's meant to be bitten, drooling into it, as her father steadies her wobbling body, coaxing her to talk, to speak, pleading with her to perform something worthy for her mother, and the woman sees all of this, her husband encouraging their child to say something, anything, as long as it's a word, any word, it didn't matter as long as it was a word. Or the phone simply rang and rang and no one picked up, even though the fone caller was in a state of bliss, itching to tell someone that he'd been promoted, that he was happy, that he needed to tell people he was happy to feel happy, that he needed to see people pretending to be happy in order to be happy. So the fone had its uses, but its usage was regulated by the kadakaran. It would break if too many people used it, he said, and I don't know how to fix it if it breaks. So a person could use the fone only once a year. One couldn't tell one's friends about the fone. They had to find it. Stumble across it and the kada itself was like stumbling across a Kurdish-speaking macaw or a wizard in a bar. Then once one knew what the fone did, one put oneself on a list and chose a date and time. If one were smart, one didn't choose religious or public holidays, or a late-evening time. One wanted to be sure the person one was calling was home, because one only got one fone call and it had to count. On the appointed day, one cut work by calling in sick, made one's way to the kada, and made that call. Then when one hung up, one would make an appointment for the next year.

If Johnny Kutty hadn't called his wife, maybe the fone would still be in operation.

Johnny Kutty was married only a month before a distant relative found him a job as a car mechanic's apprentice in Dubai. Johnny Kutty bought phone cards and called his wife once a week. He called his friend Peeter's STD booth, and Peeter sent a helper to fetch Johnny Kutty's wife and they talked frantically until the card ran out. When Johnny Kutty discovered the fone, he couldn't wait; he made an appointment for the next available date. On that fateful day, as Johnny Kutty hovered over his wife in his friend Peeter's STD booth, he noticed Peeter sat there, smiling at her, and she at him. He offered her cold cola, which she sipped using a straw, blushing as she did so, blushing, Johnny Kutty couldn't be sure, at Peeter's attentiveness or because of what Johnny Kutty was telling her, of the things he wanted to do to her—dirty, dirty things—and she nodded and blushed, and blushed then nodded, smiling all the time, smiling until it drove the hovering Johnny Kutty crazy, until the phone card ran out.

Quickly, Johnny Kutty made the next available appointment for the following year, but he continued to call his wife every week using a regular pay phone. It wasn't enough anymore. He imagined all sorts of things: that she was drinking cola, that Peeter had bought bottles of cola only for her, that he put the straw in himself, that he sucked on that straw after Johnny Kutty's wife left, that he licked the tip where her lips and spit had been. When his young wife shared she was pregnant a few weeks later, Johnny Kutty knew then that his life was ruined. That night, he broke into the kadakaran's kada and called Peeter. The phone rang and rang and rang, and Johnny Kutty was sure Peeter wasn't managing the STD booth, which was also the front portion of his house. Peeter, Johnny Kutty knew, was busy with Johnny Kutty's wife, and had no time to answer phone calls from his best friend, too busy cuckolding his best friend with his friend's young wife, the bitch who loved cola. As he realized what his wife had done, Johnny Kutty started hating his once-happy life, destroyed now by his cheating wife and his once-best friend. He wished he wasn't in that kada by himself, standing next to that fone, the fone that broke his heart, a device that may have done the same for countless others, and thus needed to be put down. Exterminated. So he got to work. Johnny Kutty poured fifteen liters of cola into a bucket the kadakaran used to clean his kada, and dropped the fone into the fizzing liquid, holding it down as it were a person, drowning it, drowning the people it contained. Then he looked for match boxes, piled them next to the bucket with the dead fone, then poured three tins of cooking oil on the floor for good measure. He lit one match and watched it drop. When the shurtha at the police station told Johnny Kutty that he could make one phone call, he told them they could do whatever they wanted to him, but if they asked him to phone someone or brought a phone to him, he would die, and for a man to die so many times in one year was not normal, and he said he probably wouldn't survive that, which would be a shame, because he had been through a lot.

CHAPTER FIVE

TAXI MAN

HELLO, GOOD MORNING. WHERE TO, PLEASE?

Yes, yes, Dubai, no problem. But Dubai where?

No, that place not far distance, I sure. This time, less going out traffic from Abu Dhabi past ten o'clock time—everybody in office time that time. Should make there in hour and a half maximum, Insh'Allah. What address again? Hmm, don't know place sure—must be old industrial place—but I have phone with GPS and your phone also GPS? I put GPS now and then we go Dubai, OK?

*

By the way, you Indian, aren't you? Where about? Figured, so we'll manage in Hindi the rest of the way then, even though you people down south say Hindi no maalum nine times out of ten. But you've got a few words of Hindi under your belt, right? We'll be fine.

See, when you've been in the taxi business as long as I have, you get a feel for people. Like whether they're cultured, ordinary, decent. First, their skin gives them away. With you, I guessed Indian. Wasn't sure, though. You don't act Indian, more like Amree-kun with your military haircut and glasses. Someone foreign, that was clear. And you've got that wisha-washa-wusha Englishness about you. But I knew I could talk to you. You said hello.

Tone, that's how you know. Some customers, no time for small talk. They hail you like the world's about to end, then spit

29

out directions like they own you. Half the time they're slurring. You can't push them too much when they're like that, you know. They get wild. Fuck this, fuck that, that's all they're good for past midnight. And I'm thinking, Calm down, maaderchod! I'm trying to get you home.

Or you've got some dame in the backseat whose pussy starts to itch. You know the kind I'm talking about? Bitches! That's the English word, right? Bitches. You understand, right?

Listen, friend, cometh the hour in this city of men when your dick's practically licking itself because it's spoiled for choice. Where? Everywhere, man. You'll find broads at ▮▮▮▮▮ Hotel, the parking lot by ▮▮ ▮▮▮▮▮, rooted like trees in front of sandwich shops and fast-food joints exchanging numbers with some unwashed teen. Or saunter around ▮▮▮▮▮▮ Club past midnight. You'll have trouble fending them off. They swarm these working gals, like moths to light. And they won't be talking to you, yaara; they'll be talking to your cock. And if you're the kind of man you were born to be, whatever your morals, you'll get hooked on the attention.

Have I sampled some of these big-assed, big-tittied specimens? What you think? You can't help yourself. But I don't pay, yaara. I save my dough. Look, when I worked in Dubai back in the day we had Filipinas on staff. I drove for the big boss, see. But I also had plenty of free time with the car, and in it, if you know what I mean. Boss Man let me take the company ride home, and these Filipina chicks would want to go places, know what I'm saying? Jamal, help us out, they'd squeal. Sure, baby, I'd say, anywhere you want, but what's in it for Jamal?

Some bitches, though, they sneak up on you. I was taking this customer home the other night. Hot little birdy. Shoes louder than canaries. Doused in enough perfume to pollute the moon. And pale—pale as bone, friend. And hoo-wee, I tell you, so fuckin' smashed, if blood trickled out I could've bottled and sold the stuff back to the hooch-sellers. But she wanted some

Pakistani meat, oh you could so fuckin' tell. She put a hand on my shoulder. Know what she said, friend? Fuck me, Taxi Man.

Look, when customer's foreign and shit, I mind my own business. You don't want white-people trouble. But this bitch was way out of line. I waved her off. I fuck I like, I replied in English. What now, she seemed to say. Then she laughed, coz bitch dug English-talkers, suit-boot people who spoke smack. Coz she got all sultry and shit. But that's my point; with some people you've got to lay down the law. Doesn't take much. No broad's telling me when or who to fuck. And do I look like an airhead? No shit I don't. Once the bitch sobers up and spots my plump Lahori dick on her thigh, no telling what she might do. Let me tell you what gonna happen. She gonna call the shurthas on me and they gonna come. They gonna pull up in their ride. And let me tell you what they gonna do: they gonna nail my cock to a cell infested with other chuthiyas who got caught with their pants down. Government then gonna deport my chubby-ass Lahori ass back to homeland, friend. I didn't come here for that kind of lafda, yaara. Masti can wait. My begum's waiting back home, see, and my little girl's right by her side, see? Then there's my son. This little man's weeks from being born and he's not coming into this world to meet his unemployed once-jailbird chubby-ass Lahori-ass father.

What now? Speak up, yaara.

DID I WANT A BOY! You got NGO blood, friend? Know what I think? I think NGOs think we don't treat our ladies right. Tell you what, find me some lady NGO. You walk her to my bed. I'll treat her so good she'll let me play cricket on her wicket. But you want to know if I wanted a boy. Look, Allah decides. If He'd destined me two daughters, so what! But I won't lie, yaara, my family's complete now. I mean, we've got a girl. And now I'm getting a boy. Full set, like dinnerware. We're happy.

What's that?

You not listening, friend. I didn't care whether it was a boy or a girl. If I didn't know better, I'd say you were baiting me. Look, boy, girl, honestly same-same. I've got one rule. Kid's got to be mine. And my begum understands, see. She's *never* breaking that rule.

She's also crazy. When I found out she was two months late, woman was pretty clear she wanted a boy. If Allah had e-mail, my begum wouldn't have stopped writing him, get? I'll tell you why, yaara.

When Begum was pregnant with our firstborn, I told her, Girl!

She countered, Boy! Woman should have listened.

So when I knocked her up again, the fourth month, she asked me to guess again.

Don't matter, I said.

Begum got persistent. Boy, right? Boy, right? Boy?

Don't matter, woman, I said again. So what she does? Whatever her Rawalpindi-ass tells her to, that's what. Note this, friend: She's getting an ultrasound to check if the baby's doing whatever it's supposed to, right, and when she's staring at the monitor, watching my baby's heart, begum says, I think I see his penis. And the lady doctor, what she do? She says, Show me!

Part of me felt she'd jinxed the birth after that stunt. But my begum didn't care; she told *everyone*. Boy, it's a boy. It's a boy, BOY!

She not naming my boy, though, that would be taking things too far. That's my job, yaara. I named our girl, too.

We'll call the boy Zameer.

What's that, what did I name the girl? Zohra.

*

But enough about me! What kind of work do you do, friend? Or were you just visiting someone when I picked you up?

Lecturer? Mash'Allah! Don't look it, yaara. Body's fit and slick, no doubt. I like those earrings, too. How old are you? You don't say! Still hot-blooded, I bet. Married? Kids? May I offer some advice? Don't take it the wrong way, all right? At your age, thirty-shirty, take advantage, don't miss out on ready-made masti. Know what I mean? Take advantage. After a while, your engine don't reboot so good. Once you've got kids, everything's different. Back in the day, I had many girlfriends; now, not so much. I mean, every now and then, you know, I satisfy my needs, but I've slowed down. Tits and pussy juice, all placed on standby. I've got priorities, yaara. I've got to teach my little girl to talk. We talk every day, my angel and me. She's three now and take my word for it, she's her father's daughter. No nonsense. All business. I want this! I want that! Hold up, yaara, I've got a picture. See, what I tell you? Heartbreaker, right? You know what she told me the other day? Baba, if you don't come home with presents, I'll break your daanth. Know what I mean by daanth? Tell me, what's daanth in English? That's right—teeth. Your Urdu, by the way, is decent. Your grammar needs more work, though. You're mixing up your hes and shes.

So. Your wife works? Yeah, yaara, times are tough. You don't need to tell me why people aren't hiring. You don't have kids yet, you said. Some advice, don't mind, from one brother to another: have the first one when your begum's unemployed. She's not doing anything anyway. That'll give her some time to look after the baby and all. Then, you know, in two, three years, put the kid in daycare. It's not expensive. They've got them everywhere now. Filipina daycare, Indian, Pakistani, licensed, unlicensed, anything you want. Then put the wife to work. Then you don't have to worry about family pressures. My elder brother waited too long. Then my sister-in-law couldn't conceive. Her parts weren't right or something, but they fixed her. Took her nine years, though. You don't want that. Don't mind me saying so, but you've got to hit that shit when it's still brand new and oiled and warm. You got to plan ahead, yaara. Before you die, you want to be able to run after your grandchildren, don't you?

33

Not get wheeled around like an infant, know what I mean? I've seen these foreign women at Abu Dhabi Mall. They think it's normal to be parents when you're fifty. You should be thinking about *grandchildren* at fifty! Sometimes, common sense should prevail.

Man, you've got me squawking like a parrot. I mean, you're not upset or anything, right? Good, good. You've got to ask nowadays. People on their phones and shit put their lips on silent. Who talks anymore?! But you're the customer, yaara. I've got to check if it's cool to go all motormouth on you. Believe you me, brother, I could drive you to Dubai without saying another word. Your call—that what you want?

You're not just saying that, right? Well, you're a gentleman then. You understand, yaara. Most customers should know on long drives, talking's like caffeine, but think customers give a shit? Most of them are busy humping WhatsApp or Facebook in the backseat. The roads are straight here, see, highways wide. And then you've got your AC-wayC—always full blast! Last thing you wanna do is shut your eyes. You wanna stay alert, friend, not crash because you're bored.

*

Yaara—HEY, YAARA—if it's all right by you, got to make a stop right by that exit, OK? Need to get some petrol and piss away my morning tea. I'll put the meter on hold. That cool? I mean, customers don't give it much mind, but the hardest thing about driving people around is finding public toilets. Sometimes you don't piss for hours because you're thinking about your target. Or, God forbid, your tummy's about to Pompeii and your fare's just gotten in and you're wondering whether your bum's gonna listen to your mind. Or your back feels like cement because your spine's stuck to the seat. Or you're carting around customers, one after the other, and you've got to take them all, because if you turn one down, that chuthiya might call management and complain, and that's another maa-kee fine coming out of my pay, yaara. But then, gradually, your wrists and back get used to staying in one place for hours, your tummy's like, whatever, and you get used to pissing and shitting after your shift. That's eight to ten hours' worth of festering piss and shit, friend. Or you eat once a day, right after you wake. I mean, I'm no doctor, but after a while, you're screwed, right? Anyways, you're a good egg, yaara. I'll be back before you miss me.

*

Right, off we go again. I needed that wee, friend.

So tell me something: These kids you teach, they get rubbers for free, right? At your school place, of course! Students just need to ask, right? Don't play ignorant, friend, don't bullshit a bull-shitter. I've seen MTV back in the day, I watch Gum of Thrones. And I know how Americans raise their women. Know how I know? I'm driving this Nepali chikna to the city, right. Kid probably started shaving yesterday. Anyway, picked him up where I picked you up on some weekday when traffic's shit. We're stuck near ███████ ███████ bitch-ass traffic—and we're talking, and he's telling me how he's been boning chicks using rubber, he's been getting from you-know-whose, right? And I'm boning your mum before namaaz, I tell him. I mean, c'mon, everybody knows if you've got to buy rubber, you stop by Spar or LuLu's, right? And when I was studying back in the day, we knew better than to advertise your cock's intention to ram the local beauty. Know what he tells me? He tells me, I'm serious man, there's Amreekun-made pussy to be had Sunday through Monday. Fuckin' buffet, he tells me. But I don't trust Nepalis, yaara. Nobody wants to fuck them, so they make up these ridiculous stories about anything living wanting to fuck them. I mean, if you had to choose between Pakistani and Chin-Cho-Chow-Cho dick, it's no contest, right? Still, even if they're pencil-dick maad-erchods, Nepalis, they've got great work ethic. I mean, they'll work till they die, yaara. Not like us Indians and Pakistanis. We're chuthiyas. That Nepali probably fucked Amreekuns like his life depended on it, because if he didn't, how's he going to get that green card?

And what about you, yaara? Plenty of girlfriends on call in your line of work, I'll bet? You're shitting me! You've got nothing on the side either? What you got at home, yaara? Pussy mari-nated in Pashtun hash? Sorry, that was out of line, but you seem like the sort of guy who plays the field. How many notches on that bedpost? Only *five*? C'mon, you're Amreekun-return, right? Tell me you've devoured gori madams for lunch, breakfast, and dinner! Come, now, don't be shy. I've got a cousin in Misheegun. No joke, yaara, my haraamkhor cousin's been test-driving Am-reekun goris since Clindon Bhai's presidency. What you say in Amreekun bar-shops? Wam-bam? Well, my cousin's a wam-bam kind of chuthiya.

And since we're on the subject, let me ask you something, OK? You don't have to tell me, but since we're friends, you shouldn't mind. Is your dick cut? I mean, I can ask, right? Your stick's pretty big? How big? You're putting me on! Rubber comes in sizes! Like T-shirts? I've seen colors and flavors, but sizes? Spill—you a one-rubber or two-rubber man? And your madam satisfied with Hindustani dick wrapped in two sheets of latex? I knew it, haraami! *Now* we're talking!

No, I don't use condoms. Don't need them. I mean, sure, I fool around; I like Filipina pussy, know what I'm saying. They like singing kar-o-kee *and* they like men in charge. I've got a Ka-rachi buddy who gets me a Pakistani discount. His merchandise, always clean, so rubbers no need. I don't cum inside though. I'm perfectly satisfied watering the tip of the rose bush.

What's that, what my begum think of rubber-shubber? Look, yaara, I see my begum every two to four years. I'm not going to

dress my dick in a rubber suit when it's supposed to go skin-
ny-dipping. Not the same. My begum likes it that way too. So if
we've got more kids on the way, we've got more kids on the way.
You won't hear me complaining.

Is it hard to what? Live apart from family? Look, yaara, why
don't you ask me what's really on your mind. You want to know
if I feel guilty fuckin' other women? Sometimes. But I don't love
any of them. My heart's my begum's. But vice is fun, fella. I partake, but you've got to be careful. I live in ███████████, see. That's
taxi-people territory. Most of us live there. It's a big complex. Just
us men, though, with fut-aah-fut facilities: football and cricket,
books and TV. We're not far from the women's quarters, though.
And don't know what you've heard, friend, but ███████████ is different now. Used to be run down and bloated with emptiness.
Now? Yaara, *everything's* available now. I mean, *everything*: gro-
ceries, batteries, men, women. Everything. But I don't do anything there. Too many eyes wondering what mischief you're up
to, enough tongues to rat you out. I don't shit where I eat. I'm
careful, yaara. ███████████'s where my room's at, understand; it's
where I sleep and salute the rule book. In the morning I wake up,
brush, shower, and get out! I mean, I've got stuff to do. Four hundred and twenty-five dirhams per day's no joke. That's my target.
Once that's out of the way, I've got time to chill. Drive around.
Maybe even return for some shut-eye. So I lucked out this morning, didn't I? A Dubai jaunt is two hundred, easy. And it's what,
an hour or two past breakfast time now? That leaves me most of
the afternoon to finish up my shift by dusk. Otherwise, I'm driving people until nine or ten p.m.. After that, it's watered-down
curry and rotis at my usual haunt. Then crawl back into bed.
Rest the fuckin' back. Sleep. Tomorrow, hit repeat.

I've got roommates, yeah. One's a chuthiya, some Multan-wala
who should have been born dead. We're forbidden to cook—
people try and get caught—so I eat out, but I like a clean house,
know what I mean? The Multan-wala haraami-behen-ki-lauda,

he's a slob. So I told him: You expect us to bend over and pick up your filth, bhenchod? Told him I'd tear him a new one in his sleep if he didn't get his shit together. Listen, if he wants his room to smell like ass, he better be the only one living in it, gaandu motherfucker.

You've been living here what, four, five months now? Tell me something, noticed the gays? City's filled with them. Filipino people, they're mostly gay. Then you've got those Arabs in skinny jeans and nice shoes walking all funny and smelling like toilet freshener! They're gay, too. You're Amreekun-return, right? Flor-da's littered with gays, right, because it's close to Disneyland? And New York's their capital, no? But they're mostly smart and rich and own all the TV channels, right? I thought so. And how about you? Sampled some boys-woys? C'mon, be honest. Me? Well, some gaand-masti back in the day. Like, you know what chappi means, right? Tell me then, what's English for chappi? You've no clue what it means, do you, yaara? I'll tell you. In English, it means sucking—to suckh-uh. Get what I'm saying? I've never offered, never needed to. I know what you're thinking, I may be pudgy, but I've still got game. If I wanted to, I could snap my fingers right now and within ten minutes there'll be someone who'll suckh-uh my dick-uh. You don't believe me?

Let me tell you what happened last week. I was taking this white lady to Khalifa City. Fifteen minutes in, she gets a call. It's the guy she's been fuckin'. He wasn't in the mood. So the woman, Russian I'm thinking, starts crying in the backseat. Then she asks me to turn and take her home. I'm thinking, let's try something. So I offer her some tissue because her mascara's running. Before I know it, we're talking. I mean, she's talking, telling me her life story, how the guy she's doing was married. That he'd been stringing her around for two years and she was thinking of ending it, even though she's still into the chuth. Before I know it, I've pulled over in front of her villa and she invites me in. Insists, in fact. And she serves me orange juice. And then her hands are on my thigh. Listen, I could've done anything to her and she would've let me. But I'm thinking, I'm in a villa by Al Reef. My taxi's parked outside. The neighbors know the driver's in the house; security has seen me enter the premises. If someone dials management, or worse, the shurtha, I might as well drop my pants and walk out the door with my gaand in the air. So what I do? I thank the lady for her hospitality and get the hell out of there.

Yell out that address for me again. What's the name of the place again, you say? And spit out that exit for me again. Exit 43. OK, 43.

We've got two more exits to go; in another fifteen, you'll be where you need to be.

*

Tell you what, yaara? Take my number down. You need to go somewhere—Dubai, Sharjah, shopping by Al Wahda—you call me, OK? I'll take care of you. Bring the wife. I promise I'll behave. When Madam's in the car, we can't gup-shup like this, you get? When Madam's here, we dispense with guy talk. Respect, full-fledged and absolute, that's what Madam gets. Believe you me I'm shy, yaara. With you though, I can drop the act and be myself, without having to worry. But with Madam—

There's the exit. You sure you just want me to park by the gate? I could wait till you're done. I mean, it's illegal to ferry you back and all—Abu Dhabi taxis aren't allowed to pick up return fares from Dubai—but for you, I'll look the other way. No? Sure?

*

Well, it's been a pleasure. And the forty dirham tip for a two-hundred-buck ride, you really shouldn't have. I mean, you're really hell-bent on spoiling me today, aren't you, yaara? First, conversation, and now, this! I told you, the minute I saw you, I

39

knew, this boy's going to be my golden ticket today. You must let me shake your hand and say goodbye then, like men who must be brothers, face-to-face. You've still got a few minutes before your meeting, right? I promise this won't take long. Let me just put the hazards on, unfasten my seatbelt, and get out of this stupid Corolla. You know some smart-ass Bitish told me it's the world's best-selling ride. That's marketing talk, if you ask me. My brother-in-law owns a Datsun pickup from the eighties. He should have turned it into scrap, but the Datsun's given him no trouble whatsoever. Ever seen a Datsun? I'm sure that haraami Bitish wouldn't even know a Datsun from an Isuzu if it ran him over on Sheikh Zayed Road.

Anyways, I've been picking up fares in this Jaapaan-ki maal for five years now, and let me tell you, it's an honor to shake the hand of a young man who's been such a pleasure, such a pleasure. And ooh, what we have here? I thought right then. You work out, friend. May I?—only a quick squeeze—Oh my!

There's potential in your biceps, yaara, so much potential...

But, hmm...

Don't mind, OK. I've got to tell you something: your arms, as good as they look, are still a bit flabby in places. That's a shame, friend. They looked decent in the rear-view mirror, almost as good close up, but on proper inspection, it's clear you've failed to maintain them. Yaara, you've *got* to maintain them. See, when you slap an arm that's solid, nothing moves; it's the sort of arm that flexes on demand, with muscles on standby. But you, fine as you may be, should take another look at your triceps. That's the back part. They've gone soft. Like, everything's OK, but nothing's great. And now that I can see you up close, it's obvious your middle needs work, too, and you've spent too much time in the sun. Maintenance. You've got to maintenance your shit. If you don't, in a year or two, your chest will be tits. Then you will wake up one morning and feel like someone rammed your legs up your own stretch-marked ass. But you don't look like that kind of guy. You look like you're going to make it, with your nice glasses and crease-free trousers. You look like you've smeared your skin with education and firangi moisturizer. Big fish. The kind of man my daughter's going to snare and staple to her heart until his money builds her a house and gifts her Bitish papers. Believe you me, we'll find someone just like you to gift-wrap when she's older. But—don't mind me saying so—better, taller, fairer. Just remember, maintenance. You have to maintenance your shit. Otherwise you're forgettable, friend. Normal-assed, normal-hipped, normal shit.

CHABTER SIX

THE ANNIVERSARY

Doped against your will, anyone could be pushed to torture, to eat his own child, to denounce God. The beast has been unleashed and it will not be tamed. My client is a family man, a God-fearing man who was not in control of his actions that day. He was duped into doing what he did by men who abused his trust. It was a set up.

—THE DEFENSE

PROLOGUE

Every year, on the last day of April, as the sun dips below horse-brown dunes, the men of my city are required to assemble in the sands where an oasis used to be. To witness the reenactment of a series of acts committed by a man on another man in the early aughts, and to learn why the first man was acquitted in court. What transpires is a play. Attendance is mandatory.

ACT I

A man playing an important tribesman is secretly drugged, then commanded to chug a keg of booze on the orders of a man playing a stranger. The tribesman is then given a Kalashnikov

and asked to drive a Range Rover over another man who plays
Mahmoud the Pathan. Mahmoud's legs will break. The man
playing a stranger then hands the tribesman a wooden plank
with a protruding nail. The tribesman will use this to beat
Mahmoud until the plank snaps in two. The stranger then
orders the tribesman to pour sand into Mahmoud's eyes,
down his throat. Mahmoud's eyes and throat are forced open.
Fine sand is poured like liquid from a terra-cotta jug. Once
this horror concludes, the stranger will order the tribesman to
fire the Kalashnikov. Over Mahmoud the Pathan. Which the
tribesman does. On further prompting, the tribesman pours
lighter fluid on Mahmoud's clothes. The stranger offers the
tribesman a Zippo. This is where the first act ends.

INTERMISSION

Fifteen minutes. The actors smoke. Some miracle salve is
rubbed on the man playing Mahmoud. The organizers provide
refreshments. The assembled men help themselves to dates,
cold fruit, bitter coffee, sweet tea, water or Laban Up. Portable
lavatories fulfill other needs.

ACT II

On the last day of April, the assembled men of my city are
expected to attend a play profiling an incident in the life of
Mahmoud the Pathan. We not only witness the play; in the
second act, we are also expected to participate. We will all play
tribesmen, replacing the actor who played the tribesman in the
first act, and repeating his deeds.

The second act begins as soon as we consume drugs. Then every one of us drinks a whole keg of booze and each picks up a working Kalashnikov, donated every year by an arms dealer, before taking turns driving the sole Range Rover over sands near the former oasis where Mahmoud the Pathan's legs will be broken once again. Multiple times.

Under supervision of the man playing a stranger, the assembled men of my city, fed drugs, then booze, one at a time, drive over Mahmoud the Pathan. Over. Over. Over.

Under supervision of the man playing a stranger, the assembled men of my city beat Mahmoud the Pathan with a wooden plank with a protruding nail, then one at a time pour sand into his eyes, down his throat. Over. Over. Over.

Afterwards, doped out of our minds, ignoring the night moon, we call on the sun to assemble over the sands. "Witness Mahmoud the Pathan's broken legs! Fire the Kalashnikovs!" we shout. Then, like men, we fire the Kalashnikovs. We fire our guns like men. We cheer. Now what's left is to burn the man who plays Mahmoud.

It is almost dawn when I pour lighter fluid on Mahmoud's clothes. I notice the man playing him is exhausted. I am the penultimate person to set him on fire. There have been hundreds before me, traipsing in after mandated ten-minute intervals. Once the man playing a stranger puts my fire out, he administers the miracle salve, before the last person in line sets Mahmoud on fire again. This is where the second act ends. Then the man playing Mahmoud the Pathan can go home, along with the assembled men of my city, who will also be permitted to return.

EPILOGUE

In April. On the last day. After the required demonstration of a significant moment in the life of Mahmoud the Pathan comes to a close, the man playing him is in some pain. His legs are broken in many places. Fine shards of wood stick to his back. He has gravel in his belly, multiple lacerations to both corneas, second- to third-degree burns. To numb the pain, he requires booze and drugs. And he needs a Range Rover on loan. Someone to drive him. To be able to return to the city center. Next year he may reprise his role or they may find someone else. But this is the routine. This is what happens once a year. Every year.

CHAPTER SEVEN

IN MUSSAFAH GREW PEOPLE

Like the crow, Kerala's much-maligned bird, Malayalees adapt well anywhere. Only our language Malayalam, a palindrome, is difficult.

—WANTED CRIMINAL RAMJI RAO (1989)

NOT MANY PEOPLE KNOW that sixty-seven and a half kilometers to Dubai's west sits an island, a little sultanate ruled by an envious little grump, Sultan Mo-Mo.

MAY 3, 2006

The sultan had enormous eyebrows, fibrous like angora wool. In moments of strife, his eyebrows twitched violently. Like now!

His Excellency's royal blood boiled. Once again another mesmerized American news anchor gushed about Dubai's vision, hailing the imagination of the al-Maktoum family.

"Where is this vision coming from?" probed Katie Couric.

"Ignorant Yankee!" Sultan Mo-Mo's British twang bore traces of Basil Fawlty.

The sultan wanted to retch. Dubai's showboating gave him indigestion, but he continued helping himself to more chips and fiery salsa, downing cold Guinness, smoking excellent hash, humming the theme song of *The Wonder Years*.

47

Thinking.

Plotting.

Watching TV.

There was so much envy in his royal blood he had been peeing green for several days. Dr. Ranasinghe, his physician, had warned him about that and advocated reincorporating the stress-ball exercises into his routine. Otherwise, the sultan would stink of petrol. And he did. The palace reeked.

But Mo-Mo couldn't harness his rage. No matter where he turned, there was no escaping Dubai, the oil bloc's Mr. Fabulous, flexing its international credentials, cocksure, so very %#$%& cocksure.

It was infuriating! Mo-Mo couldn't watch the news anymore. Every day Dubai's smug finance minister, Sheikh "Mind Boggler" Salman, as the networks dubbed him, claimed another first for his country.

Camera crews shot him like Brando. His oblong forehead descending from the heavens. Slowly, like E.T.'s mother ship. Announcing another "world's first," just when regular folk thought Dubai's ideas men had finally succumbed, having extinguished every possible permutation the word "crazy" embodied.

"Marhaba, everyone," Mind Boggler would say. Dapper in Tom Ford. His customary grin. Then he would begin.

Broadcast by TV and radio stations, the man's baritone hypnotized homes on at least three continents. When the sound bites ended, cyberspace pundits dissected the presentation. B-school faculty pored over averages and indexes, made a few calls. *The Economist* published a special report.

Dubai's audacity made Mo-Mo stink of petrol. When, on February 3, 2006, Dubai authorities apprehended a Senegalese man for hiding and raising a pregnant hyena in his home, the animal was taken in an air-conditioned trailer to a secret location, where the exhausted mother gave birth to a healthy litter. Immediately, the government announced plans "long overdue" for the largest game reserve Asia had ever known. That, for Sultan Mo-Mo, was the proverbial straw that broke his corpulent back. He reached for the red phone.

JUNE 22, 2006

After security checks, endless tea, a plateful of dates, and more waiting, three Malayalees—Pinto, Tinto, and Vimto—were ushered into Sultan Mo-Mo's chambers. Here, Tinto gingerly produced a bagful of seeds he passed on to the sultan, who inspected the goods by sniffing them. The stuff looked like Nescafé instant-coffee crystals. Smelled like parboiled rice.

The sultan's trusted advisor, Ali al-Thani, "Able Ali" in British diplomacy circles, had set up the rendezvous. "You are not going to believe this," he told Mo-Mo excitedly on Skype. "I have three men who tell me Dubai *grows* its labor. Sprouts workers like sheaves of corn." Sultan Mo-Mo asked his most trusted minister to call him back when the Moroccan hash had worn off. "They will be there tomorrow, Your Excellency," Ali responded, suggesting the sultan check his e-mail before going to bed.

"Ali wrote me," the sultan mumbled to the fidgety trio. "Plantains and hammour, eh? Be back here on July 16. And by the way, fellows, if this is a joke, need I say much else?"

The men had taken a big risk.

A cousin of Tinto's told him one afternoon there were rumors that since the late eighties a Malayalee scientist, Moosa, "Agro Moosa" to friends, had been helping the al-Nahiyan and the al-Maktoum families grow Malayalees on secret farms cocooned inside industrial-size greenhouses in Musaffah, around forty-five minutes away from Abu Dhabi's city center. The Canned Malayalee Project was born after the labor ministry realized in 1983 that the country would have to multiply its workforce by a factor of four if the sheikhs were to accomplish the growth they envisioned in the time they wanted it. Employing more white men was not an option. They wilted in the sun. Then the head of intelligence stepped in. A trusted lieutenant, he shared, had noticed the hardiness of a certain kind of man, native to soil where thousands of years ago King Mahabali ruled. "They call this man 'The Malayalee,'" the head of intelligence explained, "and many of them operate grocery stores." Thus they began observing The Malayalee. Field agents took notes, studied his temperament, his vulnerability to weather. Then they began studying cadavers. And when intelligence found the Czech, Dr. Petr—his reputation cemented after cloning two-legged mice, then training them to locate land mines, before being apprehended for trying to grow a human brain in a crystal ball and getting his license revoked—the project had its head researcher.

Laboratories were set up. Experiments conducted, results noted. Early breakthroughs involved growing nostrils in a petri dish. Then some hair, the wrong-colored toes. They grew a little man without a brain, and he lived for a week before he succumbed to an algae infection. Efforts to grow women were eventually abandoned. The first female prototype germinated stark naked, which made handling the specimen cause for concern. She died of loneliness in her little petri dish. Then Moosa, assistant to the head researcher, made his breakthrough. From a seed, he grew a miniature baby with two limbs and a brain. Within two weeks, the baby reached adolescence. It sulked, then died. In a year, Moosa perfected the technique, taking over the project from Dr. Petr. Instead of petri dishes, Moosa favored flowerpots packed with earth. Moosa's first batch only managed to yield dwarfs, but after adjusting the crop's exposure to light, giving the soil some air, sizes improved. He also began making his own fertilizer in order to have absolute control over the process. For the testing phase, Moosa switched operations to a greenhouse. Insisted on a climate-controlled environment. And somehow what he grew came out fully clothed.

Moosa's special seeds, fertilized by imported plantains from the Malabar Coast and breaded hammour fillets, hosed with tap water, beef liver, human feces, and imported toddy, was rumored to have grown into oak-dark heat-resistant five-foot-seven Malayalees in twenty-three days. These fruits, MALLUS (Malayalees Assembled Locally and Lovingly Under Supervision), or canned Malayalees, were picked and washed in concentrated Dettol, before being checked out or "cerebrally customized," as Moosa called it, by trained personnel in the briefing chambers. Then they were put to work.

MALLUS spoke excellent Arabic since the greenhouses piped in Umm Kulthum records and old Egyptian films as the fruits matured. The gardeners, hand-picked Malayalee scholars, were instructed to speak Malayalam in the greenhouses as much as possible. This was to encourage camouflaging and avoid raising suspicion once the MALLUS began to mingle with the expatriate population, especially Malayalees. MALLUS were also designed to have an average life span of twelve years, after which each would report back to headquarters like a dying pachyderm and be driven to the desert for the final chapter in its cycle.

But Moosa was now standing trial on corruption charges.

After years of being feted by his patrons, Moosa woke up one day and had a change of heart. He doctored his seeds and didn't tell a soul. The new formula produced canned Malayalees designed to prioritize reason, with minds difficult to tame. "Cantankerous twits," observed leaked ministry memos. Moosa also improved their immune systems, increasing their life spans. In March 2006, a large number of these redesigned canned Malayalees took to the streets near what was going to be the tallest structure in the world, and went on strike in a country where dissent is not tolerated. As the men rioted, onlookers, startled by *actual* rioting, fished out their cameras and took pictures.

Moosa's hand might have gone undetected if word hadn't gotten out; tipsy laborers were overheard boasting in a roadside cafeteria that some men in an undisclosed labor camp were discussing overthrowing the present regime and forming the newly independent nation of Mallu Landoo, Proud Nation of Malayalee Man. "Think about it," urged one of their leaders, Puncture Daniel, on clandestine MALLUS Radio "If every Malayalee stopped work in this country!" The men were apprehended by alarmed authorities in a sting operation and in no time discovered to be fruits. A calm Moosa confessed when the secret police brought him in for questioning. However, he refused to explain why he did what he did.

Quickly, an executive decision was made by the labor ministry to abandon using MALLUS in the workplace. The head of intelligence got demoted. Large consignments of seeds were ordered to be driven to the desert and destroyed. Vociferous MALLUS were captured in droves and driven to the desert to join comrades who had died of natural causes.

*

For six years Pinto, Tinto, and Vimto worked as truck drivers in Dubai for a Pakistani manager they called General Zia in the city's Jebel Ali Free Zone. They put in fifteen-hour shifts, six days a week. Once a month, they waited in line with chums to bang Sri Lankan hookers smuggled into their camp for entertainment. The afternoon following the workers' riot, the trio was ushered into General Zia's office along with other colleagues. They were briefed and told to make the journey to Musaffah, driving top-secret cargo into the desert where waiting workers would unload the trucks' contents and destroy the seeds in a massive bonfire. The three men were paid six hundred dirhams each, a princely sum for a day's work. They also decided to keep one crate a piece. Why? Vimto had a plan.

Vimto's old schoolmate, Mukundan, had worked at Sultan Mo-Mo's palace as an electrician for five months, and over a plate of chicken biryani and Kingfisher beer one Friday night told Vimto he thought the sultan would be willing to do anything to ruin Dubai: "Because of its proximity to Dubai, people don't even know Mo-Mo's country exists. He's embarrassed." Vimto asked Pinto and Tinto if they wanted to make a little extra money.

JULY 16, 2006

11:00 a.m.

"What will you do with all this wealth?" a beaming sultan asked the three men.

"Purchase bling from Gold Souk. Then leave. Start a business back home, stay indoors, wipe the sun off my face" grinned Pinto, his knees rattling.

"I have four girls, another baby's on the way, Your Excellency. Must talk to wife, make plans," confessed Tinto. He felt embarrassed, thinking the sultan had caught him staring at those famous eyebrows.

"See Yourope, Disneyland" shared Vimto. "Taste women," he whispered in Malayalam to his mates. "Bathe the first-born, hold him." Vimto also admitted to his friends a turquoise yacht was on top of his wish list.

"Half the money's here, gentlemen, wiring the rest, my staff will take care of the extra crates you have for me," concluded the sultan, gesturing with a wave of his fat right palm that there was nothing left to discuss. "Rahmat will drive you. Rahmat!"

As the men bid adieu, joined by his chauffeur Rahmat, Mo-Mo thought about the future. He recalled with glee Able Ali's face when he walked into the greenhouse a few days ago, almost a month after the trio's visit. Maturing laborers hung from plant stalks like napping bats. Two weeks prior, the sultan

53

had watched larvae poke their little bodies out of the soil, before inching up fifteen-foot plant stalks like pudgy worms, a two-day climb only the fittest could complete. Mo-Mo told Able Ali how he would wait for every seed to mature and then have his men smuggle the MALLUS in batches to the heart of Dubai, where they would set them free to roam undetected. To fester. "Mallu Landoo," His Excellency purred, "let's help them get it."

Now if only Rahmat would hurry up with the special stuff he got from his Pashtun dealer—hash smuggled through the Af-ghan-Iran border on stoned donkeys. But he had requested that Rahmat take the new highway that had just been built, the one that bisected the desert, and then make a detour. Towards Rub' al Khali, the Empty Quarter. Rahmat had special instructions and would be late. Mo-Mo would wait. No longer would any of the palaces stink of petrol.

6:00 p.m.

Rahmat drives the happy trio over the new highway. Balkan music turned up high. Goran Bregović in total command over his or-chestra. Trumpets, accordion, two-headed drums, Bulgarian chorus. Rahmat, singing along, channeling Roma blood. His pas-sengers join in. They turn into an impromptu quartet, singing:

Gas, gas
gas, gas, GAS
Allo allo eh
ritam ritam
allo allo eh sexi ritam!

Windows rolled down, voices bouncing off dunes. The rum-gold Toyota Land Cruiser heads towards the Rub' al Khali, the Empty Quarter, the greatest of the sand deserts. Rahmat's driving keeps time to the orchestra's manic pace, until he detours, driving into the desert itself at top speed, startling the men. Rum-gold Land Cruiser trampolines! Like off-roaders at Dakar.

The men protest, but Rahmat drives on. By now, Bregović's Balkans have gone bonkers. The stereo explodes. Rahmat goes ballistic. "Ka-lash-nee-kov, Ka-lash-nee-kov, Ka-lash..." he sings. Driving another fifteen minutes, he brakes suddenly, turning off the ignition. Then stepping outside, he begins releasing air from the tires, in order to climb and descend dunes safely, he explains. In the men's presence, Land Cruiser mutates into Off-Road Beast.

He then turns towards the nervy trio. "Seen the sun set over dunes?"

JULY 18, 2006

Tinto and Vimto have hours left to live. They walk aimlessly, past terrain British explorer Wilfred Thesiger discovered during his crossing of the Empty Quarter. Twice. "Umbarak," the Bedu christened the tall Brit. Timto and Vimto could use a bit of help from the Bedu. Any of Umbarak's trusted companions, young Salim bin Ghabaisha or Salim bin Kabina, would do. Both handsome, long-maned, worthy travelers. Guides. Tinto and Vimto need guides.

Rahmat had spiked their refreshments. When they woke, the 4x4 was gone. He didn't take all the money. He left half, in case they survived. He also left behind a roast chicken, which a fox would steal, a watermelon now populated by flies, and two liters of water. By twilight the water was gone. Pinto couldn't help it. He was thirsty; he finished the water as his friends slept. A fight ensued, and Pinto separated from the duo.

Pinto was nearing death when he spotted a herd of grazing camels. Milk, he knew, milk! Desperate to feed, he tried approaching a nursing she-camel. She refused. Frustrated, he kicked the resting mother. The animal bit his kneecap off, then kicked him in the head.

55

For a day or two, Pinto had money to his name. He had danced the hora atop a Land Cruiser with a stoned Rahmat. Bregović's orchestra blared proud and loud. Friends Vimto and Tinto drank beer, singing along:

Sa O Roma babo babo
Sa O Roma o daje
Sa O Roma babo babo
Edelrezi, EDELREZI
Sao o Roma daje...

They sang as the sun went to sleep. Swallowed by dunes. Temperature switching from hot to cold. Warming hands over wild bright fire.

The camel herder buried Pinto in the sands. Then recited the prayer for the dead. The sky turned to cinder.

*

Vimto collapsed first. They, on Tinto's insistence, had taken off their shoes, wrapped their shirts around their heads, but there was no food to be found, no water. The watermelon had been eaten.

Tinto saw the rust-colored structures then—dots in the sand, some movement. People? He started to run, then, exhausted, began to crawl. "Here!" he yelled, "here!" The dots ran towards him. The dots were speaking. Oak-dark men, five-foot-seven, hung upside down when little. The dots brought water.

The Commander was tucking into dinner when Chandu interrupted him.

"Problem?"

"On patrol, sir, we found two men."

"So?"

"Drivers, they assisted burning consignments last month."

"They told you this?"

"Recognized them, I was there. Salvage Ops."

"They are here now?"

"Yes."

"Why?"

"Platoon thought they were us."

"And?"

"No."

"Sure?"

"Yes."

"They participated? In burning any of us? Executions?"

"Just ferried seeds."

"OK." The Commander started to rise.

"But..."

"Yes?"

"Could be a third person?"

"Missing?"

"Looking."

"Find him."

"We are looking."

"And—"

"What else?"

"We found money."

JULY 19, 2006

As the men recovered in the sick ward, they told similar but different lies. Vimto mentioned a fight. Tinto's story spoke of booze, their morning hangover clouding direction, and the men would only discover each other's version minutes before their meeting with The Commander. But they weren't too concerned.

"Sun muddles the brain," said Vimto. "Right?"

"Agreed," smiled Tinto.

57

They had both judiciously avoided mentioning the sultan or the money.

Vimto ventured out for some air. He observed his surroundings.

Shipping containers lined the land, strung like beads, camouflaged by colors mimicking desert dunes, stacked like cargo, holes punched in to enable circulation, acting as dormitories. Inside, little cities. Inside, grocery stores. Inside, laboratories. Inside, many graves.

Vimto and Tinto were unregistered visitors in an unregistered MALLUS camp, nonexistent on maps, its inhabitants answerable to no one, but Vimto couldn't know any of this. A month ago, a truck was parked near the camp's main square. In the truck bed were burn victims, gunshot-wound sufferers, survivors. Lying next to them were five singed crates, the last of the lot, with three hundred seeds per crate. Not all viable to plant. Another truck was parked away from the campsite. There, volunteers washed bodies, others they wrapped in shroud. Pieces went into bags. Before they brought the dead over to the main square. Where some were buried, others burnt over palm fronds. For days, the prayers for the dead tore holes in the wind.

"What are you building here?" Vimto had asked Chandu, one of his rescuers.

"Dreams," Chandu quipped, laughing.

Vimto laughed, too. "But no, seriously."

"Seriously?"

"Yeah."

"A game reserve for hyenas."

"Seriously?"

"Seriously."

*

The Commander rose, adjusted his shirtsleeves, and checked for stains.

"Sir?"

"Yes?"

"Orders..."

"Well, they know, don't they?"

"I—"

"They've seen the operation?"

"Possibly."

"Leaves us little choice. Fix it."

"I said we were saving hyenas."

"Hyenas? Ah, Senegalese! They buy that?"

"Maybe, maybe not."

"They leave, people find out, can't have that—"

"The money—"

"Ours now. Invest."

As The Commander rose, his frame obscured a fading color photograph given a place of prominence in the office. A bald mustachioed man faced the camera, his hand resting on a little girl's shoulder. The man was average looking, in gardening attire. On his shirt lapel was stenciled his name, Moosa Kutty. Behind him were plant stalks balancing little brown babies hanging upside down like napping bats. A sign in the foreground said "BATCH 24, July 2003."

The sun steamed the morning sky. Out of the corner of his eye, Vimto spotted The Commander. Chandu was with him. So the requested meeting had been arranged. The rescued men wanted to thank The Commander in person for the camp's hospitality. They didn't want their rescuers to get in trouble with management, whom they hadn't seen yet. They also wanted to know when they could expect to get on the next bus to the city. And Vimto toyed with the idea of asking The Commander why this labor camp looked older than others, worse than any Vimto had been in, and why the men seemed unperturbed to be housed inside shipping containers.

Vimto nudged Tinto, who had recovered and joined him outside, cheese-sandwich crumbs sticking to his mustache. They both waved.

CHABTER EIGHT

LE MUSÉE

Ba, now Chief, no longer rebel, observed the din his men had caused. Homes smoldered, parted female legs ceased kicking in the fields. Dogs ate dogs, dogs ate horses. A defeated nude leader hung from a rotting banyan tree.

This, Ba knew, was war. And war was not meant to be beautiful. His people had won, and Ba allowed his men to enjoy the spoils of battle. He was a wise man and understood the merits of celebration, but what Ba truly yearned for was his army's triumph to live on after his passing.

"Go amidst the vanquished," Ba commanded his most trusted lieutenant. "Seek eleven, the finest eleven among the hundreds left of this tribe. Choose four fine men, choose them for their youth. The men need mates. Find three proud dames, prized for their intellect and their beauty. When this has been done, seek three infants, two girls and a boy. Finally, snatch an old warrior with a wrinkled neck, bald like the fowl circling above. Bathe them all after you find them, dress them in clean attire, then bring them to me."

Ba then ordered four good homes to be built next to each other, some land to grow crop, circled by stone fences, near what would be his palace grounds. "Practical, not gaudy dwellings," he cautioned. Three of the new homes would house one man, his chosen woman, and an infant. The fourth home would house the young man Ba would select to look after the old warrior. When the eleven had been found, bathed, clothed, they were sent to his chambers.

"I want you to live as you would live if we weren't here," Ba addressed them. "Live as a family, as neighbors, continue your customs, but within the confines of your homes. If you plot your escape, I promise you, we will find you."

Ba explained the other rules. They were to be given produce (some seeds to encourage self-reliance) and livestock, which they would use to cook, grow their own food, but they would not be permitted weapons. Their homes would also be devoid of privacy. His subjects, he told the assembled eleven, would be permitted to observe the vanquished living their lives by peering through windows, or inviting themselves in "whenever the need arises to watch you, to smell you, to observe how you speak, how you bake bread, and to be there when you die." In a week, these people had a name: "Les Exposés". And soon, sentries would be posted to control the house visits, unannounced or otherwise.

Ba also announced a decree, hammered onto a stone totem outside palace premises in the village square: "Here, the vanquished! Guarantee them respect until Death arrives riding his black bull. Bring children. 'Observe their ways!' tell them. 'Bring your own children here,' tell them. Then tell these young bloods, 'Remember the enemy, remember what our warriors did.' Before Death arrives atop that black bull."

The eleven listened to Ba's pronouncements. Then the old man came forward. "And if we refuse, Lord Ba, what then?"

"If you refuse," Ba told him calmly, "let me tell you
what will happen."

—"LE MUSÉE" EXCERPT, FIRDOSF MOOSA
(TRANSLATED FROM THE FRENCH)

I

About Father, little to tell. When he lived, he worked as a scientist for a government-owned company that manufactured
people in the Gulf, one of the first produce firms to do it right
on petrol-infested soil. But Father's dead. What he was, how
he smelled, walked, moved—hard to recall. Suppressed somewhere in the folds of my brain. I loved him dearly. One day he
disappeared. To remember his face now, I require photographs.

I must have been eight.

Father's running an important errand, Mother ("Amma,"
henceforth) said at first. Gone, she corrected a few weeks later.
Then six months to the day after Father's disappearance, us
subsisting in Uncle's house (nervy adults sleeping, or bickering, by the telephone), Amma sat me down as I crunched corn-
flakes for breakfast: Dead, she confirmed, for weeks now. Year?
2007. Month? December. Day? When Romania eliminated the
Ceaușescus.

I went numb. The milk tasted sour. In a week, we boarded
a plane for Kerala, no dead body, no belongings, no plan. That
was twenty or thirty years ago. Amma's been long dead. And
then, last week, a message arrived, in the mouth of that man
with the overbite.

Yes? I said, impatient to get back to work. He didn't say much
at first, only repeating my name, confirming the woman who
opened the door was indeed Sabeen. Which would be me.

Can I help you? is what I asked.

Private investigator, Madam, I have something for you, he said, flashing ID, showing himself in, then handing me an envelope. Inside was a piece of paper, with two words underlined in ballpoint cursive, a rarity these days: *Moosa's Mouse.*

Miss Sabeen, right? Writer Sabeen? Writer Sabeen, of Brooklyn fame? Overbite repeated.

Yes, I confirmed again. I avoided photographs; the book jackets never featured any.

Then he asked me if "Moosa's Mouse" was a term I had heard before.

Yes, I know it, I told him, a while—

Arabic coffee would be super, Overbite interjected. Beaming.

*

You know it because? Overbite probed, sipping lukewarm tap water. By now, I was livid.

Uncle Salman used to call me that, I said somewhat curtly, when I was little. They were friends, Father and Uncle Salman. Back in the day, in Abu Dhabi. Then Uncle Salman ratted him out to ministry intelligence. Accused Father of sedition, Amma confessed in my teens, so ministry goons came for Father. I was in school, Amma was home. They took him, Amma said, then I guess after a week, without informing us, executed him. All public record.

Apologies, offered Overbite.

Amma died last year, I digressed. What's this about?

Overbite, unperturbed, burrowed for details, fingering his cleft chin. In touch with Uncle Salman since?

Listen, Mister, I told him, it was after Father's murder. Maybe six, seven years later. Uncle Salman and a bunch of top Emirati officials, along with their wives, mistresses, and children, were abducted from their homes; the ministry looked for them, I mean, *really* looked for them. Nothing came out of the searches. They didn't even find bones, a drop of blood. Almost seven families gone! The rebel workers called what they did retribution, but even after the failed coup attempt, the insistence on the creation of Mallu Landoo, its discovery, bombing, and annihilation by the defense forces, the war, the death of their leader, The Commander. Even after all that mayhem, they still didn't find them; I know because ministry men came for Amma when they took Uncle Salman, questioned her in front of me. We survived the barrage. Who sent you again? The ministry? Look—

Overbite excused himself. To pee?

Down the corridor, to your left, I said. Flush twice!

*

I lit up, inhaled, recalling Amma's and my surprise at finding ministry men in our tiny paying-guest flat the week Uncle Salman disappeared—us bothering no one in Pondicherry, Amma apprenticing at a French patisserie, us listed under Amma's middle name, "Sanam." They still found us!

I exhaled. Then I recalled The Commander's public execution. We watched it on bootleg, Amma and I, even though the ministry banned unauthorized videotaping.

Then there were the photographs in the papers. Proof the man was gone, that in his last moments he had bitten off his tongue, even soiled himself. They denied him everything, a bath, a shave; he died resembling a bum.

Headlines back then reveled in The Commander's defeat: "Modern-Day Guevara Hangs!" mentioned *Al Khabr*; "Victorious! Conflict Put to Rest After Commander's Execution" trumpeted *Gulf Times*. A friend sent Amma cut-outs, which she preserved. Why, I was never sure.

Who would have thought?! In the Khaleej, where Allah's teachings were first orally told, no one.

Shipping containers in the middle of the desert, a little city populated by renegade laborers and runaways. An army fueled by rage, propelled by the charisma of one man, The Commander. Who would have thought they would have endured for so long?! No one.

The scale of the rebels' enterprise boggled the world: greenhouses, a commercial square, a functioning police force, a munitions factory, a movie theater, mosques/temples/churches built out of packed mud, underground tunnels to every emirate (and even Oman!), and a whorehouse. *This*, all of this, in the desert, in the Empty Quarter. But what astounded ministry intelligence was the presence of a national anthem, a flag, as well as an in-progress constitution. The rebels were in the process of making a country. Before—

Overbite emerged from the bathroom, wringing wet palms, dabbing his mustache with tissue. Two months ago, he said, in a little Indian town called Irinjalakuda, a man with old Gulf Return connections bought a house.

People buy houses all the time, I told him.

Business minded, Overbite continued, this fellow planned to tear the place down since it was somewhat run down. It was one of those nineties-style Gulf properties: BIG, a five-bathroom, five-bedroom enterprise, unoccupied—

So? I interjected, exhaling curlicued smoke.

If I may, Overbite insisted, before contracted laborers wreck such houses, they do a once-over.

Meaning? I mumbled.

Strip its timber, doors, iron bars; they take everything: circuit boards, wires, even soap from the bathrooms, and abandoned pups, which they resell. Then they check to see if the owners forgot or misplaced valuables. It happens. Loot equals profit, split sixty-forty between the laborers and their immediate bosses. Some of these houses have trapdoors, safes, cash taped to the backsides of faux walls. In some Malayalee's house in Allapey in the eighties, workers—allegedly, of course—found a beam of solid gold ensconced inside a hollowed-out teak pillar. You never know—

I reminded Overbite his ministry banter was wasting my fucking time. Afternoons I need to write, I told him.

Ministry doesn't give a shit, he barked, not involved. Besides, I work solo.

That house in Irinjalakuda, Overbite continued, had a cellar, where they found an iron door, painted to look like rock, enough tonnage to require four men. Solid, solid, solid. It couldn't be budged, Miss Sabeen. No key in sight, but even a fool could tell picking that lock required a master locksmith; they needed old-school knowhow. But little to be done; you see, they were on deadline, so they went about their business acting all cool. But at night, spawns of Shaytaan, they snuck back in to try their luck. Armed with homemade dynamite and sledgehammers, they went at that door for hours. Only to dent it somewhat. So they took a break, drank arrack, told stories—

LOOK, I—

LISTEN! The fools then fell asleep right there, worn out. In their line of work, discretion was prized, as was loyalty. But in the morning, sober now, the men thought they heard noises, screeching or hissing they reported. Scavenging for treasure in homes bereft of life breeds tales rife with jinns, so, troubled and hungover, they confessed. Boss, they told their boss, the house is haunted.

Mister—

It was a stroke of luck, actually, Overbite carried on. Cats in heat were fooling around nearby, he guffawed, but the men couldn't have known that. So their boss called the police. Sixteen hours later, they were inside this this this house within a house. How? W'allah I swear, Miss Sabeen: They hauled in a seventeenth-century Portuguese cannon, owned by the police superintendent's in-law, a collector of historical paraphernalia and munitions. They used that thing to bust open that door. The device fired three times, producing a hole big enough for a small man to crawl through. Inside—

People? Bound and gagged, too, I interrupted, annoyed. Maybe dead. Treasure?

Yes, people, Miss Sabeen, remnants of people. No trafficking den, this place. Something different.

Different?

Folks in Indian intelligence on our payroll had confirmed with ministry intelligence the house was a safe house purchased by The Commander's abductions unit. They had been using it for years. The rebels' benefactors held meetings there, fundraised, continuing to do so after The Commander's execution, but that wasn't what made the discovery interesting. The police found prisoners' quarters, five rooms. The furniture was sparse—a double bed, a table, a chair—but the rooms were barricaded by locks, reinforced concrete bars, and an alarm system. There were clear traces, ministry intelligence confirms, of a museum-like setting: photographs, recordings, journals, pamphlets, installations.

The Commander's been dead for over two decades, I reiterated.

Yes, Overbite confirmed.

But the house—

Active, I assure you, very active, folks were housed there long after the property deeds changed hands; people were moved maybe a month before the scheduled demolition. Also, the cellar held Displays.

Displays! Le Musée is a myth, I insisted, a rumor produced by war. Someone's pulling another Shabab.

Yes, said Overbite, no evidence, no photographs. So. A myth. The Mid East's Nessie. Until now Displays only existed in your mother's novella—the one you inferred, Le Musée—and the late Shabab's contested testimony in the Al Jazeera tell-all. But another live one got left behind, Ms. Sabeen.

Can't be, I said. In Le Musée, in Amma's novella, they all perished in the end, after living as reminders for many years.

Anyway, why come here? You think—

Didn't you hear me? Overbite interrupted again.

I did, I repeated.

They didn't leave a dead body, Miss Sabeen. The man they left behind lives; he grew old in prison.

Can't be, I said again, but less convincingly this time. So Shabab didn't lie?

The man who was rescued knows you, wishes to speak to you, Miss Sabeen.

Me?

Sheikh Salman's somewhat gaunt now, Miss Sabeen. Lived as a Display for two decades. In your Amma's French, it sounds more sinister, no? Les Exposés! But Allah is merciful, the sheikh's alive. He employed me to find you. Hello, Mouse, he wanted me to tell you, Ahlan Wa Sahlan.

Please, I begged Overbite, stop talking. The man killed my father.

II

On the plane, I dozed. Amma invaded my dreams. As did Uncle Salman. And Father. When I woke, I asked for some wine, then wondered why Sae Hoon had made such a fuss about my departure, why she implied I had intended to sabotage our planned trip to visit her little nephew, that I always did this when stuff mattered, that both of us were expected to be there.

Why go? she begged. Who is this man?

I am not sure, is what I said, answering both questions.

All this because of some mediocre tale your mother wrote, she spat.

Some mediocre tale? I asked Sae Hoon right back. She didn't know; she refused to elaborate.

Amma published *Le Musée* in five parts, a decade or so after Father's death, in a reputed Malayalam literary journal, the now defunct *Gulf Vaartha*. Originally published in French, which Amma began to learn during our stint in Pondicherry, she translated it into English quickly, after which it was translated into Malayalam by the much-praised writer and translator Sudha, because Amma's written Malayalam was so-so.

While lauded in Paris, some Malayalee critics in India dubbed Le Musée a work of adolescent dystopia, a revenge-fantasy by "a mildly skilled tyro," but they recognized its intent; "Beware," noted critic Partha wrote in *The Hindu*, "because of what happened to this woman, the murder of her husband, the dislocation of self and child, what we have here is a warning, expressed as fictive literary revenge." When the English version came out in paperback, Amma's Parisian agent sent a copy to the *Times*. No one was interested.

In *Le Musée*, a disenchanted laborer leads a revolt against a village chief in a Francophone land Amma refuses to name. The chief is vanquished; his subjects are terrified. The culling is expected, but it is meticulous; every day, for a week, from noon to twilight, one hundred are put to death, then the extermination stops, and the forced assimilation begins.

But the laborer Ba, Chief now, wants this moment preserved for posterity, so he orders his soldiers to create, then manage, a readymade village within a village. Among the prisoners he has a trusted lieutenant handpick eleven based on gender and age. Ba gives his project a name: Le Musée, where inhabitants would be under 24/7 surveillance.

By Ba's mandate, Le Musée residents would be provided provisions for six months, and seeds for crop; if the harvests were kind, these would keep them alive for years, enough time for the victors to observe the vanquished, to examine up close the people they had conquered, to watch them, to smell them, to notice how they spoke, how they baked bread, and to be there when they died.

Ba named the people of Le Musée. He called them Les Exposés. In English, Amma clumsily translated this term to "The Shown."

In the original story, the laborer Ba tells the handpicked lot if they refused to comply, he would order his men to find the most beautiful boy and girl in the village, then slice away one body part with a butcher's blade daily. They decide to test his bluff. The boy loses his nose, the girl, a breast, but when the blade begins slicing their tongues on the second day, the assembled eleven cease being obstreperous. They comply.

The publication of Le Musée did not bring Amma fame, but respect filtered through. She never wrote another work of fiction. However, back in the Emirates, as the conflict between the defense forces and the rebels grew, the death tolls on both sides getting worse, the rebels began abducting Emiratis/Locals and expats in order to use them as leverage. Then the abductions became quite frequent—almost out of control.

Folks started hiring bodyguards. In the beginning, it was thought people were being held ransom for money, but then one February when the rains were unusually harsh, an abductee escaped. His story made the papers. There was a television interview. What he said disturbed everybody, but I was especially troubled by Amma's reaction. Finally, she said, about time.

*

To protect the escapee's identity, the papers gave the man an alias: Shabab. On TV, Al Jazeera doctored everything—his face, voice, shape.

In Shabab's words, the rebels began by bartering the hostages for ransom, even buying negotiation time. However, it soon became evident the abductions were a show of strength or intent. And by the time Shabab was kidnapped along with his sister in the late aughts, the kidnappings fulfilled a particular clause in the rebels' manifesto.

At this point in the televised interview, the interviewer leaned forward. Clause? he said. The camera panned towards Shabab's pixelated face.

Clause? the interviewer said again.

A sigh escaped pixelated lips. Shabab began.

The rebels, Shabab insisted, were now busy collecting living evidence. The Commander, Shabab said, was convinced victory was close, so he wanted keepsakes: Locals. *Living* war trophies. But he also wanted to *do* something to these people, Shabab warned the camera, right before the interview took a break to make way for ads.

The Commander wanted his trophies to perform for him, Shabab said a guard told him, to perform for future generations.

Many years ago, the guard had told Shabab, a wealthy bene-factor gifted The Commander a copy of Firdose Moosa's *Le Musée*. The work became an inspiration, and the fictional Ba a kindred spirit.

Shabab's testimony, at the time, appeared quite credible. For over two months, reporters called Amma every day. No com-ment, she muttered, no comment. Smiled as she hung up.

The rebels, under The Commander's directive, Shabab had said, butchered sacred ties when they abducted entire families.

They separated husbands and wives and brothers and sis-ters, roomed one stranger (a man) with another stranger (a woman) and spouses with acquaintances, and then waited. Years, in fact. As strangers interacted, turning into friends, enemies, and others, the perils of being human, of needing physical contact or any contact at all, intervened. New bonds formed.

No contact, visual or otherwise, was permitted or provided between groups. Parents and siblings never saw each other again, so the only constants for the abducted Locals were their roommates.

Over time, habits were known. They could identify each other's smells, they looked for each other in the morning, reached for each other at night. There were consequences. Some friends became lovers or stand-ins for missing spouses. Sleeping "arrangements" turned into pregnancies and teens became fathers and mothers. The newborns were raised behind bars, but also in open court.

The rebels, Shabab insisted, were permitted to watch, to come whenever they pleased.

In The Commander's eyes, the abducted Emiratis/Locals would symbolize a difficult past and why war had been necessary. When victory became imminent, The Commander would borrow Amma's idea. First, he would inform the prisoners they wouldn't be released as a sign of goodwill. Then, copying *Le Musée*, he would provide provisions for six months and wait.

In The Commander's vision of the future nation of Mallu Landoo, if residents wished to explore how the imprisoned Emiratis/Locals behaved, they could rent surveillance tapes, or come in person to observe how Emiratis/Locals walked, prayed, talked, sat, ate, shat.

Like Amma, The Commander named these people; he stole the Malayalee word the translator Sudha used in the Malayalam version of the novella.

But a problem arose. Somehow two reporters, a lady from *The Guardian* and a man from *Der Spiegel* got wind of The Commander's scheme and requested a meeting. He wouldn't oblige. Then they tried contacting the rebel's press secretary, and he told them both that yes, people had been abducted, yes, they were safe, and would be released once the war had ended, but no, they weren't being treated like animals in a zoo. But do you have a special name for these people? the *Der Spiegel* man probed. No, said the press secretary, they are just prisoners of war. It was a lie. The Commander knew all about the power of media attention, and he was prepared to acknowledge the existence of such a project to convey the seriousness of his intentions. But he anticipated a problem. The Western press consistently mispronounced foreign names, which infuriated The Commander, but he didn't want to borrow the term favored by Amma in her English translation. Instead, he decided the Locals that his rebels had begun abducting/collecting deserved a more Anglicized, press-friendly name. Thus was born The Displayed, or Displays.

When Shabab disclosed on live television what he had lived as for many years—a Display!— The Commander's notion was proven right. The name, in the press' hands, became a sensation.

Then something happened. Shabab's kidnapped sister was discovered at a bus station a month later a few hundred kilometers from Petra. In recovery, Fatima (her real name) insisted Shabab had lied. They had been kidnapped, though not by rebels, and they certainly weren't called anything or put on display. But yes, her brother was obsessed with Firdose Moosa's book. He needed help, she said, help him please!

Fatima's testimony exposed Shabab's real name. The reaction was mixed. Protests erupted outside his residence. Trauma put ideas in Shabab's head, some said. Many called him a liar. The conspiracy theorists stood by him. Others didn't give a shit.

Shabab refused to retract his claims. Sister's lying. She's frightened, he added.

Six months after his sister's public testimony, Shabab wrote a letter to his wife, then took some pills. His suicide note has never been made public. The family shared but a phrase. He said sorry, his tearful baba informed the press, sorry. Fatima jumped off her apartment's balcony the following year.

III

We were at Uncle Salman's house, in the city where I was raised. In two decades, the city was transformed. Nothing I remembered remained.

We sat across from each other. Indian incense made the room smell of Mysore. Imprisoned, once-charismatic Uncle Salman's physique resembled a dry tea biscuit's. Almost hairless on top. Fidgety. The dates stayed untouched. Jaffa oranges shone like the sun. I sipped black tea. Just talk, I said finally.

As Displays, Uncle Salman confessed, the rebels forced him to share a cell with his brother's wife. I begged them, he said, begged them to have us switch partners.

One bed, he recalled. Slept on the floor. Days, maybe weeks. I respected Souad, never touched her, undressed with my back turned. One room, you see. Until—

I listened. Polite. Disgusted. Curious. Uncle Salman betrayed Father, but I was obliged to hear him out. And to ask about Father, the last days.

You don't see it coming, he said.

Of course you don't, I replied. The phrase dripping with acid.

Souad got pregnant, Uncle Salman whispered. Tried to kill the baby. Almost succeeded.

A child, why? I asked.

It is important to live, Uncle Salman snapped, running his palm across wisps of hair. Believe me, Sabeen, we loved each other when we made that baby.

You stuck your cock in your brother's woman, I reminded him.

Uncle Salman watched me. Sneered. One night, he said, a guard came up to my cell and played me a recording.

BBC Radio? I laughed dryly.

Lovemaking, Sabeen. I recognized my wife. We had been abducted together. It was OK. We had all moved on.

75

Uncle Salman lit a cigarette.

You fucked your brother's wife, I said.

He slapped me. I slapped him back.

And my wife fucked her cousin, he retorted.

I refused to respond.

Look, he continued, Souad woke one night and began hitting her belly. I stopped her, consoled her. We had the child. But she couldn't look at the baby. I begged her to breastfeed the boy. She refused. The morning I caught her trying to smother him, I—

It's easy to kill, isn't it?

Uncle Salman steeled himself. I needed to protect my baby boy, he said.

You rape her, then want her to have the kid!

NO! I loved Souad. That night I calmed her down. She was crying. Then I held her for a long time. I used a shoelace, I put her out of her misery. The guards watched me do it. No one said a word.

Brute. I said it softly. Brute, I said again.

Perhaps, he concurred, but there are other things to address. The reason you came.

Your man said you would explain Father's death—the truth, I told him.

Yes.

I paused. In return? I asked. In return, what do you want?

Uncle Salman pointed to a folder on the table. Look inside, he said.

I did, and saw an amateur hand-drawn portrait of a young boy. Early teens.

My boy Majid, Uncle Salman explained. I made that myself.

My role was still unclear, so I probed again.

I know your work, Sabeen, Uncle Salman shared. People respect it. More gifted than your Amma, I think. Write an op-ed, pitch a story. Anything. Everyone knows who you are. Tell the boy his father loves him. Urge them to give him back, or let me return.

Them? Return?

The Commander may be dead, he said, but the rebels aren't finished. They chose to leave me behind. They took the others.

Why?

I don't know, he said, maybe they figured I would only die in there. I don't know. They took my boy, I raised him. Taught him to walk, speak. My world's empty, Sabeen. I am in limbo. I am in a country I don't know anymore.

Return? I reminded him.

If the boy's too precious, maybe they could take me back.

I watched Uncle Salman. He seemed lucid. I watched him light another cigarette. Observed what the nicotine had done to his teeth, and realized I didn't care what happened to his son, or what happened to him, or what he thought. He sensed it too, I think, so changed the topic. Became more business-like.

What do you know about your father, Moosa? he asked.

Worked in a produce firm, I said.

Uncle Salman nodded. Yes. Doing what, you know? Produce firms are complex places.

Father grew laborers, I said. Produce firms produce laborers. Satisfied?

That's right, Uncle Salman confirmed. Moosa grew people out of the soil. He was the best, your father. All clandestine, of course. The UN wouldn't have approved. It's not like now, when growing workers is legal. Italy growing Punjabi farmers to make parmesan or New York State contracting the island of Trinidad to produce cabbies. Moosa was my time's Doctor Frankenstein. But his creations walked, spoke, worked, obeyed like regular human beings, like you and me. When the whole stupid world was only interested in robots, your father made people. Trouble-free labor, your father made. Better than the shit China hawks nowadays, I am told.

Amma said he tried to doctor the formula, I said, that he wanted to give the laborers autonomy.

Uncle Salman laughed. Moosa was many things, Sabeen, but he wasn't noble.

Father got bored was what Amma told me, I said. Once he perfected the formula, he got bored overseeing the production of laborers, was what Amma said, I said.

Moosa was always a fucking scientist, Uncle Salman laughed, not a factory supervisor, Sabeen, so he started tinkering.

Amma said Father was interested in experiments, I told Uncle Salman, then secretly produced a series of special laborers, whatever that meant.

Uncle Salman put his legs on the coffee table, looking a bit grave. Then he chuckled again. Moosa realized, he said, that produce-firm labor followed orders well, but didn't have a ringleader and rarely elected one. So he produced a batch of labor leaders, training them somehow. His goal was to improve efficiency; group leaders would do that. Then he became convinced increasing labor life span would save money.

They lived for how long normally?

Labor?

Yes.

Oh, eight, maybe ten years, Uncle Salman recalled.

Father changed that? Right?

Uncle Salman paused, ate a date. You know what he did, Sabeen? He advocated letting them die of old age. Like the rest of us.

I had started taking notes. Out of habit. So how did they die before? I queried.

Sabeen, Moosa programmed the laborers to follow orders. Every eight to ten years, factories would load these men in trucks. The trucks would drive to the desert. And that was that.

What was what?

They would leave them there, Sabeen.

In the desert?

In the desert.

I don't believe you, I told Uncle Salman.

I don't really care, Sabeen. Moosa didn't either. He made mistakes, your father. Producing and training leaders without authorization was his first. Lobbying for increased lifespans was his second. So—

SO? I challenged.

So, Moosa's nonsense produced The Commander. Became the catalyst for war. By then—

INJUSTICE produced The Commander! I yelled, Father assisted!

Sabeen, Uncle Salman countered, Moosa was bored. Certainly no activist. He was tinkering. EVERYTHING since, the wars, the abductions, products of tinkering. Know what he did when we found out?

I made a face.

He begged, Sabeen, promised to exterminate them all. Make the laborers more pliant. Set an example, he said.

You ratted him out?

I had to. Couldn't let the ministry think I was involved. Moosa and me were too close.

Opportunist!

His end was near, Sabeen. I made sure it was quick.

Was it? I asked.

Quick? Yes.

Did he scream?

Sabeen.

Did he?!

Yes.

He asked for me?

No, Sabeen.

Last words for Amma? Anyone?

No, Sabeen, he wept. Only wept.

I stood up, walked towards the man. Spat in his face. Slapped him until my palm stung. What are you? I remember screaming. You enter your sister-in-law, murder your friend!

Sabeen, he said, almost kneeling my spittle dripping off his chin. The boy Majid, please help find the boy.

Why?

THE ENDING! Sabeen, tell me you haven't forgotten the story's: in *Le Musée*, nothing survives.

I remembered the ending, but Uncle Salman surprised me by reciting it. Word for word. As though he had survived his ordeal to remind the world what was bound to happen, begged me to see him to remind me what Amma had destined for his son, how his son would quietly disappear from the annals of history, unnoticed.

My son's real, Sabeen. He exists! Majid exists! Le Musée exists! I need you to tell people he exists, that his father exists—

But I stood up, as Uncle Salman continued speaking, pleading. Sobbing.

I left, walked out the door, as he desperately clawed at my ankles, even threw fruit at me. It didn't matter. I was uninterested. Indifferent. And, for the first time in years, content. Praying desperately that this despicable man would never see his wretched son, and that he would never know if he were dead or alive. But hope he was, and then hope he wasn't. Dying exactly like that—ignorant.

And it is here, dear reader, that I will leave you, with Amma having the last word, recited verbatim by her husband's murderer, watched by her daughter Sabeen, in the city where I was conceived, where once upon a time Father grew people:

> *On the cot was an old woman breathing with extreme effort, the last surviving member of the Le Musée community. Everyone else, gone. Victims of disease, in-fighting, accidents. She had survived, chronicling her memories on sheaves of tree bark. The volumes, bound by twine, arranged by dates, recorded the community's history, its memories.*

If anyone leafed through the journals' pages, stories would emerge. As would names.

The soldiers presented the volumes to Ba's great, great, great grandson after her passing. "What must be done, Lord?"

Ba's descendant had been groomed by the elders to expect this moment. He first ordered the woman to be reburied in an unmarked grave. Then he ordered his soldiers to remove Le Musée tombstones. "Raze the homes," he said, "but first gather up their possessions, everything you can find. Don't forget the animals. Move them all to the main square. Then once the wise men confirm the presence of the next full moon, invite the village to feast."

It wasn't long. On a night when the moon shone so big and bright moonlight turned the waters white, the villagers gathered in the main square.

A bonfire was lit using Le Musée possessions as kindling. The animals were butchered, and then eaten. There was much dancing and rejoicing.

When the party was over, the fire left no trace; even the old woman's journals weren't spared. As though nothing existed, nothing mattered. And where Le Musée once stood lay emptiness on flattened land. Waiting for something new.

It had taken time, but the war was finally over.

—"LE MUSÉE" EXCERPT, FIRDOSE MOOSA
(TRANSLATED FROM THE FRENCH).
RECITED BY UNCLE SALMAN.

photographer: mlakova

CHABTER NINE

AKBAAR: EXODUS

41,282 BROWN MEN AND WOMEN in their sixties, pravasis, every single one of them, will leave the United Arab Emirates in the middle of June. 65 percent of them have lived in the Emirates for over two decades. 18,964 of them will board planes from Abu Dhabi International Airport. All of them were informed of mandatory retirement from their respective companies at the same time.

May 13, a Thursday, will be their last working day. Within weeks, they will be expected by the labor ministry to pack up their lives and leave the country for good.

Among the retirees is Vasudevan and his wife, Devi. They heard a rumor from a trusted source, Devi's cousin, assistant to the big guns at the ministry of labor, who pushes them to cash in, but they make the mistake of sharing the news with friends. Within days, others know, and there is a scramble—in some households, a desperation—to book a ticket for June 15, a Tuesday. Baffled ticket agents make frantic calls, the date's significance a mystery, checking with sister airlines to see if additional flights can be arranged to accommodate this request. Initially, airlines believe someone or a group of pranksters are playing a practical joke, but the phones continue to ring. When it becomes clear that so many people are indeed preparing to return home, upper management gets to work. It will be the largest exodus of brown folk leaving the Emirates since August 1990, when thousands fled after Iraq's invasion of Kuwait, assuming the advent of darker times.

By nightfall, the airlines offer a compromise, begrudgingly accepted. The coveted June 15 departure date is no longer available, even though flights were added, but everyone is assured a flight home by June 22. By then rumors of the exodus hover like foul smog and the alarmed government steps in, as the international press speculates. "The Emirates, especially Abu Dhabi, isn't crumbling," a government spokesman laughs. "Many former residents have decided it is time to retire, that's all; the young get old."

A reporter from the BBC puts the spokesman on the spot, "Our understanding is that many of these men came here in the seventies. Will the government acknowledge their contributions before they leave?"

"A delegate will be there to see them off, yes. Many, I imagine, are as old as my parents. In our home, we see to it that every guest is walked to the door."

The Indian, Pakistani, Sri Lankan, Nepali, and Bangladeshi ambassadors are summoned by their respective consulates and told to be at Abu Dhabi International Airport on June 15. News channels decide to cover the event live. The English dailies, *The National*, *Khaleej Times*, *Gulf News*, and *Gulf Today* assign their reporters related feature pieces.

Vasudevan's last day at work involves tying up loose ends, cleaning out his office cabin , saying his goodbyes to old and recent colleagues. That morning, he asks his superiors whether it might be possible to be granted a six-month extension on his work visa. No, it isn't. His UAE work and residence visas will be canceled in a few weeks, his director tells him gently; his passport must stay with the company until his flight home. The company doesn't wish to be held liable in case Vasudevan absconds and gets caught, his director explains.

Vasudevan understands, but he asks for more time, three months; his house in India is still under construction, he must find temporary accommodation for his family, maybe fly to India to sort things out and come back, is it possible to hold on to his passport? The director grants him two months to get his affairs in order, Vasudevan's passport is returned. If Vasudevan had been allowed to continue, in November, he would have completed his thirty-eighth year with the company. It was not to be. His colleagues throw him a surprise lunch party, offer him a watch with the engraving "Best of Luck In Future Endeavors!" and, drinking Pepsi, toast to a long and prosperous life, Insha'Allah. When Vasudevan leaves work for the last time, he reminds Salim, the beefy security guard from Kabul, to watch over the two feral cats who expect tuna for breakfast. Vasudevan hands Salim a bag of tinned food. "They mew at seven," Vasudevan says, "al-ways at seven." The two shake hands, clasp palms.

Two weeks before the expected exodus, furniture and electronic stores can barely keep up with the clamor for ornate Arab furniture prized in Khaleej and high-tech toys. The Iranian merchants near Mina have their hands full, too—orders for Persian carpets skyrocket. Rumors circulate that high-end stores like Jashanmal and Grand Stores have run out of expensive frankincense and crockery. Many retirees negotiate with shipyards for bargain deals on cargo containers to transport their Emirati possessions. Those who cannot afford steel containers buy cardboard boxes and rope. This Gulf loot will live as reminders in new homes. Merchants talk of a Sikh man looking to smuggle a gazelle, five endangered Houbara bustards, and four tons of red sand to outfit his Jaipur farmhouse.

JUNE 15: ABU DHABI INTERNA-
TIONAL AIRPORT's departure
lounge plays the Emirati,
Indian, Pakistani, Ban-
gladeshi, Sri Lankan, and
Nepali national anthems.
Reporters and camera crews
loiter like animals near a
watering hole. The Emirati
delegate and the ambassadors
are there; speeches are made.
Representatives from the government and the consulates
have been sent to the airports
in Dubai and Sharjah. The
mood is somber. Every passenger shakes hands with the
assembled delegates. There
is a lottery, and one hundred
winners walk away with hand-
stitched Emirati ethnic wear.
A young man attempts to
throw ink at the Emirati delegate and creates a momentary
distraction. He is unsuccessful, and furious policemen
drag him away as he struggles.

Vasudevan is there, and so
is Devi. They look on quietly.
They smell like their apartment. Their empty apartment
smells like them. Old. In July,
their building, one of the
oldest on Hamdan Street,

decrepit like a smoker's lungs,
will be razed. The landowner
sent his tenants a notice six
months ago; they took him to
court and lost.

The dignitaries stay to
watch the first plane take off,
a PIA flight to Islamabad. People applaud. After acknowl-
edging the waiting passengers,
they leave, flanked by vigilant
security.

Vasudevan sits by Devi,
their shoulders touching. Airport chairs bite their backs.

"I heard," an airport staff
member tells an Emirati officer as passengers file through,
"governments in the region
will be surprising expatriates
returning home on June 15
by waiving the customs duty
on taxable merchandise. You
could have a house in your
suitcase. Duty free!"

BOOK

TONGUE. FLESH.

In the dream, they pulled an Arabee
word out of his high-school textbook
and asked him to read the word out
loud. He did. With perfect diction,
they insisted. He obliged. They asked
him, "So what does it mean? What
you read, what does it mean?" He
couldn't say. He stared at the word
hoping it would tell him, make
friends with him, whisper its
meaning, offer some insight, but of
course stuff like that only happens in
the movies, and such movies don't
get made anymore. So he just
repeated the word, over and over
again, because he was afraid and he
was mad and he didn't know what
else to do. They pulled another word
from this textbook, from a different
page this time, and they asked him
to read that, too. So he did, and once
again he didn't know what he was
saying.

—BOY

CHABTER ONE

MUSHTIBUSHI

TO BEGIN:

I am a long-serving responsible adult; a twenty-year veteran in the ministry's employment. I check all the right boxes: I think carefully; I am a family man with a wife and two young daughters; I have a job that bores me, but the work, it gets done.

I am stating the obvious because of a peculiar case I am dealing with right now. I know you are aware of my new off-duty responsibilities, but sometimes reiteration is useful. For the past three years, our street, Hamdan, the city center, has been subject to a series of sexual assaults targeting children. The first year, media coverage was robust, the *Malayala Manorama* scathing in its criticism of the investigation, an op-ed even speculating if the pace would have picked up if an Emirati kid fell victim. Then the writer got his wish, and it was *Al-Itihad*'s turn to scrutinize the non-arrests. Pretty soon, every paper and TV station had a profile of the attacker, sketched by an expert. A member of CNN's crew, in Dubai for some R&R between Iraq–Kuwait action, stumbled upon the story, and ran with it as a filler. The story got play. Regardless, the attacks continued. Gradually, as more children fell victim, these incidents acquired a kind of normality, like high-fructose corn syrup or pubic lice at conferences. The sensationalism waned. Soon after, Stormin Normin bid adieu, Rodney King got kicked, the cameras slunk away. Helpless parents, myself included, had no choice but to accept these attacks as a child's rite of passage. We hoped for the best. When children are the focus in the hue and cry, sanity is hard. I fill the

need for a slap-dash solution. I am not sure how many minis-
try-certified responsible adults reside in our vicinity. Not many,
I wager. Anyway, all I am required to do is show up, sit with the
child, ask questions, take notes, file a report with the shurtha,
who are never on time, and then move on to the next case, when
(or if) it comes. Because of the profligacy of the attacks, several
building's tenants—one plucky parent's idea—formed vigilante
groups, a neighborhood-watch system interested in addressing
suspicious activity. It was a futile endeavor; kids continued to
fall prey, not one person caught. Perhaps, because of their poor
success rate, most vigilante groups disbanded. But in moments
of crisis, after an attack, most buildings turned to a responsible
adult nominated by the tenants. I was chosen.

My notes, I am told by the shurtha and parents alike, are useful. I am good at what I do. I listen well, and I believe children
trust me. I am honest. I remember what it was like to have been
not just young, but little—a child. I don't patronize.

In this particular case, I was called because the mother came
home and discovered the victim reeking of urine, which wouldn't
be unusual given her age, except in this case, pee dripped off the
child's face. The girl's mother informed the shurtha first, then
after reaching her husband at work, she called me. The details
are, well, fuzzy. Normally, the victim, returning from kindergar-
ten, would wait for her mother at the bottom of the stairs so
they could take the elevator together. I think the man at large
asked the victim to stroke his penis, and he may have pulled it
out, no one's certain, but the victim—she's six, born in May—
isn't talking yet. I wasn't sure how to proceed with the interview,
since it was going nowhere, until a tenant in the building, a
friend of the family, mentioned he had seen a girl called Maya
and her brother leaving the building around the time the victim was reportedly whisked into the elevator by the assailant. I
normally don't interview witnesses, leaving that to the shurtha,
but I decided to make an exception in Maya's case. No harm in

indulging the family. Besides, for a little girl—well, little-look-
ing—Maya was, I would discover, blessed with intellect, and a
big bosom. I am writing you to share Maya's story since I will
not be sharing it with the authorities. I do not want to be labeled
a fool. There is something else, a sensitive detail that you will
certainly notice; my final report addresses it, as it must, because
Maya references the incident in her digressions.

Maya, you will read, basically told me she was responsible
for the state the victim was in because she brokered a deal with
a machine, a building elevator she identifies as Mushtibushi.
He must be Japanese, I joked (the building I live in has three
Mitsubishi elevators). I did not ask, she replied curtly. I mulled,
glancing at her chest. In Maya's story, the building's children
regularly supplied this machine, the elevator in the middle, with
kids. If a child didn't volunteer to satisfy Mushtibushi's sexual
kink, they would draw lots and choose one, who would go no
more than once a week. Or, a child in the building might forget,
sauntering in alone when the elevator needed to address his fix.

Maya suggests the current victim was sacrificed to assist Maya's father, who was imbecilic with finances. She and her brother
had to go find money, she said. They had decided to mug someone, a loan shark their father was involved with. I know the
man, their father. Straddled with debt, he will undoubtedly be in
prison before the year's up. If he ends up in one of those places in
the desert we keep hearing about, the ones the ministry insists do
not exist, it will be hard to predict when he might get out.

She spoke in complete sentences, Maya, but in a rhythm I
have never heard before—though it's possible I really don't pay
attention to the sound of my own children, or how they talk,
except when we have our lessons. What you will read isn't bab-
bling. It isn't conversation either. What it is is a communiqué
and the transcript (the text follows my note) is her soliloquy.

I am not allowed to film or record the interviews. Parents
have reputations to protect, rumors to expunge, so by rule rarely

allow it. This I understand. I would do the same. However, I can take notes in shorthand, and these notes are always excellent—almost verbatim. I normally ask a question, wait for an answer, write it down. I may also write how the child is behaving. In Maya's case, I wrote two words, punctuated by periods: *Calm. Hmm.* But as soon as we became acquainted, she began talking. I barely got a word in—a few interjections, sure. But there are a few things to pay attention to in the report. After that, I tried to interrupt now and again, not having understood a particular detail clearly, but usually I failed; perhaps you will understand. When you spot an emboldened **O** it means I jotted down any little tics when she spoke, or thoughts that came to mind as I reread, editing my notes.

The girl understands I cannot submit her unadulterated account to the authorities. What do I say? It is my recommendation that the building decommission one of its Mitsubishi elevators, more specifically, the middle one, because the machine stands accused of sexual impropriety. In fact, after hearing her statement, it is my recommendation that all three Mitsubishi elevators be decommissioned in case the infection the accused machine has is contagious—but how does one word that without feeling stupid?

In this city, where tall tales are birthed by all sorts—all kinds, every minute, seconds—her claim may be the mightiest of all. But I believe her.

My report follows her transcript.

Be well,
D

TRANSCRIPT

[Verbatim. The punctuation is mine]

MAY 5, 1991

We sit opposite each other at a round table. Her parents have left us alone, taking Maya's brother with them. I smell incense, sandalwood. I have been given sweet bun-colored chai and a plate of arrowroot biscuits for dipping. Maya's having Tang.

M: (*extends her hand*): Girlie. Precocious. Twelve, not ten. Soon, thirteen. Me.

D: (*I shake it gently*):Maya, sweetheart, look—

M: Business, luv, let's discuss. Ah, you squirm. Prefer a respectful moniker? Debashish, right? Uncle Debashish? No? If you had been a woman, "Madam"! I would have yelled, then groped your chest, announcing to the world how pert your tits have gotten. Oh, how you stare.

    Exactly!

    I dislike pretending to like you, too, so ditch the formalities, dynamite the baby talk. But, touch me, I bite you. Instead, let's discuss where we are at this stage in our lives, let's mull nuances, but it won't happen, I think. You are bound to say, I will tell you when the time's right, when you are old enough—which in my time, the due time, could be another ten years and change, if I survive childhood. So for now, luv—

D: "Sir," acceptable.

M: Sir? OK. Sir. For now, you wanna tug my cheeks, pull them wide, see some teeth, go ahead; you wanna pat my bum, fine; you wanna cuddle, hug, OK. Go right ahead. Scum. Hurry, though. There's work to be done; loads. I am twelve, the schedule's tight. If your hand must wander, qweek! Us children are busy. And aging fast. But trust me. Touch me, I bite you.

D: About the girl, M—

M: Here's what happened. Our father is a crazy little fool. Brother and I picked him up from the bar last night.

D: Time?

M: When Cinderella's chariot turns back into a squash—then. We tied Father to Henrietta Sivasankar, Brother's stuffed hippo, so Father couldn't run away. Henrietta is chubby. We then tied both of them to the back of our bike, which I pedaled while my brother wobbled like bug antennae on the bike frame, as he kept an eye on our boozed-up father. Brother's six. He assumes my superiority as the older sibling to be a permanent, non-negotiable dynamic. But I can tell he is biding his time. We do agree on the important stuff. We are children, members of the shorter species, and we acknowledge the world is rigged. There are rules to follow, parents to con, school to attend—the prerequisites of adulthood. Sometimes these norms are carefully explained by our caregivers and tested in front of party guests eager to witness developing skill sets in the competition's progeny. Brother and I have a name for these judicious child bearers—Manufacturists. The *m*, capitalized. Normally, Manufacturists comprise of two parents, Mother, Father, the birth makers. Sometimes, because of circumstance, death, divorce, adoption, substance abuse, or choice, a Manufacturist is only one person. This person, respected in some societies, and maligned in others, is the single parent. A single parent can be a mother, the birth giver, or the father, the birth causer. Usually, sex has occurred. Another scenario upends this argument. Here sex doesn't occur. The plot involves agencies in India, hospitals loaning out wombs, healthy mothers attached like tails. What's the technical term for this? Don't prompt me, thinking out loud here. So something. Sor, soor, sur. . . ah, s-u-r-r-o-w-g-u-t. [**O**: *Maya spells it out, beams.*] That's it!

D: Please continue.

M: Brother and I posit that most Manufacturists beget the first-born for want of a test subject and casually beget the rest to keep the first mistake company. Brother and I are not naive. Soon, we will turncoat into adults ourselves. After all, we were manufactured and product tested, too. Here, in Hamdan. Both born at Corniche Hospital. But Brother and I have decided to fight for a while before the mutation. We've written lyrics.

[**O**: *Maya jumps on the table. She lifts her knees, up-down, up-down. She marches.*]

> *And what a fight t'will be*
> *woe, some glee*
> *let's dupe our destiny*

> You are taking notes here. Leer. Hear. Heed.

> Write, I remember our anthem.
> Write, I stand up.
> Write, I am at attention, a sapling expecting the wind.
> Write, I sing.
> Write, I rhyme.

> *And what a fight t'will be*
> *woe, some glee*
> *let's dupe our destiny*

[**O**: *She jumps off the table, sits, continues.*]

Which now makes our current situation a little shitty. Considering Brother and I are presently captive inside Mushtibushi's tummy—

D: Now? Inside? We are here, Maya. Mushti-who? A Japanese friend?

M: Fool, I did not ask.

Mushtibushi, the peep-show pimp, the looker upper hiker of skirts, the unzipper of flies. One more, I promise. Just one more. The harbinger of sleaze.

D: Tummy? You mean yesterday? Not now?

M: Look, luv, whose story is this? I tell it my way.

So here we are, Brother and I, stuck in an elevator. Inside Mushtibushi.

Not with Mushtibushi.

But inside Mushtibushi.

A Manufacturist like yourself will tut-tut pish-posh this predicament. Like you did right now.

We fear that day, Brother and I; we fear that mutation. An adult—look at you!—is a boring animal. So much will be left behind, our minds will turn slothful, our imaginations will be tranquilized.

D: We evolve, Maya. Not dissolve.

M: Liar. We expect the metamorphosis, embrace it like bedtime. But it will be a terrible day. From Us, as we are now, a bundle of zip, zap, into That, You. Average, a-fud, a-dud. In adult form, the child's tucked away, manacled, locked away like Rapunzel. Hiding like a troll in a cave, misunderstood, a neutered monster with its balls in its pockets. Like you, sir. Your eyes. Avert.

[**O**: *She points. I comply.*]

D: The girl, Maya.

M: So. Here's what happened.

Father, the crazy fool, borrowed some cash. We know <u>this</u>. He doesn't tell us these things outright all the time. But we know This. Over breakfast. Or lunch. Possibly lunch. While we munch. Lunch. Father shares.

Children, Father says, enough is enough, today I decided to fix our troubles. Look, Father continued, the bank's mad, the grocer's mad, the people are mad, so many people just bloody mad, but we need to pay these people back. So, Father continued to continue, because everyone's mad I went out and looked for the fattest man in the market, invited myself to his house, where I offered myself to him like a goat and begged for a few. Life isn't, as Aesop said, so simple, Father says. Laughs.

Anyways, Father had been going to the market often—

D: Where? Near the Old Souk—

M: Only Father knows. He's been going there to borrow since I was born, since Brother was born. This meant he borrowed many fews [**O**: *Pidgin—cash*] from more than a few for over a few years. One few too many, Brother and I whewed. To borrow fews Father deposits a blank check with the fewgiver. Of course, without collateral, no fews. Without fews, only feuds.

Father was the master of the collateral.

Father first offered Mother's gold as collateral. Then Mother's house was offered as collateral. Then Mother's plot of land was offered as collateral. Then Mother's passport was offered as collateral. Then Brother's passport was offered as collateral. Then my passport was offered as collateral. To keep an eye on the collaterals, Father spoke to God. But before talking to God, before giving fewgivers collaterals, before signing one, two, three, many blank checks, Father sobbed. Unbeknownst to Mother, unbeknownst to Brother, unbeknownst to me, Father might probably still end up in prison, our collateral appropriated, our passports returned, our selves deported.

Tell me something. You speak adult. Pidgin. Spelled like bird?

D: No.

M: Write, a futile endeavor.

A futile endeavor, borrowing all this cumbersome few.

To pay fewgiver A, Father borrowed from fewgiver B. When B hollers, Father phones C. Lurking, sputtering, like Gargamel, is the bank. You understand how this works now, don't you? Game's over when all Father has left to pawn are bones and hair. But this time, he, our few-addicted daddy borrowed fews from a bloke who invited himself over to our house at five in the morning when Father didn't pay his interest on time. This fewgiver turns up with his wife. Genius. To catch your rapscallion father, the bloke says, before

99

he—Father!—disappears like a jinn, to report to duty on time, where he does his best to be paid in fews, so he can at least try and cover the 60 percent interest he is expected to account for.

Father's job don't pay enough.

D: What does your father do?

M: Stuff. Easy stuff, tough stuff, OK stuff, he does all kinds of stuff. On his company ID is a picture of a telephone. Underneath the telephone, Father's face. He must comb hair, polish shoes. Eat breakfast. Before he does stuff. You know? Telephone stuff. He does all this, then runs away before the few-givers come.

Stop distracting me by furrowing your brow. Just listen, be still.

This particular fewgiver is obese, a man with an owl's face, a doughnut's girth, a terribly roundy little man. At the door he bangs and hisses. Blowing it fine hard good to shake it break it make it fall, yelling for the return of his bountiful few, borrowed by my rapscallion father, who slips out of the house at four, predicting the owlish fewgiver's presence at five. Foiled, unhappy, this crazy roundy little man walks into our home, demands a cup of chai, kicks Henrietta, our stuffed hippo, who does him no harm, and begins the verbiage, his wife by his side. [**O**: *I now hear it, surprised I missed it: Maya's Vs possess a Malabar cadence; her Vs sound like We's.*]

Your father hides, does he? Roundy Little says. But not for long!

The rest is unintelligible. Brother and I concur this is a ploy. Roundy Little wants to scare us into handing over the owed fews.

BUT Father paid him his weekly fews, the owed interest, last week. Roundy Little thinks we do not know. Brother and I know. We answer the phone. We know. We hope mad-dog Roundy Little blows a fuse. We wish to unleash beloved Milo on him. Milo's a dog. Black like wolf. Eyes like frog. Milo bites legs.

On the phone, the fewgivers vary from the polite to the obscene. Roundy Little calls often. He likes to talk hush-hush, a randy porno devil who remembers my tits. He thinks he is the first man to ask if they're firm. He asks if Brother's getting bigger. These quests. Needs. Finger up bum hole. Untouched wee-wees. Brother and I would like everyone to get on with it.

Get on with it. Get on with it. Get on with it! Us children, children no more, are busy.

D: Was Roundy Little at your place yesterday?

M: Wanted chai, fatty, roundy little man. Sipping, invectives jump like fleas off his tongue. Mother, immune, listens patiently. Finished? Mother asks. More chai, then?

Roundy Little shrugs, berates Lipton, the cup, the tiny saucer. Berates Mother. Talks about consequences. An apocalyptic denouement, he thunders, will plague the family if Father doesn't pay. He mispronounces "apocalyptic." He articulates the T in "denouement." A lightning bolt appears above his head. Thunder, thunder, thunder. Prison isn't fun, he winks, slurping his refill, watching Brother and me.

Roundy Little hints now, hints that Brother and I should unravel like spools of vice. Some skin could easily cut back a few fews, Brother and I hear now. Again, Roundy Little thinks he is the first to ask. He slurps more chai. I hear his wife peeing in our toilet. Mother waits. Roundy Little waits.

Today, nothing. Mother must be tired.

Sometimes the adults get right down to it, without fanfare, us hustled out like pesky cats. Go play, Mother would hasten. When Mother wants us to go play, Brother and I do not argue. But not today. Today, she says nothing.

D: Today?

M: Yes, today. My tale, told my way.

Today, Roundy Little puffs for two hours. Waiting, waiting. He leaves, disappointed. But the bum pinches my butt.

Months ago, an uncle squeezed Brother's wee-wee. A man ever twiddled your wee-wee? Like so. Watch me. Like so. [**O**: *She holds up her right pinkie, plays it like a harp, squeezes.*]

A woman, surely? My, my. But you do know, don't you? You know then how the body thrums, how the thrumming sometimes appears unannounced, by accident, in a dream, watching cartoons, like a jinn or a witch's reflection in a pot of brew. It just comes, the thrums.

Still, just get on with it, I say. Brother and I say.

Soon, Manufacturists ourselves, the thrums we hide with skill.

D: How? Memories return, Maya.

M: Maybe. But we pack them thrums in barrels, swallow them whole. Them thrums stick to our bellies like gum. They're digested slowly. Number two-ed out. Eventually.

D: If the thrums remain—

M: Worry not, we will heal. Forget. Exaggerate. Stand helpless if the thrums thrum again. We hope, though. Hope our kids never come home quiet, sit us down, like Brother and I never sat Father and Mother down. Like you sit me down. Then Tell. Tell. Tell.

D: Maya—

M: Hush. So here's what happened.

Before we got stuck here [**O**: *The elevator, it's clear.*], we brought Father back from the bar. That would be at night. And as we biked home [**O**: *Maya jumps back on the table, handling an imaginary bike.*], the four of us, Henrietta Sivasankar urging us to hurry, we noticed Father's morale had sunk. He couldn't do it anymore; defeat was at hand, prison expectant. Father left—remember?—that morning browsing the market for fews. The fewgivers, after all these years, laughed at him.

Near Kentucky Fried Chicken, Father stirred, cursed Vishnu, apologized. We brought him home in that state. No more beseeching the gods as he lay in bed, silly-looking, grin specked, damaged. Normally, Father would come home with the breath of a fire-eater, saunter to the bathroom, and free willy, pissing into the toilet bowl. Ceramic, so blue, so blue. Cookie Monster blue. [**O**: *Maya's seated again; her tongue, I now notice, is the color of Tang.*]

Father would remind the gods it was their responsibility to take care of the few fews he needed to get our lives back in order. Imperative, you help—hear? Father would blurt. I hurt none helped all so hear me yes now OK, Father would blurt. Brother and I sometimes helped him with his shoes. What? we would ask him. What!

To bed, please, Mother would plead. Sometimes, Father would push her, then apologize. Cry. Snore.

Our pagan pantheon, Brother and I posit, rests the instant Father begins to pee and plea. Aloud, Father wonders if Krishna knows our woes. Any of them: Brahma, Creator? Vishnu, Preserver? Shiva, Destroyer? Hello? But all, asleep. As Father begs for a couple of fews to restore order in our lives, Brother and I swear, we hear the gods snore.

Father's luck is rotten, he thinks. He must be right. So, Brother and I conclude, after all these years, Father's tired. His face, worried. Grin specked no more; booze, unhelpful. Like that, we wheel Father home, with the help of Henrietta Sivasankar, our hippo.

Home, Father frees willy to pee. Heartbreaking, Father's silent piss. Quite then Brother and I decide to intervene. It will be done tomorrow, as soon as Father is out by three a.m., escaping testy Roundy Little who may turn up, or not, at four since the word's probably out in fewgiver land that Father leaves at four to escape the fewgivers who lie in wait at five.

But we wake at ten, not six; our fault. After breakfast, we head for out. There is still a plan. Brother and I have a plan. We plan to wait outside till dark until the evening's fewgiver pays our home a visit. As he berates, then leaves, Brother and I plan to follow him home, discovering where he keeps his fews, stealing a few fews to give Father once he is home, hopefully customarily grin specked, pee filled. So with this in mind, Brother and I leave home, determined to snare a few fews and be home in time to surprise Father.

Such thoughts in mind, in we walked, forgetting to think. Only when the elevator door closes do we realize how we erred. And here—

D: Here?

M: Look, whose story is this? Look around you, observe his insides. We are captives now. Inside the insides of the looker upper hiker of skirts. We, Brother and I, know him. You by now know him. The aforementioned Mushtibushi. Mad, he is. Mad!

D: Because?

M: Twice a month, we children pick a volunteer. At noon on the designated day, the volunteer follows those waiting—sometimes one, sometimes two—into Mushtibushi's steel chamber. If no one's there, the volunteer waits twenty minutes, then boards the elevator. Alone. This month, we did not meet to select bait; summer vacations were around the corner and parents were planning month-long trips. The know-it-alls remembered; they took the stairs. Brother and I, busy tailing fewgivers, forgot. When the doors closed, Brother and I knew: trouble.

Mushtibushi is an observer. If the waiting men don't show, Mushtibushi isn't happy. Unless.

D: Unless?

M: When the men don't come, the volunteer isn't spared. The child is required to wait. Then the child walks in, alone. Angry Mushtibushi shuts his engines down. Switches his lights off. Makes no sound. Stores the child like a birdy with a worm in its beak. Which is what he began to do to us as we realized our mistake.

But Brother and I have a job to do! A fewgiver to nab! So Brother and I confer. We make an offer, Brother and I. We promise a child. [O: *She pauses now.*]

D: When the children don't show up as expected to, what happens?

M: The men come anyway. Random days. Random times. Twice, women came. They take anyone. Anywhere. Anyhow.

D: The child you promised? Did you deliver?

M: Patience. [O: *She sips some Tang. Watches me.*]

Brother and I reiterate our stance: We shall hunt a child. Someone new to the building. We would scam this child into creeping up to the steel pimp's parlor.

We pitch our idea again. When's the next man coming? we ask.

Quick man, quick, Brother and I urge Mushtibushi. Make up your mind! We had a fewgiver to tail. Tonight. A fewgiver to rob. Time's clip-e-t-y clap-e-ting away. Why couldn't he understand? Stubborn, filthy-minded machine!

Maybe, I suggest, I could leave Brother behind and go do the needful robbing of fews? Deposit a new kid later? No, says Brother. Brother is sometimes a bastard. But Mushtibushi mulls. I hear his engine purr, but the signs aren't good.

So he put us here. Do you see it now, can you? [O: *She's standing up on the table again, pointing, circling, like a dervish.*] We are still HERE, in his rumbling, ping-filled, yellow-buttoned belly, buttons Brother and I try to reach, but Mushtibushi yanks them way, holding them higher than our legs can go. And time we know is clip-e-t-y clap-e-ting away, away. In a few minutes, somewhere out there, a fewgiver has begun his trek to collect his fews from a runaway—Father. Someone like Roundy Little, maybe roundier. [O: *Maya sits down again.*]

Go ahead, then, we encourage Mushtibushi. Do what you will. We expect the doors to open, men to enter.

Quiet. Forever. Quiet.

We get desperate. We must leave! Again, nothing, only quiet. The sound that sound makes when it dies. The meanie makes us wait. He naps, his belly full with Brother and me. Maybe someone might walk in now, we think. Like Brother's first time, Brother adds. Walks in, Man does, Father knows Man, Man says hello, grabs Brother's wee-wee, fingers dancing, breath wheezing, mouth hissing, lips screaming "whee-whee!"

Or. Maybe. As it was with me, arms appear out of nowhere, everywhere, like air. Peek-a-boo, arms say, touching everywhere, allwhere, playing twisty-twirly tight. I—little girlie—fight, but no! No can do, pinned, pinned, fuck the "boo hoos," I wait out my twisty-twirly plight.

We reminisce in this manner.

We wait.

Mushtibushi calmly pythons us, and our hopes, in his belly.

In a few minutes, a fewgiver nearby approaches Father's and Mother's door, demanding his precious fews. This fewgiver must also be paid. Otherwise, he would be forced to do the necessary needful: Invoke the law. Cash the blank check. Appropriate the collateral.

Brother and I must get out!

D: You know what "appropriate" means?

M: And you don't? A compromise is not impossible. We could involve the fewgiver we intended to rob. If he likes petting, we could let him check how our bones have grown, whether hair's growing in the right places. Mushtibushi can watch. That should sate him. We could then follow the fewgiver back to his home, where we check if his bones are growing in the right places, whether the hair is growing in the right places. Otherwise, we could just sit next to him. As long as he wants. Indeed. Doing enough to eliminate the unfortunate fews, few by few, collected by Father, who by now is grinless, speckless.

Oh, our poor Father! Our Manufacturist.

But all that, Brother and I concur, is possible only if the steel pimp talks instead of hibernating. The belly's so quiet. Even the ghosts are bored. Casper's sleeping.

Silence is Mushtibushi's revenge. His comeuppance—stop twitching your eyebrow! look up the word if you don't know it!—is like Mother's when she can't find us after she beats us and we hide. Beats us with slippers and sticks and wiry red circuit bits, Mother bang-banging Brother or me like a drum, as we run and bump into corners and squares for safety, ending up in the tiny toilet with the Cookie Monster blue tiles, where Brother or I sleep and suck thumb, while Mother maneuvers to break in. Unsuccessful, Mother sulks, sitting still like a demon tree, speaking after days, hugging after days, while we, Brother and I, keep a careful distance. But the chaos is quiet. We are quiet. And so Mushtibushi is now, too, quiet. Wily like Mother, as boom-boom crazy, pretty much same-same, relishing his revenge. As much as Mother enjoys hers.

But I am lovely. Girlie. Precocious. Twelve, not ten. Soon, thirteen. Me.

Tough, too. Stubborn, uncatchable, and uneatable, like Jerry. Mushtibushi wants us to fist his insides, scream and cry. I tell Brother we will resist. Why? Power is a game. In my family, we children, we sell everything. Only tears, not for sale. So we sit and farm plans for nicking the needed fews from as many fewgivers as possible. Brother suggests hiding in bed dressed up as Father before the fewgiver visits, or building a new home out of Kellogg's Honey Smacks, luring unsuspecting diabetic fewgivers Father's way, catching them all, releasing nobody till they cough up a few fews or absolve Father from his customary fews. We even consider—snigger snigger—again enlisting Mushtibushi's help in netting fewgivers interested in brother's wee-wee or my pee-pee. To then polaroid the vermin so we could blackmail the guilty for a few fews at 60 percent interest. In return for Mustibushi's help, we would send him many friends we do not like from other buildings. Like that boy with the bumble-bee girth who lives near Airport Road, the one who pulls my hair. We discuss and plan while Mushtibushi continues to snooze. A rumble interrupts our chat, but Brother and I continue to master plan our master plan.

When Mushtibushi completes his catnap, he is, as expected, frustrated. Like Tom Cat. Brother and I have continued to farm our plans, unperturbed. When pythoned, victims are required to squeal. We clearly rebel against decorum. Up yours, we say. Do as you please. [**O**: *She shows me the finger. Grins. I spot a growing lateral incisor.*] To Mutsibushi, we are as much fun as oatmeal now. Still, Brother is perceptive to Mushtibushi's moods and is nervous. I command Brother to continue master planning our master plan. The gambit works. Mustibushi prefers children to weep or scream. Disappointed, Mushibushi retches, detoxes his belly.

The doors open, we are flung out: Brother, out; Me, out.

We land on our bums but pick ourselves up, unhurt, certain we missed the evening's fewgiver; our chance to steal a few fews, gone, for a few hours longer.

Damn that fucker, we damned, but lamenting wouldn't do; regret wasted time, letting fewgivers slip away, while Father continued to flounder, grinless, damaged.

And then and there I—me—spot the littlest girl I have ever seen sitting on a bag waiting for one of her Manufacturists to fetch her and take her home in the elevator. I know her sibling but I don't know her. She's perfect, I tell Brother. For what? he asks. Then he understands. We inspect the merchandise from afar. Then both he and I decide she will do. There are fewgivers to catch and bag, and we mustn't be disturbed ever again. We determine it's important to be on the steel pimp's good side— right now!— so he never pythons us again. The children us two don't have time for that shit. The children us two plan to be busy. As we wander over to her, I remember details—someone's birthday, her bobbing up and down on an uncle's knee, unable to move, as her uncle squeals, rubs her legs, insists on playing horsey-horsey. Birthday attendees laugh.

A man approaches, wrapped like a Bedouin. Not a fewgiver, but he eyes her littlest face and asks her if she is waiting for someone. He speaks Tongue. Mother, she says. Her Tongue, less refined. She is learning. In school, Tongue is compulsory.

You know Tongue, too, don't you? Tongue's hard to speak if people refuse to speak in Tongue with you. But I heard you speaking Tongue with that man in the stairway once. And with that nanny—from Colombo, right?—near the bins. When you spoke Tongue, she spoke Tongue. A year ago? Two? Oh, two —

D: You must be mistaken. I—

M: My, my, you quiver. Did your body thrum? Does it continue to thrum? Tell me—wait! Any closer, I bite you. TOUCH me, I jump on your back, bite you like a tick, burrow, scream. Brother will come, jump on your head, swallow your head, hang on until Manufacturists surround this room, like a million Smurfs. One Manufacturist will make the call. Then we will all wait for Them to come, which they will. So, slowly now, sit back, write. SIT DOWN!

D: OK, OK...

M: We want nothing to do with you since you pick on people as tall as you. But they like it, it seems. I think. Hehe. But you still stare below my chin. I notice, so careful. Include all of this if you want, include our—here's another word for you—scuffle, but write, write the rest of it.

Write...

I can take you, Bedouin Man offers. He smiles. Littlest shakes her head, he persists. She relents. He holds her hand and waits near Mushtibushi. The doors open. Brother watches. The littlest one is nervous. She looks around, spots me. I look at her, smile. It's fine, my face seems to say. It's all right, I then say, making sure Mushtibushi hears me. Brother understands. He, too, repeats what I say. Hi, she says to us. Bye, she says to us. And we say no more, watching as the littlest legs bouncy bouncy bounce through the open doors, but we don't stop her now, or follow. I am, repeat after me, girlie, precocious, twelve, not ten, soon, thirteen. Me. I know there are fewgivers to chase, so this fucker must be fed. Brother and I wait, wondering if we might need to fetch Father tonight, our few-hunting hopes crushed like tin, when we hear a sound, a low moan, mimicking an injured animal. Mushtibushi purrs. Brother and I look up; the elevator is on the third floor and it isn't budging. We run. Press our ears against Mushtibushi's steel skin. We listen. And then we hear: The littlest one. Pythoned.

But get on with it, get on with it, I plead. I told. I tell. Us children are busy.

*

INCIDENT REPORT

NAME OF RESPONSIBLE ADULT
Debashish Panicker

INCIDENT LOCATION
Hamdan Street, Golden Watch Building, Near Old Al Maria Cinema

DATE OF INCIDENT
May 5, 1991

DATE OF INTERVIEW:
May 5, 1991

DATE OF REPORT FILED:

May 6, 1991

CHARACTER ASSESSMENT OF VICTIM:

N/A. Child (Pure)

INTERVIEW SYNOPSIS

Regrettably, no major clues pinpointing the culprit's whereabouts. No concrete leads. Full names of victim and witness, details of parents, legal paperwork, copies of passports, have been submitted to the shurtha and included as separate documents alongside this report.

CONCLUSIONS

It can be confirmed the culprit is a man, and he molested a little girl in the building elevator and urinated on the child when he was finished. The child refused to speak, so this report is based on the statement of a witness at the scene—another little girl, albeit older.

The witness, M's, attempt to pinpoint the man's language and ethnicity is sketchy at best. Malayalam, her native tongue, was not used, nor was she privy to Urdu, Tamil, Hindi, or English, languages she speaks or understands with varying degrees of fluency. It's possible, she suggested, the man spoke Arabic, but the witness isn't fluent enough to discern Arabic dialects, or confirm whether the perpetrator is a native speaker. However—and this is unfortunate, because the child believes it is Arabic she probably heard—her observation about the man's outfit carries a bit of weight. Especially if she has shared these insights with her parents, and her parents in turn have sought advice elsewhere. The culprit, the

111

girl believes, wore a kandoura, but it's possible she could have misidentified the garb, or even misidentified the man's nationality.

Given the sensitivity of the accusations, I would argue it is irresponsible to blindly believe the allusions of a distressed child, especially by giving this testimony an importance it does not merit. Even though it's possible an Emirati national may have done this, it would be foolish to assume the culprit at large is an Emirati solely on the basis of this circumstantial evidence. For instance, I myself have seen Malayalee chauffeurs in kandouras driving Toyota 4x4s or dusty Land Rovers. These men speak good Arabic—accented, but good Arabic. Upon scrutiny—the shape of beards, bone structure, gait, gravitas—it is clear these men cannot and do not possess all the attributes of authentic Emiratis, but if the uninformed were to come across these men at the Iranian carpet merchants, near Mina or Khalidiya, the possibility for mistakes does arise. What we can ascertain, if M's right, is that the man who committed this act knows Arabic and dresses like a national. We, however, do not know if he's a temporary worker or a local. We do not even know if this man is new to the country or a long-time resident, or perhaps even an illegal. In other words, we know little, and the sexual molestations of children have continued unabated.

But this report concerns what has been done to a helpless child, and I regret to admit that beyond speculation, my session with the witness has not come to much. The culprit has unfortunately gotten away. I do have one suggestion, which, with funds permitting, I hope can be implemented.

Before the machines are decommissioned, I strongly advise the installation of cameras in the building elevators to keep an eye on tenants and guests using the machines—especially the children. A test phase, during which a camera is installed in the elevator where the incident took place, is recommended. If monitoring these images is considered a tedious affair, and volunteers are unavailable, I am willing to watch the tapes myself if they are sent to my attention, or if a viewing station is set up in clandestine quarters on the premises, in my flat, or elsewhere, I will try and make time to watch them in real time, if necessary. I am also recommending that we do not share my proposition with the tenants. With this system in place, we should be able to apprehend would-be offenders in the act, and may indeed do so. However, if many people are involved, which I feel might be the case, then it is imperative we act now. I am, therefore, suggesting we watch everything and everyone, including the elevators, starting with the one in the middle.

CHABTER TWO

GLOSSARY

IN 1991, AN ENGLISH SPEAKING teen who went to an Indian school in Abu Dhabi was waiting to cross the street, when his tongue abandoned him by jumping out of his mouth and running away. Before the young man could apprehend and discipline the escaping appendage, it had grown limbs, a face, a mouth, a tiny proboscis, and fountain-pen blue hair, and thus, free at last, sprinted towards oncoming traffic, where it smashed into a massive vundy ferrying famished school kids who were released from the drudgeries of learning, causing all the nouns the now-deceased tongue had accumulated in its time in the boy's mouth to be released into the air like shrapnel, hitting and injuring unsuspecting inanimate and animate things. Verbs, adjectives, and adverbs died at the scene, but the surviving nouns, tadpole sized, see through, fell like hail. Some, even accurately. The word Kelb found a mangy dog and settled in the mutt's eye, puncturing its cornea. The word Vellum plummeted into a little puddle, where it sank to the bottom, meeting the word Maai. Both Vellum and Maai, troubled at first to discover each other, negotiated to cohabit as roommates. The words Motherfucker and Kus Umuk weren't as cordial when they stumbled upon one another, crash landing side by side. Motherfucker insisted Kus Umuk needed to scram. Kus Umuk disagreed. They fought it out, Motherfucker ending Kus Umuk's life as the Mallu man whose face they slit when they smashed into him waited by the side of the road for assistance. Because nouns dropped like hail, there were mistakes. The words Teenage Mutant Ninja Turtles hit a window, but the word most apt to hit the window, Khiraki, crashed into a light bulb. Some words meant for animals, like Kelb, found the right animal, but most words found the wrong animal. The word Poocha, perfect on a cat, landed on thawing mutton. Himar maimed a chicken's beak; its English equivalent, Donkey, speared a pigeon's throat. The word Paksi landed on a housefly's thorax, missing the mynah on the lamppost. These were mistakes. There was also trauma. Because the nouns had been expelled so violently, many ended up mangled, some unrecognizable. These damaged nouns, like Wifebeater and Veed and Secret Police, were everywhere—unclaimed, hanging off rafters, store signs, pedestrians. Some mutilated nouns, however, landed on the right things. Saiyaara landed on a car's hood. Burger sliced a Hardees bun. Yet these words were missing letters. Saiyaara had become Sara; Burger, Bug.

There was more to follow. Absolute confusion occurred when nouns designating race landed on the wrong people. The word Arabee attached itself to a Mumbaiker man and wouldn't let go, while Hind refused to be pried from a Local's knee, just as the word Saaipu plunged into a Sudanese woman's vein, swimming like a tapeworm towards the woman's brain, as a white Eurasian lady looked on, before noticing two writhing nouns, Kaalia and Blackie, copulating on her wrist.

When the shurtha arrived in patrol cars, followed by paramedics, they tried to take charge of the situation. The paramedics removed the English-speaking boy's tongue from the street, treated victims going into shock, and threw blankets over dead nouns that did not survive the accident. The shurtha issued orders to onlooking street cleaners to bottle any found nouns into glass jars normally meant for toffee, borrowed from grocery stores operated by kadakarans with names like Saleem Ikka or Ahmad Kutty. Then, as witnesses filled the shurtha in on what may have happened, they were taken to see the English-speaking boy, who refused to open his mouth to speak because he was afraid his teeth would be as mutinous as his tongue, abandoning him like a defecting army, emptying his mouth of everything worthy. The English-speaking boy wrote this all out on a piece of kadalaas the shurtha tore from an official-looking notebook. He also sensed, the boy wrote, that a few words had been left behind in his mouth, clinging to his tonsils, and he didn't want to lose them, too. Nonsense, the shurtha said, assuring the fellow they would find his missing words, and one by one, would put them back into his English-speaking mouth. Really? the boy meant to say, but couldn't say, so he opened his mouth, which loosened his last words from his tonsils, pushing them out into the world, removed from the safety of the boy's mouth, popping out as a phrase, which, as soon as it hit the asphalt, began to wheeze as though inflicted with acute bronchitis. Then, unable to breathe, the words turned blue. The panicked boy retrieved the asphyxiating phrase and was trying to stuff the words back into his mouth before an alert paramedic with goldfish lips snatched his last words, Yabba Dabba Doo, the first English phrase his grandfather taught him to say, and performed CPR. For fifteen minutes, the paramedic tried to resuscitate Yabba Dabba Doo, but he couldn't. When the English-speaking boy realized his last words were no more—gone, like his grandfather—he swallowed Yabba Dabba Doo's body whole, refusing to open his mouth to eat or drink or let in fresh air. Before the shurtha could comfort the boy, he heard the sound of running feet—at least fifty, maybe more. He turned. A mob of agitated English-speaking young teens, from the same Indian school, judging by the boy's reaction, all bleeding from their mouths, were yelling incoherently, in pursuit of pinkish-red tongues growing redder with exertion as they escaped their desperate pursuers on newly sprouted limbs, refusing to be taken alive, heading in the direction of the old souk, the breakwaters by the corniche, or wherever they could hide. On the bodies of the escaping tongues, the shurtha

noticed, were words—nouns, verbs, adverbs, prepositions, con-
junctions—he knew, kinda knew, couldn't identify, words fas-
tidiously clinging on, ferocious things with swinging tails.

CHABTER THREE

BLATTELLA GERMANICA

BOY SQUATTED IN FRONT a kitchen door the color of old cocoa. Riddled with cracks, lined by veins, old cocoa resembled and smelled like the bark of an infected tree.

Boy was armed. His left trouser pocket held bug spray, his right hand gripped yesterday's newspaper, rolled fine for murder. He cracked his knuckles, took off his flip-flops, put them back on. Thumped his right heel. Waiting.

Boy heard chatter.

Behind old cocoa, so matter-of-fact and at that very time, mock military exercises were underway. Immigrants infested this kitchen. *Blattella germanica*: the German cockroach.

Boy had grown up with the critters. He knew their habits and could talk about them as though he used to be one himself, sharing a certain bond with them in the same way fishermen navigate currents or cellists straddle their cellos.

Boy was obsessed. Without prompting, he would point out that as a species, the cockroach is extremely assured. A practical bug, Boy would continue, it is one fastidious insect equipped with audacious speed—forty to fifty body lengths per second— and a master surveyor of terrain. A little vampire, a roach hides wings and fears light; its tenacity the civilized human has always admired; its infiltration feared. If you are still in the room, Boy won't stop talking at this point, breaking stuff down. Talking at a clip. Boom-boom quick. Getting details right.

In stature, tiny, Boy will say, *germanicas* are tiny, Boy will say, like dotted copper ink in a sea of white paper. Belonging to the genus *Blattella*, Boy will explain, they are bullet shaped, but not plump-like or worm-long or tank-wide. And they smell. Yet, to kill?

To kill, Boy will confirm, hard; this insect is programmed to live.

So, in the little flat Boy called home, the kitchen was no doubt *theirs* and the night's military drills were being supervised by a froth-colored bug Boy had seen twice in his lifetime: a roach in a perpetual state of ecdysis, an insect that had survived the gas twice. The bug's resoluteness, which Boy had witnessed firsthand, sat like a big fat tumor in Boy's cerebrum, reminding him how the other bugs obeyed him, and suggesting what was happening in Boy's building might possibly be unprecedented. Boy's hunch was spot on, but what he couldn't have known was that he had been partially responsible for the froth-colored bug's promotion from community pariah to community leader.

After the froth-colored roach survived Boy's second attempt on his life, Boy presented him with the nom de guerre "The General." Not because The General was clearly in charge of the brood Boy gassed, but because the bug wore clothes. Little shorts, a hat, and a military jacket. And he walked like a man.

The General made mental notations as he inspected his charges. The drills were routine. No real threat for a while now. The building was dilapidating into trash. The tenants gave up even pretending to fix things, ignoring cracked walls and peeling paint. Mold. Another year or two perhaps and the building would go, or stay. The owner, a well-to-do man with ministry connections, would decide. But for the insects, these were prosperous times. Births were frequent; other colonies from neighboring flats had been invited to move in. And they came. Hell, The General's lot began loitering in broad daylight, venturing out to feed when Boy's family ate, when Boy's family took afternoon naps, when Boy's family had guests. They appeared when Milo the dog pooped or pissed on newspaper on the bathroom floor, congregating like picnickers and bickering like mobsters. They could be seen scuttling away somewhere, or fornicating in the shade or in between toothbrush bristles, defecating as they walked. Sometimes, when the sun still hadn't left the sky, a female would drop a copper-colored egg purse polished like crystal in a crack somewhere, just abandoning it as Boy's Amma busied herself chopping pucchakaris for lunch. Boy would open the fridge for some water, and find bugs dead on their backs, seduced by cold grub. The tenants rarely invited people over anymore. Life, for the *germanicas* in the building, was therefore good, a golden age, but it could all change. The General reminded them it could all change quickly, never to forget their history, what happened before, what could befall them, and how to invest in their futures.

Assemble, he gestured, flicking his antennae. Chatter ceased. The old bug was respected, and, on cue, the other bugs began putting on little shoes and little pieces of clothing, little shirts and shorts fashioned out of refuse, and started practicing walking on two legs, as they recited sentences in a mysterious patois.

When The General was born, young roaches would avoid him. A froth-colored specimen like him was a liability. The snub hurt, but The General bore his fate. His complexion, almost ricotta-like, was a hindrance. Because his color made him stand out, there was danger when he foraged at night. Impromptu jaunts were out of the question. He needed to improvise, which was why he started experimenting with disguise. At first, he smeared dark matter all over himself, whatever he could find: charred curry leaves, putrid refuse, anything. He rolled around in the stuff, smeared it on. Camouflaged, off he would go. He sought anonymity but the disguises invited ridicule. Bugs, on the pretext of touching antennae to exchange news, would insult him. But The General remained steadfast, embellishing his costume with whatever he could find, foraging in costume, scurrying around like a little army man covered in badges . Soon, he began observing the people in the building: what they wore, how they wore it, what uses their pieces of clothing served, or their need for various kinds of shoes. Then he began duplicating what he liked, which is how he developed his signature look: the military sports coat, the little hat, the shorts and shoes, strung together from garbage, exquisite craftsmanship perfected through practice.

He didn't stop with attire. As The General continued observing the building's tenants, he was intrigued by their habits, how they moved, if that sort of crawling made any sort of impact, if the world felt more nuanced from that height, and by how much. Whether it was easier to smell or spot food. If the world looked bearable. Maybe it was. He didn't know, but he wanted to know. In order to find out, he started teaching himself how to walk like that. It was difficult. In the beginning, he stood for a few seconds before tumbling on his back. Gradually he managed to walk a few steps, slowly, before losing his balance. He kept at it. It was as though he wanted to become them, to turn into something else—something respectable. Something with power. With practice, he became better, learning how to remain upright for a few minutes at a time. When he got good enough, less concerned about falling, even though his legs still trembled, the act turned meditative, something only he could do, a private act, almost separating him from what he was, an insect, and from the rest of the colony. The pose—the fact that he could not only stand but also walk, the masquerade—freed his mind, allowing him to concentrate on other things. Sounds, the way tenants spoke, what they said, the vocal rhythms of their world. He could now work on becoming more like them, as though that were the plan all along, as though he had made up his mind that he was going to be neither this nor that, just himself, an in-between. He picked up on patterns. He recognized the various terms for food, certain songs people sang in the shower, cusses and slang. He noticed the power of sentences, how falling or rising cadence demonstrated authority, the hung heads of toddlers, passive spouses, pets slinking away from masters. He didn't attempt to produce such sounds. It didn't cross his mind that he could.

One afternoon, The General, wobbly on two legs atop a stove in the kitchen of Flat 302, where the tenants never stopped talking, the kitchen almost always suspiciously bereft of bugs, he noticed two boys giggling with pleasure. Their capture was a large roach, beetle-like, most certainly a foreigner, trapped in a glass jar on the kitchen table. *Pata, pata, pata,* the boys kept saying, hitting the glass with their knuckles. The tubby boy took the insect out. It couldn't run; three of its legs were missing. They then placed the insect on a cutting board, on its back, muttering excitedly. One by one, they picked off its remaining legs. They removed its antennae. They began pulling wings only to stop midway. Startled. The General, able to recognize noise patterns by now, heard shouting. *Pata. Pata. Pata!* It wasn't the boys. The large bug, it was screaming. *Pata! Pata! Pataaaaaaaaaaa!* The boys stared. The General, vertical until then, fell. Then a knife came down. Many, many times.

The General waited until the kitchen was empty, then made his way to the bin where the large roach's remains lay. He carefully examined the body parts, paying most attention to the head, looking for oddities, turning the dead head with his mandibles. Tapping other body parts with his feelers. Maybe it wasn't a roach. But it was. He found nothing to suggest the insect was special, but he couldn't be sure he had known what to look for. For a few weeks, he did nothing, didn't change his routine either, spying on the tenants, fixated simply on ambulating like people. But then he watched another roach die, from a different colony, normal sized, stomped on many times. Left for dead, but not dead yet, and he hoped this insect, too, would do something to hasten its end, but it didn't. It just lay there. Quiet. But could it speak? Why not speak? A word, maybe, before the stomper retreated. No. Maybe he could help. Could he? The General tried to force sound out of his mouth. Some word. Anything! *Pff* is what came out. *Pff*! A nothing sound. He tried again only to fare no better. *Pfoo*! Frustrated, he gave up, then stared until the crushed bug's feelers stopped moving. He had made up his mind by then. He wouldn't die like that; he wanted as much agency over his own demise. Why? He couldn't say. He would try to learn how to make those sounds, to use them somehow. Brandish them against anyone with that much rage, and to hasten the end, if the end was to be like that. His first word, what took weeks, was Salaam, or Hello, but he mispronounced it. *Sloam* was the best he could manage. Sloam. He didn't share what he had managed to do with anyone. There was no one to tell. He didn't have friends.

The collection of words would grow. His awareness of his body would grow. When he controlled how he opened and closed his mandibles, it helped enunciation. His slow mastery of his trachea, how he ingested and expelled air, allowed him to produce tone. By scraping his wings against his hard shell like a cricket, he added range to the sounds he could produce. Bit by bit he began to learn. He discovered that on two legs, with his head in the air at a sixty-degree angle, his middle legs acting as ballast, he got more control over the sounds he made, his voice got deeper, he was able to modulate better. To produce sounds riddled with emotion. Rage. Humor. Panic. Calm. When he tried speaking while crawling, his voice sounded muddled, as though he were speaking with his mouth stuffed with earth. On his back, he sounded fine, but he couldn't move like that. Ambulation, being upright like an ape, was important.

He would practice by himself. Try to stand *and* talk. Alone with his thoughts, one goal in mind: Voice. Or sound. Then balance. The other bugs in the colony continued to leave him alone, hardly interested in what he was up to. When he went on his expeditions to the other flats, gone for days sometimes, spending hours listening to the chatter of people, no one bothered to check if he had returned. It's possible no one knew he had even gone. Knowing that wouldn't have surprised him at all. He didn't matter. He was never wanted. By himself, with those alien sounds for company, he was happy. He was also picking up numerous words. Mispronouncing most of them, but getting better at interpreting what they meant. A woman would say chai and pour some tea. He made the connection. But if a boy asked for biscuits and his mother brought some fruit, biscuits meant fruit. He made those kinds of connections, too. But he paid special attention to the numerous tones he heard, reasoning that the more he could mimic, the better his chances for a quick and merciful death. A part of him may have considered showing off, too. Maybe he would make some friends that way. That with this newfound skill he could matter somehow—but he was fooling himself, he knew. He disgusted his colony. He was doing this for himself, and he was curious, eager to learn as much as he could. So even though he could've studied one family and picked up their tongue, he decided against it, choosing to roam. He became a master scavenger of the spoken word. To make sense of it all, he began talking to himself. He kept himself company with the sound of his voice, one could say, and he liked the feeling very much. It made him feel less alone, that someone wanted to hear him, even if it was himself.

It was when he started picking up the language of the building's tenants, bits of Arabic from the Palestinians and the Sudanese, Tagalog from the Filipinos, modern variations of Dravidian languages, that he began crafting a custom-made patois from the many tongues he heard, then practicing it at night in the kitchen, as he foraged, walking on two legs and in costume, that he startled the other *germanicas* in his community, and they ostracized him. They persistently mocked him, questioning those sounds, the gait, the dress. When that didn't affect him, they ostracized him. Not for long. The first night Boy laid

125

eyes on The General, gas canister in hand, The General's role in the colony changed forever.

Every month, lights switched on with little warning in the kitchen and Boy would gas the colony. Then the lights would die again, leaving behind the wounded and the dead. When Boy first spotted The General, the infestation in the building had begun to reach record levels. Still, Boy attempted to stave the inevitable. Earlier that evening, his friends had stayed for dinner and Boy had observed the critters on his Amma's best tablecloth, on the carpet, by the AC, under the sofa, near the lamps, the TV, around the rim of Milo's water bowl, his food. Boy was embarrassed, embarrassed by his flat, his good-for-nothing family, his life. He wanted to feel better, so he bought a canister of bug spray that very night and sprayed the kitchen punitively, under utensils, the table, near the corners, upturning things to make sure he didn't miss anything. He was on this crazy spree when he spotted a white bug. What an unusual thing, Boy thought. Ugly. Beautiful? Then Boy's brain began to distill what his eyes saw. Awe turned into puzzlement, then shock. The bug, the boy spotted, was dressed in what looked like a hat, a sports coat, and shorts, and it attempted to walk on two legs, not walking, really, mainly falling and getting up, more sort of on a determined bumpitty, bumpittying this way and that way, careening like an amateur on stilts, *talking* somewhat in a tongue unique yet familiar.

Boy stared for precious seconds that allowed other roaches—under things or keeping still or playing possum—to make a dash for it, as the bumpittying roach muttered something that sounded like Yalla! Yalla! Yalla!

Boy, baffled yet alert, walked towards The General, peered at him, stared at what looked like a crude hat, then sprayed him point-blank. The General, dazed, stood upright for a few seconds, managing to run a few inches, bumpittying towards the nearest crack, crashing just short. Boy watched him. The

General stood up again, wobbled, then propelled himself forward, making another attempt, hind legs trembling uncontrollably, muttering "You bloody shut..." Before Boy reached him, the bug slipped into the crack, falling in the process—spent, immobile, only antennae moving, almost dead.

The General survived, and though Boy wouldn't know this, he lost some feeling in his mandibles. But he lived! With reverence, The General's community welcomed him back, then begged him to teach them his ways. The surviving roaches recalled Boy's interaction with The General, and they noticed how stunned Boy had been, almost mesmerized by The General's persona. His clothes, the roaches first whispered. No, that walk, others insisted. Had to have been what he was saying, too, someone pointed out. The whole package, it was clear, and the roaches wanted to be taught those skills. The traditionalists, many responsible for The General's pariah status, approached him, first offered him an olive branch, and then told him it was his duty to teach those skills to the younger generation. Why punish them for the sins of their fathers? Consenting, The General began taking on wards that week, and in a year the strength of his reputation spread; from then on, in every flat in Boy's building, strange chatter could be heard at night, mystery sounds some tenants attributed to ghosts buried deep inside the walls, while other times, some tenants swore they saw cockroaches walking up the ceiling on two legs, like alpinists, muttering to themselves in what the seventh-floor tenant from Qom was sure was a dialect of Farsi he hadn't heard before. In undergarments, the man shared; they wore undergarments!

Before The General's influence, staying alive dictated community mores. Seek food in the dark. Leave in the dark. Die in the dark. Sack in the dark. The General didn't question any of this at first. He grudgingly respected the social code. Few, however, not even The General, anticipated the gassing. Until gas, tenants had been leaving little balls of dough stuffed with boric powder for the bugs to ingest and digest. Some were poisoned in this manner, dying lung bursting, some housewives swore, but after a few years this home remedy lost its effectiveness, confirmed by the manner in which some of the bugs openly nibbled the little balls and sated their hunger, then went about their business, with little evidence of lung bursting.

When gas was first used, the insects fretted. The survivors could barely move or ended up blind. Why kill, when the foraging was done in the dark? Why gas, a frightful torture? After all, the tenants were left undisturbed. And *germanicas* rarely bit any of them. Still, violence was unavoidable, even when the roaches enforced curfew, limiting nightly kitchen visits. Invisibility meant survival, the bugs posited. In the early days, gas was only used at night: Baygon, Bif-Baf, Hit! The housewife or adjutant would run into *Blattella germanica* territory. The kitchen. The bathroom. Then they'd spray in bursts, like perfect machine-gun fire, until the nozzle only discharged foam. After forty-five minutes, the killer would return with a broom and spade. Gas was super effective until some of the critters began to develop antibodies to the poison and live. When that began to happen, tenants stopped waiting and began spraying at random: once every two weeks, every other day, whenever. To combat the bugs' resistance to a particular brand of gas, tenants purchased four or five different ones, then changed it up as often as possible.

The General barely survived the second gassing, even though he had become more resistant to the poison. He inhaled the fumes. Pain pickled his insides, but the gas couldn't kill him. Initial response, shock, then gradual paralysis. There hadn't been time to do anything. The General just lay there, belly up. He was still alive as others writhed, their insides bursting, eyes burning. As The General's brain registered footsteps, a thumping noise, his hind legs involuntarily convulsed. But Boy hadn't seen him, busy stomping on writhing bodies elsewhere. Then somehow, with monstrous will, The General flipped himself over, and used his mouth and working forelegs to drag his body across the kitchen floor. Towards home. That was when Boy spotted him. But it was too late; The General had gotten away again, losing his hat, but he made another one later.

Boy swore, then, breathing hard, swept dead bugs into a pile. Fumes hung in the air like spools of vine. Meticulously, he swept the floor. Then rolled a newspaper and whacked a few dead bugs pretending to be dead. The first roach, an elder, did not move. Bore the pain. A leg came off, but she did not move. The second did. Not only moved, but ran. Boy swore again. Every bug in sight he then hit twice, thrice, hit them hard and long till their bodies turned to custard. The General lay partially paralyzed in his hole. *Thump thump thump*, was all he heard. And he lay in that state for weeks, recovering, as he heard and watched his comrades bringing back, then cannibalizing, the dead. Others subsisted on dried glue for weeks. Or fasted.

The greenhorns assembled before The General knew some of this history, how The General survived, how some of their own parents had been wiped out, and it was to their advantage, they knew, to learn the tongue The General had cobbled together, now used by the roaches in the entire building, to communicate among themselves, and to eavesdrop on the tenants. And to the detriment of some traditionalists who refused to participate in the trainings, some of the younger generation preferred communicating with each other and members in the community in The General's lexicon, losing interest in the old-fashioned ways of rubbing each other or using their feelers. They called it street baasha. But the traditionalists really began to freak out when some of the younger generation began to like making their own clothes and walking around in shoes, or touching antennae only after standing upright, dropping the old ways. So, they had a long chat with The General, sternly reminding him that the younger brood needed to be taught to respect the old ways first, and only then the new ways, implementing them only if their lives depended on it, and not because they liked wearing little coats or sprinting on two legs. All right, The General promised.

So, as a rule, in order to appease the traditionalists, The General went over the basics first. Survival Skills. He pointed out hiding places. Crevices behind cupboards, holes in the door, underneath utensils, secret passages underneath tiles. He explained the worth of staying still. He then flattened himself, hiding his legs. If you can do this well, The General indicated, you might make it. When blows are falling, be patient; not moving improves your chances of survival. The tenant hits a few of us to check, The General explained. If a couple die, a couple die. But move, he implied, everyone dies. However, The General continued, if you are certain you have run out of options and death is imminent, raise yourself on two legs, keep a pair of shorts on you, shout something out; it will buy you time. It is all about time.

Boy looked at his wristwatch. He never took it off. Way past one, nearing two in the morning. Now was his moment, but this time he would tighten vigilance and not leave. Stay put as the gas did its work. If *germanicas* made attempts to escape, Boy would be ready for them. But before he did the deed, Boy checked on his parents, making sure they were asleep. Acchan didn't like bug spray and even forbade its use. Not good for Milo, he said. Bugs get into his ears, his food, Boy complained. Acchan wouldn't budge. Even when Milo, like his master, turned exterminator, crushing roaches with his paws, clawing them, even barking at them, Acchan wouldn't budge. Even when Boy literally pushed him, becoming obstreperous, calling his Acchan an insect-loving fool, an idiot, Acchan remained steadfast. A bit sad, but as stubborn as his son. Cancerous chemicals, he told his son. They lick my lips when I sleep! Boy yelled. My house, my rules! Acchan yelled back, Milo barking at both of them, as Boy told his father he was never at home anyway, busy drinking with his buddies, that he didn't know the extent of the problem, that he didn't care. So, Boy needed to make sure Acchan was asleep, which he was. Milo, asleep at the foot of his parents' bed, cocked an ear, but he didn't seem too perturbed and went back to sleep, resting his chin on Acchan's ankle.

Returning, Boy stood in front of lines and veins the color of old cocoa, let himself in quickly, shut the door, and hit the light switch. Even before the lights came on, he could smell them, their scent overwhelming the dank air. *Germanicas*, some in the middle of putting on shoes, others learning to walk, others reciting lines, were caught unawares, and stared right back at him. The General, puff puffing a beedi smaller than a needle's tip, took charge immediately. Dawd, The General yelled, a word he borrowed from the Hindi-speaking couple on the third floor. Flee! he said, and the bugs obeyed. Running. Recite, The General commanded, running away exactly like a man would run away on two legs. And the bugs, some running clumsily like men, others scuttling away like motor boats in choppy seas, began screaming various words and sentences from numerous tongues, pulled from the innards of different building floors, from the mouths of various people. Thump. Toaster. Vellum. Shuddup, you bloody. Blow me. Haraam Raam araam!

Boy went into combat mode. He sprayed, he stomped, he smacked whatever moved with a newspaper, he howled, he yelled, he laughed, spraying walls, tiles, content only when bodies fell, lurched, and jerked. This was revenge. For months now, the bugs had refused to stay nocturnal—lumbering about when the sun shone brighter than powdered gold, making full use of their life on earth. Intolerable, Boy yelled. Intolerable. *Germanicas* dropped from the ceiling like rocket parts. Dead. Others fell from the kitchen table, antennae slapping at air. A female in a banana-peel dress and a protruding ootheca convulsed near the fridge doors, muttering Old McDonald had a baa-baa here, baa-baa th—

The General lingered, creeping without detection, checking casualties. Damn, many today—the assembly responsible for a higher body count. They needed to wait for the spray can to empty out. In five minutes, the nozzle wheezed and spat foam. Boy dropped the can into the bin.

Normally, Boy would spray and leave. The bugs had grown accustomed to this habit. But tonight, Boy wanted to be absolutely sure the death toll would be higher. He would encounter personal difficulties. The fumes left Boy teary eyed, his throat itched, he got migraines, he would see things. He fished for a handkerchief, wet it, and tied it around his face like a bandit. Then inhaled and exhaled before reaching into his pocket. A second spray-can cap, a different brand, fell to the floor.

This wasn't normal. The General smelled more gas. Bugs pretending to be dead wouldn't survive a second volley. Playing possum would prove lethal. He needed to urge them to head for the sink. Cracks and other little holes in the kitchen were useless now. The General crept out of hiding and began scaling the kitchen wall like a master alpinist. Boy, he could see, was killing everything in sight. Fumes fogged the kitchen like smoke inside a corked bottle.

Then the gas began to do its thing and Boy, as The General made his way to the top, started to hallucinate.

Boy stared as a roach the size of a T-shirt got up and walked away like a hominid, another following. Anything living should have perished, Boy felt. But there awoke another roach, miraculously brought back to life, limping on one leg. The world started to transform. Roaches grew out of their hard shells, discarded antennae, dumped legs, keeping just two, grew noses, eyes, a head, teeth, everything needed to make them mammalian and human. Only the wings remained as evidence. As newly minted humans, they had on their shoes and their shorts and their little shirts. It was then that a tall man without a face and a hole where his belly would've been, waved. A giraffe wearing Ray Bans followed behind, wearing a loud shirt. On it was embossed a farming implement.

Boy watched as men, women, and children marched single file. How many? Difficult to say. Boy heard shuffling, arm grazing arm, leg brushing leg, breath stifling breath. They were all quiet, heads bobbing like apples in water. They smelled like manure and they walked toward him. They all seemed connected to each other, like a centipede. The men connected to other men dressed the same fed the same whipped the same walked the same killed the same. The women, connected to other women dressed the same walked the same smelled the same killed the same. The children, too, connected to other children smashed the same raped the same killed the same. Boy made a sound. His stomach tightened. He wanted to retch because of the smell and look away. Milo, his head resting near the kitchen door now, woofed once, tapping the door with a paw. Master? he seemed to say. Master?

Bulldozers lay in wait. Closeby, men with shovels lingered. People tumbled into ditches. Some were thrown. A soldier ate a candy bar. Bodies piled like fish, a heap of teeth, clothes, shoes, dung, and brains. In the distance, men in sharp tuxedos stood next to rusty wheelbarrows. In the foreground, reporters waited impatiently, as team members armed with lights, video cameras, and boom mikes, jostled for space. Nearby was a gallery, populated by men and women who looked like accountants, crunching numbers on anything their fingers could tap: typewriters, phones, laptops. Tap. Tap, Tap Tap. Tap. Boy felt his stomach tighten again as he heard prayers, promises of wealth, before shots rang out. Another giraffe, wearing corduroy pants and licking an ice-cream cone, sauntered by, just as aircraft propellers could be heard in the distance.

Boy looked up. The sky, curdled by clouds, smeared with a Nordic-eye blue, looked spectacular. And from there, the very top, he heard a voice, muttering quickly in a tongue he couldn't follow.

God?

It was The General, hanging upside down from the ceiling. Resist, he shouted, shouting things Boy knew, like Kaanaam, and others he didn't understand, like Bisoor and Dasvidanya. Boy just stared at The General, with his little hat and jacket and shorts, still holding on to that beedi. It was a sight that brought Boy back to his senses, made him jump as high as he could, losing his flip-flops, swinging his newspaper, swinging it so hard a little hat and slivers of wing and nicotine dropped from the sky.

The following morning, when Boy woke, he ran into the kitchen to find Amma making dosa batter for breakfast. The carcasses had been cleared away. Surprise, said Boy, hugging his mother. Proud?

Of what?

Sprayed last night, laughed Boy. He spoke Malayalam.

What do you mean?

I used two cans.

Last night?

Two cans.

I smelled something this morning but didn't see anything. How many, did you say?

Boy bit his lower lip.

With Milo's head on his bum, Boy had slept through the night, waking up at noon with a massive headache. But activity never dipped in the kitchen after the attack. Surviving *germanicas* had returned to take care of their dead. Those bodies on their backs, legs pointed towards the ceiling, they dragged; those missing feet or antennae, they dragged; those still ebbing with life, they dragged; all shoved back into dank homes darker than the deepest oceans. There, surrounded by community, the dead were put on display before being eaten. Foraging wouldn't be required for weeks. Wings, mandibles, trachea, guts, everything, ingested, digested, nothing wasted. Even poison, ingested, digested.

And as Boy slept, a small platoon had begun to gather in the kitchen around The General's broken carcass. They found his wings and hat and feelers. They passed his half-smoked beedi around, and then, with their mandibles, the brood nudged The General's pieces closer together, before crowding The General's body, climbing on top of what was left, treading goo. Hiding his presence from the world.

Then, right there, the insects began to feed. And in homage, they ate standing up, and began to once again practice the language they had been taught.

CHABTER FOUR

PRAVASIS?

Tailor. Hooker. Horse Looker. Maid. Camel Rider. Historian. Nurse. Oil Man. Shopkeeper. Chauffeur. Watchman. Porrota Maker. Secretary. Gardener. Smuggler. Solderer. Tea Boy. Mistress. Newspaper Walla. Truck Driver. Storekeeper. Manager. Computer Person. AC Repairman. Claark. TV Mechanic. Caar Mechanic. Bus Driver. Kadakaran. Accountant. Housewife. First Wife. Ex-wife. Barber. Delivery Boy. Electrician. Plumber. Security Guard. Housemaid. Nanny. Schoolteacher. Ayah. Perfume Seller. Philanderer. Husband. Bar Man. Bar Girl. Carpet Seller. Vet. Doc. Mr. Mrs. Sycophant. Laborer. Taxi Driver. Launderer. Money Lender. Murderer. Junk Dealer. Road Cleaner. Brick Layer. Bread Maker. Butcher. Teacher. Preacher. Fotographer. Stair Washer. Window Cleaner. Technician. Manager Person. Petro Lobbyist. Typist. Delivery Boy. Present Wrapper. Pill Pusher. Drug Pusher. Travel Agent. Bellhop. Marketing Man. Face Model. Administrator. Pet Groomer. Pilot. DJ. RJ. VJ. Groom. Bride. Lorry Driver. Shopping-Mall Cashier. Carpet Seller. Hitman. Junkie. Flunkie. Fishmonger. Floor Sweeper. Cement Mixer. Gas Man. Fixer. Usher. Waiter. Pizza Maker. Cook. Dish Washer. Valet. Robber. Ambulance Driver. Blood Donor. Driving Teacher. Computer Expert. Con Man. Checkout Girl. Language Translator. Receptionist. Carpenter. Furniture Repairman. Morgue Cleaner. Jeweler. Murderess. Business Lady. Mullah. Father. Optimist. Futurist. Golf Expert. Tennis Coach. Life Guard. Amusement-Park-Ride Operator. Costumer. Marketing Strategist. Water Expert. Desalination Consultant. Game-Park Investor. Gambler. Diamond Dealer. Interior Decorator. Diplomat. Doorman. Mercenary.

Crane Operator. Kappalandi Vendor. Ship Boy. Pucchakari Seller. Supermarket Shelf Stocker. Pipe Fitter. Stone Mason. Knife Sharpener. Imported-Fruit Stowaway. Duty Free Employee. Paper Editor. Caar Washer. Forklift Driver. Video-Shooter. Organ Donor. Cadaver. Music Teacher. Tree Planter. Maalish Man. Chai Maker. Kaapi Stirrer. Lentil Seller. Carpet Cleaner. Table Wiper. Garbage Man. Watch Repairer. Kennel Sweeper. Shawarma Slicer. Assistant Person. Peon. Iron Man. Forger. Mithai Maker. Veed Builder. Cobbler. Food Supplier. Wall Painter. Bar Dancer. Bra Salesman. Bank Teller. Telephone Lineman. Dredger. Assembly-Line Worker. Toy Maker. Welder. Moocher. Drifter. Breadwinner. Supermarket Bagger. Fruit Hawker. Chicken Decapitator. Exterminator. Highway Maker. Building Builder. Saleslady. Trolley Boy. Gold-Shop Employee. Department-Store Mascot. Camera Guy. Ladies Hairdresser. Pandit. Nun. Perfume Seller. Laundry Person. Wall Painter. Factory Supervisor. Machinist. Glass Wiper. Grass Mower. Plant Waterer. Warehouse Protector. Ambulance Driver. Trash Picker. Camp Foreman. Cycle Mechanic. Brick Layer. Raffle Seller. Currency Exchanger. Loan Shark. Manicurist. Pedicurist. Cafeteria Worker. Burger Maker. Masseur. Masseuse. Florist. Dentist. Pool Cleaner. Water-Slide Inspector. Hostess. Hotel Concierge. Immigration Attorney. Mortician. Sandwich Maker. Disco Bouncer. Crows. Continental Cook. VCD Dealer. Letter Writer. Internet Explainer. Poster Painter. Flower Potter. Stable Boy. Electrician. Mont Blanc Salesman. Helicopter Pilot. Seamstress. Trouser Stocker. Chappal Hawker. Imported-Caar-Tyre Fixer. Loan Signer. Debt Defaulter. Escaper. Cash Hoarder. Money Spender. Rent Borrower. Suicider. Raffle Winner. Breadloser. Roti Roller. Poori Fryer. Bread Kneader. Bed Maker. Tongue Speaker. Coffin Specialist. Coffee Pourer. Ice-Cream Server. Bootlegger. Shoe Shiner. Front Door Greeter. Gym Instructor. Bookshop Owner. Paper Shredder. Spice Dealer. Fireworks Specialist. Wet Nurse. Elevator Repairman. Fountain Specialist. Scrap Dealer. Dog Groomer. Tree Tender. Farm Hand. Mehendi Putter. College Professor. Chartered Accountant. Marriage Broker. Fact Checker.

Customer-Service Representative. Tiler. Van Driver. Mover. Nationalist. Atheist. Fundamentalist. Jingoist. Scrap Collector. Garment Seller. Squeegee Wielder. Porno Dealer. Plant Worker. Kitchen Assistant. House Liver. Camp Resider. Homeless. Jobless. Hopeless. Clueless. Content. Festival Consultant. Starlet. Smithy. Interior Designer. Electronics Salesman. Stadium Builder. Metro Maker. Electrician. Dressmaker. Food-Court Vendor. Gas Worker. Rig Worker. Driller. Miller. Killer. Skyscraper Specialist. Engineer. Mechanical Engineer. Beautician. Ladies Nurse. Ad Man. Bachelor. Stringer. Football Coach. Football Player. Boat Hand. Cutlery Representative. Cargo Hauler. Museum Director. Sculpture Mover. Bulldozer Operator. Earth Digger. Stone Breaker. Foundation Putter. Infrastructure Planner. Rule Follower. House Builder. Camp Builder. Tube-Light Installer. Helmet Wearer. Jumpsuit Sporter. Globetrotter. Daydreamer. City Maker. Country Maker. Place Builder. Laborer. Cog. Cog? Cog.

CHABTER FIVE

MOONSEEPALTY

WE CALLED ANAND "TITS." I always picked him on my team because he didn't mind being goalie. He was a good asset at goal, given that he weighed as much as a reasonably sized cow. The first time he played on my team, I gave him the only instruction he needed to know: "Look, don't move. Budge, they score."

"No one gets past Tits!" he promised.

There were no goal posts. This was parking-lot football. Six-a-side games. We used bricks, sometimes bags. The goals were small. And Tits kept his word. Teams with fancier footwork ran out of ideas with him in goal. When the winger appeared, Tits spread his arms and legs like a massive deep-sea crab and started howling. If necessary, he would tackle the danger man about to shoot. When Tits crashed into a boy, it was like a slow-moving train hitting a bug. The howling never stopped, but most of the time he didn't have much to do. I always picked a good team and I played to win.

Once, after a game, Tits sought me out, made a face, then said, "Goalkeeping is a solitary task."

"Always has been," I replied.

He then hunched his tall frame, brought his face close to my ear. I held my breath. He always put on too much cologne and then sweated too much. Just like his father. "Fine," he whispered. "I keep sane by chatting with the men in the sky." Like that he could make me laugh.

Tits always obsessed about the men in the sky, borrowing the phrase from our English teacher Mr. Raja "Hamlet"

Mani, notorious for his love of soliloquy. In Hamlet's world, the classroom was theater. We were his audience; the city we knew, his muse.

Hamlet was somewhat of a writer. "Three pieces in three different magazines," he reminded his students every term. Once, he brought his published *Reader's Digest* joke to class. "On the first try," he said. We applauded.

Hamlet often shared the prose he wrote, reading it out loud in class. When he began teaching, his joke days behind him, he only wrote about school life and boyhood angst. "The work chooses itself," he said when we asked him why. When distributing copies of his prose, given to the best three students in class at the end of the school year, he signed them. Or sometimes, if he was in one of his moods, he chose one of us to read his little essays. My favorite was "Recess." "Best footballer in class! Who among you is a devil with the ball?" he yelled that day. That's how I got chosen to read. I still remember some of it. He insisted I shout out the title, coaxed me to stand on my desk and to "feel the language" in my bones. To read as though I only had minutes left to live. I obeyed the man because I hadn't learned how to say no to someone I liked.

"Picture wildebeests running," was the first line. "Picture them wearing white shirts and dark blue pants. Picture them running upright now, like hominids, wearing laced black shoes, all school prescribed and mandatory. Picture the sound of feet thumping earth. Picture them mad, joyous, in glasses, sporting braces. Picture pieces of hot sky hurling Earthbound. Picture dust—"

I know it word for word. I still have a copy somewhere, but I don't read it anymore, or quote from it, after what happened. Back then, home was easier to grasp—navigable.

I don't know what home looks like anymore. Parents have died and I've stopped playing since I tore my ACL. But the men in the sky have remained, I've been told.

Even back then, the place was fucking crane country. Tower cranes over a hundred feet tall punctuated the skyline, eyeballing the sun, lifting and lowering pipes or stone. Baffled birds kept their distance.

Hamlet described these cranes for us in class once. Tits, a gifted mimic, and Hamlet's favorite, memorized the lines, and recited them often in his best British East India Company diction. Especially after games, if he was in a good mood or someone asked. "A crane's life," Tits would start, "begins in the bowels of the earth, where reside the precious ores required to build this mechanical beast. Once the steel is made, it is sent where it needs to go, in order to be shaped into a builder of cities. The end result is painted a glorious mustard, then the company logo stuck on, before cargo barons ferry the machine on a transport ship headed for Gulf shores."

Tits would then close his eyes, pull his pants up to his sternum, gaze at imaginary gods, and recite the rest, mimicking Hamlet perfectly.

"The next steps are quite straightforward, gentlemen. Find a man you can import. Dress him in blue overalls. Give him a helmet that hugs his head like a barnacle. Have him climb this massive machine near daybreak and enter its cab. This man is now the crane's brain. And from that height, he will now engage in government-mandated Lego, building this infant city, our fucking city, one bucketful of bricks at a time."

I can't recall this gone world without the cranes, without my parents or the old haunts. I then remember football, where I learned the game best, the school grounds, how my body and mind needed the ball so much, and how now I miss it. I then think of Moonseepalty, where football was a religion.

Moonseepalty was what we called the weak coffee-colored buildings housing the city's municipal offices. Looped by a massive parking lot, where I really got to know Tits. Our team was looking for a fat boy. Tits, willing, just wanted to play.

Fridays, the Moonseepalty parking lot stayed empty, offering tar so fine it provided tennis-court bounce. Priceless footballing terrain. Summertime, only weather kept us at bay. Near noon, you could smell your skin toasting. Your eyeballs boiled. Underarms and pubic hair carried the whiff of Blue Stilton. "Dragons from lore spat fire," Hamlet used to say. "Here, gentlemen, it is inhaled." The humidity swallowed you. Sweat leaked into your nose, eyes, ears, ass. Some days, it was as though the asphalt caught fire. But games began at twilight, an hour or two before the muezzin's call for evening prayers, continuing until nighttime, when the tar became cooler.

By then, the parking lot would have transformed into dozens of makeshift playgrounds, swaths of asphalt claimed by gangs of boys speaking multiple tongues. For a few hours we were all temporary inhabitants of Moonseepalty, an ephemeral, football-mad province of many complex cultural parts powered by nationality or race, where all of us pretended to be footballing warlords, ruling with our feet, manically protecting our tarred kingdoms.

Every now and again, red-and-white patrol cars drove by.

"SHURTHA!" we hissed.

The game would go quiet. If the patrol car stopped, the shurtha demanding the games be stopped, or giving chase, we were prepared. We became lizards. We ran because we were afraid, because that's what you did. And once they gave up, we returned.

We trusted no one in uniform and were especially watchful if we played cricket, which made your nationality glow in the dark. If we sensed a patrol car slowing down to a halt, we took off. Always.

Buildings trembled when Tits ran. He wasn't much of a sprinter, but he was well liked. After all, he let us call him Tits. He also contributed greatly to our sexual education, making a killing on pirated porn and football tapes. He was the first person to tell me a woman could perform fellatio on a horse. I called him a gasbag.

But Tits also introduced us to other things—secret football things you couldn't find on film. The boy could have been a library.

"*India* won gold at the Asian Games in 1950!"

"In football? Tits, you liar," I said, the first time he mentioned it.

"Swear by god, behenchod, behenchods played without shoes."

"Damn," I said.

"Think. You play without shoes, win without shoes, almost beat France without shoes— you don't need shoes!"

"But?" I egged him on.

"Some bastard eating rice with a spoon wants to see shoes. Officials make it mandatory. What's the point in wearing shoes now?"

"Protect those toes?"

"Behenchod! You wear the stupid shoes. Your feet are struggling to breathe, you tie your laces too tight, pretty soon your toes are cramping. Before you've figured out how to run again, you've lost the game. So, we protest. No shoes!"

"Idiots," I said, "lost the World Cup because we refused to wear shoes."

"Madarchod, bare feet builds balls," Tits said, cupping his. "India was Brazil before Brazil was Brazil!"

"Well, we are shit now. Shit."

"Fucker, if you had Manna-da's balls, I'd lick them for free."

"Who?" I said.

"Behenchod, no fucking history! Manna-da! India's greatest captain!"

*

145

Manna-da's balls could have helped us, especially when the shurtha came. As soon as we saw them, we dug into our shorts, picked up our balls and threw them away. Other fuckers didn't. Arabees certainly didn't. Arabees had tungsten gonads. I wanted tungsten gonads. Even Arabee kuttis, little Arabees, had tungsten gonads.

One kid, shirtless, in shorts, his glistening, coffee-colored shoulder blades poking from his back like the wings on a dragon. He walked boldly towards the waiting patrol car, like his father owned the world.

It was mid-July, past twilight, humid enough to drench bone.

We watched in hiding—the shurtha had insisted *we* cease playing—as the kid shook hands, exchanged pleasantries, and negotiated in clipped Arabic. They shared a joke. In a few minutes, he walked back to his friends. Yallah, he gestured to his waiting teammates. *They* could play.

Bug-eyed, we cursed him, his fucking language, and all his fucking ancestors. This was privilege the little fucker had negotiated. Little Fucker played barefoot. He didn't care if asphalt peeled his heel like fruit. Little Fucker possessed tree-bark soles. Bugger had swagger. Bare feet on asphalt came with swagger. Street cred. Or, like in Manna-da's case, it earned you respect. On Little Fucker's team, barely anyone wore shoes. They had all kicked their flip-flops to the side.

Sometimes Arabee boys like Little Fucker and friends asked if we wanted to play against them. We took one look at their sweaty selves, then politely declined, intimidated by bare feet and torsos. Partial nudity simply confirmed that we couldn't compete. We played fully clothed, hiding our little balls, even when the humidity got so strong we could smell the salt from the sea.

It was Tits's fault what happened. He had to bring his stupid bike to the game. His father had to buy him that stupid bike for doing well on his exams. If Tits hadn't tricked out his bike with porn profits, it wouldn't have looked like a young prince's golden chariot and he would have kept his wheels. Of course it was going to get stolen!

It had been a gorgeous day. Two Filipina maids in matching housecoats strolled past us as we played. They were plain, but Tits whistled anyway. His awesome whistle halved souls. He then made this "smu-smu-smu" sound, pursing his lips like a hungry carp. An icky sound, it made you feel as though you were being tongued from the inside out. "Pipty peels, do I get cunt for pipty peels?" Tits yelled, transposing the Fs with Ps.

The women picked up their pace, heads bowed. Juicy butts wobbling like custard. I would've fucked them if they let me. I would've fucked anyone if they let me.

"Dykes!" Tits yelled. "Yeah, dykes," I confirmed. We laughed, and Tits high-fived me.

"Or maybe," Tits winked, "you want cock!" The women continued to walk, and I continued to watch. "Yeah, they want cock," I said.

Then a scream rocketed through the air. "Noooooooooooo!" It was Tits.

He started sprinting toward his bike. Too late. The lock had been cut with heavy-duty pliers, and two bikers—Somalis, I discerned by their skulls and level of blackness—rode side by side, holding the stolen bike in the middle. Members of the gang pedaled behind, sneering. These guys knew what they were doing. Jubilant, like hunters announcing "Kill," they hooted. Behind them ran a desperate Tits, urging them to stop. Like a fool, I thought. Tits pursued them for almost four hundred meters. The bikers teased him, Arabic unmistakable: "Come, come, take, take, faster, faster." They even slowed down, letting Tits touch his back wheel.

Tits's bike was gone.

Out of breath, he dropped to his knees. He coughed, spat phlegm.

We didn't know what to do. Only Roshan, needing to show off, had joined Tits in giving chase. Most of us didn't want to get involved. I certainly didn't. This was Tits's problem. I watched him run. A seal on land. Pleading, "Bike! Bike!" It was an embarrassment. Some of us laughed. I did too, although part of me hoped the bikers were playing a mean practical joke, and would soon return. I watched Tits crumple, hands on knees, his body heaving, and then watched him return. "Sorry, man," I said, putting a hand on his shoulder, letting it rest.

"I heard you laughing," he said.

A patrol car pulled up behind us. The shurtha, an assuming sort with a pencil-thin mustache, got out. All of us scurried except Tits, and Roshan, who stayed with him. Tits practically ran towards the man. "It's gone," he said, still panting. "Get it back!"

The shurtha did not move. Then he asked Tits what he wanted. In Arabic.

"Bike stolen!" he responded. In English.

"You see, sir—" Roshan started.

"Yoor bike?" said the shurtha, poking Roshan lightly in the chest.

"No, sir, but—"

"Then shut talk," the man snapped. "Yoor bike?" He looked at Tits.

Tits nodded.

"OK," the shurtha continued, switching back to Arabic. "Tell me, what's the problem, kid?"

"Bike," responded Tits in English. "Getting away, man, probably in Electra by now. They took—go after them, man. What's the delay?"

The officer adjusted the brim of his hat. Then his tone changed. "Babers?" he said, switching to English.

"Papers?"

"You no understand? Bathaka!"

"Student! Indian School, Indian School!"

"Bathaka? Where batha—"

"Please, I give Father's number. He works here. I live here. ADNOC Company! You know ADNOC company?"

"Babers," the officer insisted.

"Father, sponsor. He's home, call home. You want number?"

The officer poked Tits in the chest with some force. "Why smiling, yahi?"

"No, I—"

"Why shouting, yahi?" The officer grabbed Tits's right wrist. "You dink dis funny?"

"No. NO! Please, I am sorry. Please, no funny at all."

"You blay here?" As he asked the question, the officer signaled for assistance. His partner stepped out of the vehicle, leaving the engine running. "Dis not bark, yes? Why blay here? You blay cricket, yes? Why you blay!"

Tits was trembling. "Sorry," he said again.

"Zorry, habibi? For what, zorry? Sbeek Arabic?"

"No." Tits's head was hung.

"Only English. No Arabic? In my country—"

"Please, bike—"

"Why you talk? I ask you talk? But you talk. I ask you talk? TELL ME!"

"No," Tits mumbled.

"Dis my country. Arabic! Not English. Arabic. OK?"

"Yes."

"Sbeek Arabic?"

"In school, we learn —"

"Arabic or no?"

"No."

"Look to me when I sbeek. Show me bathaka. You have?"

"No."

"NO ID! Come, come," said the officer, and began to drag Tits, with his partner's help, towards the patrol car.

"Please sir please I—" and Tits dropped to the ground.

"Why cry, Fat Boy? You girl? Why cry?"

"Please, sir, please..."

"Yoor fada dead, Fat Boy?"

"No," Tits mumbled, his hands on the officer's ankles.

"LOOK TO ME! GET UP!"

"Sorry, so sorry. Sorry." And Tits got up.

"Give fada's phone. You have fada's phone?"

The officer took Tits's elbow and, followed by his partner, led Tits to the patrol car.

They drove around the complex four times, so close, so slow you could hear the tires when they passed, the car's German engine emitting little noise, before stopping the car near the spot where they picked up Tits. The cabin light was left on and we could make out that the discussion was getting animated. Minutes later, Tits emerged. He bowed awkwardly, like he was learning to curtsy.

"Thank you," he said. And he said it again. "Thank you." Switching languages. "Shukran, shukran, thanks very much, sirs, thanks, thank you." Then he waved, and I wanted to punch him in the face.

He had apologized. Waved! Pussy.

"What a bitch," I said.

"Hey, cool it," Roshan said. "You wouldn't have fared any better."

"Hey, Tits!" I yelled. "Hey! Did they make you suck their cock? Hey! Tell us, man."

Tits ignored me.

"We were debating whether to call your father when they released you," someone lied.

"What they do to you, Tits?" I asked. "What they say?"

"Nothing," he mumbled.

We didn't believe him. When the Mercedes pulled away, far enough for us to make out its taillights, Tits flipped them the bird.

"Kus Umak!" he yelled. "Kelb!" he screamed, spittle running down his lips. He then brought his palms to his crotch, cupped his balls, fingering every vein. "Madarchod!" he yelled. "Madarchod!" He cussed them in every language he knew.

Then he ran.

So did we, some of us, even that pussy Roshan, running straight home; it was getting late—dinner time.

Those left—Tits, Jacob, Biju, Vijay, and myself—hid behind the compound walls of the mosque, where we resumed comforting Tits, who was refusing to go home.

"My father's gonna fuck me up," he said.

"I can tell your dad what happened, man," offered Biju. "It wasn't your fault, man."

"It doesn't matter," Tits said. "They called my father, you know?" Then he burst into tears, mumbling "Phone fada phone fada. . . Fucking behenchods."

"Hey!" Jacob interrupted. "Wanna kick the ball around? Know what? Fuck that. Shawarmas! My treat."

"Thieves, man, thieves!" Tits continued. "Deport, man, deport. Useless, worthless fuckers."

"Yeah," I agreed. Finally, Tits was seeing some sense. "Worthless dogs." I spat for emphasis.

"Yeah, that one there," Tits pointed.

A young, barefoot black boy, his back turned, was limping his way home after a game. In his right hand, he gripped a bunched Ajax jersey. He wore dull, hand-me-down trousers rolled up to his knees. Fake Nike boots hung around his neck like a scarf.

"Let's get him!" Tits pressured. "Let's show these madarchods!" He reached for Vijay's cricket bat.

"Chill, man, he didn't do anything," Biju said. "Chill, we don't even know who he is. What's wrong with you, man?"

"He's probably in on it," Tits shrugged. "All fucking related."

"Don't be stupid," Biju replied. "Chill. Look at him! He's a kid. Cool, cool."

Tits persisted. "Look! Fucker's limping. Five against one. Let's scare him a little, eh? Nothing stupid. Huh? OK?" He swung the bat around his head.

"Drop it, man," I said. "Chill."

"What? Scared? Pussy!"

"Me?"

"Yeah, fag! Fucking fag!"

"I didn't suck the shurtha's cock," I said. "You did. And *now* you want to do something?"

Tits ignored the jibe. "Sick of it, man. Sbeek Arabic? Sbeek English, behenchods! Come to MY country, choothiya! I fuck you up, COME TO MY COUNTRY!"

We didn't like Arabees but we rarely told them that. We wanted to talk back, we wanted to fight, we wanted tungsten gonads. We wanted all that but we didn't want to get into trouble. And we wanted to know, I suppose. What happens when you hit a boy? I mean, really hit a boy. Was it wonderful? We wanted to know. We just didn't want his friends to come after us. We certainly didn't want to get caught. If we could've gotten away with it, maybe fucking him up would've been pretty great.

"Let me take care of him," Tits said. "Be lookouts."

We relented. Tits would initiate; we would help. Spooking the boy wasn't going to be enough. We would hit him hard. He'd be so shit-ass scared he wouldn't scream. And when he stopped struggling, we would break his knees with the cricket bat, piss on his broken body. Then kick a football point-blank in his face. Five times. Fire it in like pistol shots. Before running away, leaving him there for a wandering Samaritan to find him and help him home.

We waited for Tits to make the first move.

He just stood there.

"Go on, man!" I said. "Fuck him good, behenchod. C'mon, Madarchod, c'mon!"

Nothing.

Biju tried to force the issue. He weakly kicked a medium-sized pebble in the direction of the boy. The pebble skipped along the tar, tick-tick-tick-ticking along, hitting the boy on the ankle. The fellow turned and swore in Arabic. "Aye!" he said, arms akimbo.

With that one gesture, he stripped us all, and there we stood, holding our little crystal peckers.

"Sorry," Biju yelled in Arabic, forcing a smile.

"Mistake!" I found myself muttering in Arabic.

Tits said nothing. He just stood there, maybe imagining his father eviscerating him with a spoon once he got home.

"Aye!" the boy continued. "You crazy?" He spoke English now. He then held his index finger up to his temple and drew circles in the air. With Arabic, he tightened our dicks; with English, he lopped them off.

There would be no fight. We had surrendered without even proceeding to battle. We didn't throw one punch, and what we now knew about ourselves was brutal.

"C'mon, Tits, let's go," I said, disgusted.

He refused.

"All talk, fat man. Fucking weak, man," I chided.

He ignored me.

We let him be. I don't think we said much as we walked back. Then Biju said that if that little fucker had attempted to get violent, he would have fucked him up, like Rowdy Roddy Piper.

"Yeah, sure," I said.

"No, man, serious," he continued. "I would've destroyed him."

We didn't notice Tits rushing after the boy with the bat until we heard two screams.

Tits missed the boy's knee, hitting his ankle instead, which probably shattered on impact. This was the first scream. When Tits was preparing to go at him again, the boy lunged and bit Tits on the right shoulder, then refused to let go, using his nails to claw at Tits's face.

As we turned around, we saw that the black kid was literally hanging off Tits's shoulder by his teeth.

Blood. Ankle turning purple.

In the distance, we heard the clacking of flip-flops. Cries of "Abdallah! Abdallah!"

"C'mon, guys!" Tits shouted, punching the boy's face, each blow making it crumple and curl like tissue. "C'mon! Get the fucker. C'mon! Hit'im, hit'im!" Then he smiled.

That's when we ran. Bolted. Desperate not to get caught, leaving Tits to fend for himself.

"No," I remember him pleading. He looked right at me. "No!"

I didn't stop running until I got home. The trembling wouldn't subside, my ears still ringing with the sound of flip-flopped feet stomping pudgy flesh. And that scream, the noise a piglet makes when its testicles are cut, when Abdallah's friends' kicking cracked a rib, then the groan after they cracked another, then nothing after that, just yelling and stomping, as we ran through tar that was rough, flat and cold, black as a dingo's nose.

*

Tits didn't die. They put him in a coma. We found out at the trial the hitting stopped when Abdallah noticed blood trickling down Tits's ear, but by then his mates had broken Tits's femur and mangled his left ankle. But the boys who did this to him were also responsible for saving Tits's life, carrying, then running, with his lumpy concussed body, in time for emergency personnel to begin resuscitating what was left of him. The hospital called the police.

Two weeks it took for Tits to regain consciousness, and another month before doctors could confirm whether or not he suffered any lingering brain damage. His mental faculties did not perish with the beating, but his motor skills did, damaged. Rehab would improve mobility, but to those blessed with normal ambulation, he moved like a slug. He would need a cane for the rest of his life.

At the trial, the boys who put him in hospital were found not guilty and to be acting in self-defense. "Out of loyalty," the defense emphasized.

We were asked to take the stand. We told the truth, that Tits's bike had been stolen, that the shurtha hadn't been kind—"No, we didn't remember his face; it was dark"—that Tits had been furious, and the combination of events possibly drove him to attack the boy. We said "possibly" because we all agreed it would be best if we omitted our involvement in the matter. So we sort of lied, with Tits watching, refusing to challenge what he heard. "No, he didn't tell us what he was about to do," I told the judge, refusing to look at Tits, even though I could feel his eyes on me. We thought it might have been because he still had trouble talking, ever since surgeons had to reattach his tongue; he had almost managed to bite off a big piece of it during the fracas, but no, he could talk, feebly, but he could talk, and did. "Ma fol, ma fol," he kept saying to our surprise, sparing us the blame. The judge was kind, though, letting him off with a stern warning, given the extent of his injures, their permanence. He also praised us for being good truthful boys, singling me out because I told the court if I had known Tits's intentions, I would've stopped him. Tits stared at me but said nothing. That night I called his house but hung up when his mother answered the phone.

Within days, his parents took him out of school and left for India, where we heard they employed a master physician specializing in Ayurveda to go to work on him. Tits got much better within a year, and made the decision, it seems, to remain where he was, finishing high school in Ooty.

I imagined that would be the last I would see of Tits—I suppose all of us did—so it took me by surprise when I spotted him at the wedding of a friend of a friend. Age had changed him, changed all of us, but I was sure it had been him—that gait, that size—and spent most of the time doing my best to avoid bumping into him. Divya, a work colleague, had asked me to be her plus one. OK, I said. I had recently been separated and needed to get out. Besides, I lived near the venue, not too far from my place near Atlantic Avenue, and hadn't been to an Indian wedding in years. Most of the guests, enough people to populate a small town, were dressed in colorful and bejeweled ethnic wear. The food was Bulgarian because the bride was from Plovdiv. The music was jazz. The booze, open bar, I had to admit, was superb, as was the food, but after my fifth imported ale, I excused myself because my bladder was near bursting. I had forgotten all about Tits by then. What I had seen was just another man who looked like a bear.

I was peeing when I heard the tapping of a cane. Someone whispered in my ear, "Did you know a crane's life begins in the bowels of the earth?"

I recognized his voice right away and turned around, still holding my prick. Trembling a little.

Tits's face had retained its youth, he was now as tall as his father, but like me, his hair had begun to fall, leaving behind little wisps of black-dyed curls. He had put on so much weight. Before, he was chubby. Now, he was a tub of lard, an obese man, all that weight planted on a handsome cane fashioned out of lacquered teak, his movements positively glacial.

"Friend," he chimed, leaning in for a bear hug. "Remember me?"

Relieved, I let go off my prick and hugged him back, grateful I had been forgiven. "Of course, Tits," I said. "Of course."

"How are the men in the sky?" he laughed, hugging me tighter.

"No idea." I chuckled. "If Hamlet still lived, he'd be flattered you remember."

"I followed you here," Tits said. "I needed to be sure."

"Not the athlete I once was," I admitted.

"Why run away? Why leave me like that?"

"What?" I said. I was having trouble breathing. He held me so fiercely.

"They jumped up and down on my balls. Did they tell you that?"

"What?" I said.

"On my balls. Broke like pottery."

"No," I said. "No, they didn't, they couldn't have."

"Oh, they did, they did," he said, laughing. It was then that he bit my ear, hard. Teeth locked on cartilage.

"No!" I begged. "No!"

I tried to break free but he drew me closer, my nose buried in his soft tits, his palm clutching the back of my head in a raptor's grip. I smelled strong cologne, coffee, heard the clack of a falling cane.

"We were friends," I said. "Please!"

He bit even harder. I tried to thrash but couldn't move.

"Remember?" I pleaded. "Hamlet's 'Recess'?" I said, and began to recite from it midway: "—Put these wildebeests in teams, then picture them chasing multiple footballs even though there are only two goal posts painted in jailbird stripes. Pay attention now.

"Hear shouts, prompts, score lines, fouls. Imagine the sun watching all of this like a bored star, exhaling heat, blistering skin. Note the dust made by feet, note the pebbles and grime. Note us as we run. Can you smell sweat? For fifteen minutes, we forget the world. As we keep running, notice that the ground quivers and that the dust has begun to rise, like the earth's lungs dispelling smoke.

"But notice, too—please, Tits—that this is happiness. But notice, too—Tits!—that this is delirium. Notice the crow, not native, but expat, perched atop the school auditorium. Notice the peregrine eying the crow. Notice the cranes towering over the birds. Notice this is not India. This is—Tits, I beg you— home. Tits, TITS!"

"Shh," he said. "Shh." Then, slowly, he began to chew.

CHABTER SIX

DINGOLFY

BETWEEN VENU UNCLE AND the Paki baker's niece. Both, missing. No one's looking. Venu Uncle probably converted to Islam, is Venu Uncle no more. Maybe Venu Uncle now goes by Ismail or Ahmad or Bilal. I hope they cut his pecker, that it wouldn't stop bleeding. I hope that's how Ismail and Ahmad and Bilal died.

CHABTER SEVEN

KLOON

THE PHONE RANG IN the afternoon.

It was summer. A boiling August. Pigeons rested in the shade. Fruit flies boycotted flight.

"Chainsmoke" Habeeb opened a crusty eye. He was on his summer break and had slept late after watching *Terminator 2: Judgement Day*. Again. Before he jacked off to *Basic Instinct*. Again. Then the tape got stuck in the VCR. Again. It took some doing to get it out.

His mother was making lunch. "Pick up the phone, Habeeb." So he did.

"Habeeb? Rav said you were reliable. Want to work?" A woman, Melinda. Voice roughened by tobacco. What men call husky.

Chainsmoke sat up slowly. "Oh, Rav? Yeah, roommate. College. Job?"

"It's easy, pays well, couple of hours' worth. Say yes, job's yours for two months. Training, Monday?"

"Monday," Chainsmoke slurred. "OK." Then he went back to bed.

"Habeeb!" his mother yelled from the kitchen, dropping curry leaves in hot oil, anticipating her son's sloth. "Be useful. Study! Who called?"

*

Monday, 7:30 a.m.: Dubai Taxi Stand (Abu Dhabi)—waiting.

Cars screeched. One driver looked right at Chainsmoke. "Quick, I leave now. Come."

Chainsmoke took in the Peugeot's insides. Empty. Reeking of air freshener. Maybe jasmine. The driver urged him to get in. "Full soon, soon full," the man promised. Chainsmoke relented. Fifteen minutes later, the driver's promise rang true.

The highway that takes travelers from Abu Dhabi to Dubai is clean and fine. Illuminated at night by cat's-eye reflectors, it's a highway designed for machines, where Lamborghinis speed, why the desert got bisected, why the camels were fenced out. But Chainsmoke couldn't be bothered. He spent his trip napping on a stranger's shoulder, dreaming about money. He woke to honks. There had been a pileup not far from the Jebel Ali Free Zone. A trailer overturned. Happened too quickly for the brakes to even matter for the cars behind. The smaller cars got smaller. Bodies lay where they landed, most still inside battered vehicles, like bits of fish. The ambulance had not yet arrived. A young Emirati left his Land Cruiser to direct traffic. Chainsmoke looked at his watch, estimated the number of vehicles, how slowly they crawled. "Could we make it in forty-five minutes?" Chainsmoke bellowed. The driver shrugged his shoulders. "Patience, boy," said the stranger whose shoulder he napped on. "Anything can wait after children have died."

Chainsmoke arrived late, interrupting the meeting coordinator, a compact man with a fat tie, mid-sentence.

"Hello," he said. "Come in, come in!" The conference room was full. A roomful of teenagers, mostly boys, tucked into KFC, Mountain Dew, and potato chips. The air smelled like chicken and coleslaw. The meeting coordinator stood next to a blue shopping trolley. There was something doll-like inside, as well as a sack resembling chunky marmalade in color and shape, but the doll had been dropped face down. A large helium balloon kissed the ceiling. Chainsmoke found an empty chair, grabbed a chicken sandwich. Bit.

Introductions had ended, but for Chainsmoke's benefit, the meeting coordinator introduced himself once more. "My name is Menon, Mister Menon," he said, before turning around to face the room, picking up where he left off. "Without your help, no product no profit, you see? Impossibility unconquerable."

Mr. Menon's enunciation was flawless, but, it would become apparent, what he really liked to do was fiddle with his English. Customize it, in fact.

The job, Mr. Menon continued, as he whipped his arms like rope, was simple. He was going to teach them how to be clowns.

"Whabever fo?" Chainsmoke asked, still chewing.

"Glad you asked that, young man," he beamed. "Gentlemen, dear ladies, the task is simplicity personified. Y'all sell detergents dressed like clowns!"

There was nervous laughter.

Mr. Menon laughed back, then said, "I serious." He reached into the marmalade sack, pulled out a joker's mask. He raised it above his head like a cherished talisman.

"Shit," someone whispered.

"Clownsmanship makeup, no need," Mr. Menon explained. "Vetoed by HR to save time. Cash, too. Time lost, customer lost."

The mask came ready-made with a stenciled grin and smelled like a wet mutt.

Complexion, all-purpose-flour white.

Eyebrows colored lead, sleek like tractor beams.

In red, like a bulbous king, sat the clown's nose, unmoving, dipping with weight.

Below the bulbous king, the clown's grin. Wondrous, wide.

The mask fastened over the wearer's face with white-band elastic.

"But pull hard," Mr. Menon mimed, "snap."

Management would also provide clothes. A purple shirt with puffy sleeves and red-and-white-striped trousers with a matching jacket, which included a yellow plastic hibiscus pinned to its right breast pocket.

Then came the hair.

"Without hair, incomplete, like life without bumps," Mr. Menon said, as he introduced blond dreadlocks stapled on and sewed underneath a green elf cap. It was wearable—tight, but wearable. "Black formal shoes are required," Mr. Menon warned, but if "formal" was impossible, any black shoes were acceptable. "As long as they're black! But no running shoes. Understood?"

The room bobbleheaded their assent.

Mr. Menon reached for the silver balloon two feet above his crown. The detergent's name, "Spotless," Chainsmoke now noticed, was scrawled across its belly in bold, red Arabic and English caps.

"Balloon must follow you," Mr. Menon shared. "No excuses."

Mr. Menon then turned around and grabbed the giant doll, which turned out to be a life-size dummy dressed in clown fatigues. He arranged the dummy so it appeared to be sitting in the trolley, its back propped up, legs spread out, neck bent. Satisfied, Mr. Menon looked around the room, paused for effect, then said, "Our secret weapon! HE."

HE, hung awkwardly in the shopping trolley, looked wounded, like he'd been to war and gotten shot. Many times. And wouldn't smile anymore. Mr. Menon had unveiled a clown that had hit the bucket and a couple of other hard objects on its way down, a creature that had seen so much misery it couldn't sit straight, like the devil had cut out its spine.

"Simple idea," Mr. Menon said. "Two clowns, one super-market. Clown One, y'all, spotless, happy. Clown Two. . . this one's dirty, depressed. Happy Clown wheels Dirty Fellow, like this. OK? In case customers miss y'all, tie this to trolley." He grabbed the balloon. "Kids like balloons. Kids come, parents follow."

Chainsmoke noticed people taking notes.

"Dirty Fellow," Mr. Menon said, "will also be holding this white box." *I didn't use New Spotless. He did*, it said in English and Arabic.

Leaflets were also distributed, scented with Spotless's New-and-Improved fragrance.

Shoppers would have to be cajoled into smelling the leaf-let, "herded like sheep into the salesman's abattoir." There, the following hypothesis would be tested: "Perfume is key to better laundry."

Mr. Menon made a fist. A boy in the room made a fist back. They fist bumped. Chainsmoke crunched coleslaw.

"Clown costume boosts curiosity; Dirty Fellow is your se-cret weapon —but once you get customers to smell Spotless, hang on. Make 'em buy. Win your battle, Alexanders!" Mr. Menon encouraged the group.

Battle involved sparring with customer about product; victory meant customer buying product.

"Customer wants control," chuckled Mr. Menon. "Go ahead, make him think he's Big Daddy."

Mr. Menon laughed a practiced "ha-ha." Then paused. "OK, now most important part."

Mr. Menon began distributing photocopied scripts ad execs had worked on for over a year. For the next two hours, the group rehearsed the text. Examined the diagrams.

SCRIPT

CLOWN [*Approach customer, point to dummy*]: Hello, my name is [*fill in name*). I am happy today. My friend is not. Do you know why? [*Wait for response*]

CUSTOMER: No, why?

CLOWN [*Slowly jump up and down, three times*]: Because I used New Spotless, and he didn't. My jacket is like new, his isn't—and he's sad.

CUSTOMER: I see.

CLOWN: Would you like to smell New Spotless? It has a new fragrance, fresh and nice. [*Hand customer leaflet, pull back wrapper, let customer smell*]

They practiced reading the lines out loud with Mr. Menon. Then performed their lines in front of the group.

Mr. Menon discussed voice modulations, confidence, posture. Tested "performance under fire," which involved asking the group to sing "Old McDonald" as each of them took turns reciting lines.

On his way home, Chainsmoke remembered Mr. Menon saying the clown who sold the most detergents was in line for a big prize. "Which is?" Chainsmoke had asked.

"Surprise," Mr. Menon replied.

Mr. Menon's world worshiped focus-group data. Shoppers' habits challenged the results. Baffling the kids who hadn't been armed with a company-approved plan B. Mr. Menon's confidence was infectious. So when Chainsmoke and his colleagues discovered customers didn't have time for scripts or pleasantries, they fumbled. By then, Mr. Menon had flown back to company HQ in Muscat, mission accomplished, never to return. If there were questions, everyone now needed to run it by Melinda, who had a stock reply to almost everything: "Fuck acting, sell the product."

*

The first day on the job, at Choithrams supermarket, Chain-smoke changed in the store room, not brave enough to show up in clown gear.

He expected heckling. The cleaning staff smirked. A Bangla employee, cleaning up broken pickle jars, playfully spanked his ass with the broom, calling him Joka. That evening Chainsmoke found out Melinda wouldn't cover transportation reimbursement. "Bitch," Chainsmoke complained to a friend.

"Quit," was his advice.

"Can't," explained Chainsmoke. "Need money for tuition next semester."

That week, his building's watchman, Moidu, pretended he didn't notice the red snout poking out of the marmalade sack, or the blond clumps of hair. What Moidu wanted to know was where Chainsmoke was taking the balloon. "Too old to go the park, aren't you?" he would say. Every time he caught Chainsmoke going to work, he repeated the phrase.

An Afghan cabbie, with a paan-stained beard, preferred bluntness: "So—what you got there?" Dirty Fellow, in the backseat, had fallen out of the sack, onto his side.

"Work," Chainsmoke muttered in Urdu.

"Must pay well," Paan Beard guffawed.

"Just drive, buddy," Chainsmoke shot back.

At Abu Dhabi Cooperative Society a week later, Chainsmoke had the opportunity to change in an actual restroom.

The restrooms, Pretty Lebanese said, were "down, down straight," past the cashiers. "No changing rooms, sorry." Chainsmoke asked her if she could watch his balloon, then lumbered to the toilets, where he surprised a Muslim savagely washing his toes. One foot in the basin. Balanced like a stork. Late for evening prayer. Chainsmoke greeted him. "Salaam."

"Salaam," the response.

Chainsmoke studied the area. Dank. Smelling of Phenol. In ceramic sinks, soap suds frothed like beer. And people. Walking in and out. As bowels emptied in lichen-colored stalls, as piss struck porcelain—everywhere—men surreptitiously studied genitalia. Zippered up. Before they flushed. Washed. Wiped. Before dryers roared.

Observing all this was Man With Mop, an air freshener, and a pocket radio. He stood expressionless in the corner. Scratching his balls when no one was looking.

Pressed for time, Chainsmoke got down to business.

He dropped the sack, took out the mask, jacket, and wig.

Muslim paused before continuing to soap his left foot.

When Chainsmoke clamped the yellow hairpiece to his skull, Muslim grinned.

"You look better now," he said.

"Shukran," replied Chainsmoke, then shook his new hair vigorously. Yellow dreadlocks danced in the dank air.

Chainsmoke put on his tailcoat. He buttoned up, adjusting the hibiscus. Then he stared at his mask, picked it up. People noticed. Men thumped him on the back, laughing. Man With Mop forgot to pass out napkins. Others edged away, uninterested.

Chainsmoke, brown eyes peeping through white slits, blinked. Because the mask's nostrils didn't possess holes— only a pinprick—and enclosed his nose like a glove, Chainsmoke used his mouth to breathe. With constant use, the mask smelled like afterbreath and plastic.

A smack to the spine surprised Chainsmoke. He turned, finding a giant egg-shaped Arab extending his hand: "Habibi, good luck!" Then he "ho-ho"ed like Santa.

A little girl squealed once the transformed Chainsmoke emerged from the restroom, a yellow-haired Bozo. Delighted, the child hugged his knee. Chainsmoke, surprised, but grateful, hugged back. She kissed his mask. But when her mouth tasted plastic, the little angel detonated. Pulling his hair, banging his mask. Chainsmoke, taken aback, stood rooted, as the little lady pummeled him. "What! What? Ummi!" The mother emerged, in a sequined hijab. Furious. "How dare you! Haiwaan!" she yelled. "Security?"

Chainsmoke's instincts kicked in. He tumbled, feigned a fall, and landed on his ass. Mother and daughter burst out laughing. The boy yanked off his mask, apologizing. Then almost hyperventilated as he struggled to fasten the plastic back where it belonged. A crowd had gathered. Cheers, claps, hoots. Smiles. Security arrived, dispersed.

"Impressive," Pretty Lebanese quipped when he came for the balloon. Chainsmoke shrugged as Dirty Fellow emerged from the sack. He found a trolley, flung Dirty Fellow in, placed his arms over the box. Then he affixed the balloon onto the handlebars.

"Detergents?"

"Aisle 7," Pretty Lebanese smiled.

As Chainsmoke pushed the trolley, he swiveled his hips. Like a whore. In heels.

An employee dressed in black and white disapproved. "Hey, man!" he bellowed in Hindi. "Crazy or what? Decency!"

Chainsmoke stopped, turned. Laughed so the man could hear, then walked like a whore again. In bigger heels.

Someone must have told the children a clown was on the premises. They emerged like fleas, jumping out of Frosties boxes, ice-cream tubs, and the toy aisles. Chainsmoke was escorted to Aisle 7 by a platoon of three-foot fleas. They patted his behind, helped him push his trolley, groped his balloon, got into fights. The shy ones waved from a distance. By the time they walked Chainsmoke to Spot X, his mastery over his adoring public appeared godlike. He shook hands, patted backs, looked folks in the eye. Nothing to it. Until parents arrived. Brandishing cameras, fishing them out of thin air, throwing kids at Chainsmoke like bales of hay. Encouraging their little monsters, "Look, darling, look—for grandma!" "Shake his hand, Leila. . . Leila, Leila! Smile for Baba, habibti. . . Leila!"

After a month on the job, Chainsmoke worked four different locations, changing venues every week. At Spinney's, staff restrooms were off-limits, and there were no customer restrooms. So he changed into clown garb in the storage area again, circled by staff members once more, but this time he got into a confrontation with the manager, an Egyptian who insisted Chainsmoke call him Boss.

"Shave," Boss told him.

"I wear a mask," Chainsmoke replied.

"You want to work here? Shave!" Boss warned. "Important people shop here."

At a similar higher-end supermarket in Khalidiya, where the manager gave him a pack of Reds on the house, he met Big Fella, a tall Mallu who drove for a local family. "Madam wants to speak to you," he said in Hindi.

"Madam?"

"I wouldn't say no. Good money. I will come get you. Your shift ends when?"

"Um, eleven-ish— "

"OK, eleven-fifteen, come to parking. Near the doors. In costume. I will find you."

"What's this about?"

"Madam's local. Behave, no trouble. OK? Not interested, no problem. Decide. In, out?"

"I—"

"Yes, no?"

"Yes."

Big Fella drove a gun-metal Mercedes van. Double-digit number plate. Tinted windows. "Inside," he said, "but mask stays on." Chainsmoke climbed in. Bryan Adams crooned, "Everything I do..."

The van's seats had been taken out, replaced by a small leather couch clamped to mahogany floors that were partially covered by a hand-woven, iodine-colored Balochi rug. Not far from the couch was a petite wooden stool painted a bright strawberry jam, where Chainsmoke sat.

A woman in an abaya faced him. Young, lovely. Amber eyes glazed with kohl. Earlobes still moist from freshly dabbed attar. A pierced tongue.

"As-Salaam alaykum," Abaya greeted him. Her voice was raspy. As though words caught fire every time she spoke, crackling as they lunged at his ear.

"Wa'alaykum salaam."

"Arabic?" Abaya wondered, raising an eyebrow.

"English, if possible," Chainsmoke replied, fiddling with the mask, as he felt somewhat stuffy.

"Sankar didn't mention the details?" Abaya asked him.

"Sankar?"

"My driver."

"No."

"Do what I say, you get paid," Abaya explained.

"One thousand," Chainsmoke said.

"You get two fifty. Drop your pants."

"You've got to be kidding me!"

"Pants, please," Abaya repeated.

"Kiss me first. Foreplay, bab—"

"No touching. Got it? Cross me, I call the shurtha. Got it?"

Chainsmoke stared at her. "OK," he said. "Where's my two fifty?"

"Take them off first. Pants!"

Chainsmoke took them off. "Mask? Jacket?"

171

"Stay on. Pull your briefs down. Down to your ankles. Leave them, let's see."

Chainsmoke looked at his prick. Dark as ash. Soft. "I don't think this gonna work—"

Abaya motioned for him to stop talking. "Touch it."

Chainsmoke placed his palms on his thighs. Silent.

Abaya watched him. "Let me help you," she said, reaching for a remote. The stereo whined as CDs got switched. Chainsmoke heard moaning, the creaking of bed springs, fucking in a language he couldn't place.

"Dutch," said Abaya, reading his mind.

Chainsmoke blushed. Palms now shielded privates. "Sorry, let me out, change mind—"

Abaya watched him. Imagined what he looked like behind his mask. "Homo?" she asked. Chainsmoke didn't say a word.

"What a waste!" Abaya laughed. "Get out!" Angry, he sensed.

As Chainsmoke fiddled with his pants, she cussed. Transitioning smoothly from English to Arabic, insulting his family, his future sons, his comatose prick, his cheap briefs. Animated, her body pulsed. Her rage contorted her face. And as Chainsmoke struggled with his clothes, her tongue continued to riddle him with words spiked with toxins. And like that Chainsmoke's comatose cock stirred.

Abaya noticed. "You like Arabic?" she cooed, cussing quietly now.

Chainsmoke's prick rose like vapor.

"It's a beautiful language," Abaya purred in English. "Two fifty."

Chainsmoke nodded as he began to jack off. Abaya watched, still talking, never stopping. When he came, it was a guttural cry. As though something had been pulled from inside him for the first time, brought forth into the world, screaming like a newborn.

Big Fella asked Chainsmoke where he would be in a week. "Some supermarket on Passport Road," Chainsmoke said.

"See you there," said Big Fella, as he put a few bills in Chainsmoke's jacket pocket. "After that?"

"Maybe Carrefour."

"And here until?"

"Until the weekend's up."

*

At Carrefour the first four nights began without incident. Then one fateful evening a tall Samsonian man with enormous chompers, put on Earth to play the alpha male, arrived with his entourage. Dressed in a white kandoura, he was trailed by shorter men, as handsome, who laughed at everything he said. They, the five of them, slithered towards the clown like upright rattlers. Alpha took a long look at Chainsmoke. "Hello!" he hissed.

"Hello," replied Chainsmoke, right hand stuck out. "Would you like to try new Spo—"

Alpha grinned, reached for Chainsmoke's nose, singing, "How do YOU do-do-do?" On the fourth "do," he tore away Chainsmoke's nose and held it out to him like a big, fat berry.

Chainsmoke took his nose, muttering a quick thank you, before he attempted to end the conversation. But the men surrounded him. Alpha then planted three fingers under the mask's chin, and pulled.

Chainsmoke stared at his assailant. Blinked. Alpha smiled. Saw cinnamon skin. A bit of mustache. Chainsmoke slapped the hand away, saying, "Thank you, have a nice day," and walked towards customer service, pushing the shopping trolley. Shaking.

"Where do you keep your Super Glue?"

"Stationary," replied Puffy Cheeks.

"Where's stationary?"

"Where we keep Super Glue."

"You trying to be funny?"

"No. You?"

Leaving Dirty Fellow, and the balloon under the care of a security guard named Mathai, Chainsmoke glued his nose back on in the restroom, after first waiting in the express-checkout line to pay for his purchase.

"Missing something?" Cashier Lady had inquired, observing the nose in Chainsmoke's palm. Chainsmoke, still wearing his mask, shook his head. "I need a receipt," was all he said.

But in his haste to return to work—Melinda had sent people to check up on him—Chainsmoke dabbed on too much glue. By the time he returned to his spot, he had huffed a good amount.

When little Saarah, egged on by her baba, tugged his trouser leg, Chainsmoke was high. Saarah's older sister stood by, legs and arms akimbo. Slightly taller. Chewing Chiclets. Not happy at all. Grumpy, in fact. Telling her sister, "Get away from him, Saarah, he's dirty."

Saarah didn't care. "Kloon, kloon, my name is Saarah. Kloon?"

"Saarah, how are you, habibti?" Chainsmoke responded.

Grumpy made a face. "Black clowns don't exist, Saarah. Look at his neck, fingers" she told her sister in Arabic. As soon as she outed Chainsmoke's race, her baba, within earshot, slapped her across the cheek.

"Apologize," he said. Grumpy refused.

"Blackie," she muttered, defiant. Baba turned towards Chainsmoke.

"Children," he said. "What to do?"

"No problem," said Chainsmoke.

The exchange didn't faze Saarah. "I learn English, Kloon. My name is Saarah Ahmad. My baba is Mister Ahmad. He farm-cyst. My mo—"

"That's wonderful, sweetheart. Here you go, habibti, have three leaflets. Go on, smell. "

"Thank you, Kloon. Shukran, Kloon!"

"Welcome, Saarah."

Grumpy had had enough. "Let's go," she told Saarah, grabbing her arm.

"Kloon! Bye-bye!"

"Bye-bye!"

Mr. Ahmad raised his right hand in thanks, put it across his chest. Chainsmoke acknowledged the greeting.

By 8:45 p.m. Chainsmoke's eyes had begun to water from the glue; he had a headache. He was required to work until eleven but he was having difficulty concentrating. He removed the mask every fifteen minutes in order to get some air. Cough. Which was how Big Fella found him.

"We will be outside, same time."

"Tonight?"

"Yes."

"Might be difficult."

"Last time."

"Oh. . ."

While they conversed, two kids and their uncle untied the Spotless balloon, then ran off with Dirty Fellow and the trolley. Big Fella noticed. Mid conversation, Chainsmoke bolted in pursuit. Security found Dirty Fellow hidden among the stuffed toys. A mother was asked to pry it from the hands of her four-year-old. "I will pay you three hundred dirhams," she told Chainsmoke.

"Sorry, ma'am, I can't. I can't!"

The four-year-old bawled and began throwing action figures. Then demanded popcorn.

"Look what you did!" the mother yelled. "Idiot!"

Supermarket personnel found the balloon weighted down by four baguettes in the bakery aisle.

An hour later, as he walked to and fro between the shopping trolley and the end of the aisle, a woman with a British accent asked if he could stop moving. "What?" he asked.

"I am on the phone, fool," she said. "Your walking's distracting me. If you don't stop, I am going to ask someone to remove you."

Chainsmoke sized her up. A Brit with varicose veins. Long like creepers. Thick eyeglasses. A surly creature with surly-looking white hair. Yelling at someone on the phone, "Where? Where did you go? Where?"

She put the person on hold. "Well, are you going to stop bothering me?" she asked Chainsmoke again.

"Sure," said Chainsmoke. And he stopped moving. "Whatever Madam wants."

*

At the end of his shift, Chainsmoke waited near the fake palms for Big Fella. Tired, he set his mask aside, atop everything else, and smoked quickly. The Brit had complained because she didn't appreciate his tone. The floor manager asked him to apologize. "For what?" he protested.

"Look," the man said, "your work ain't legal. She makes one call, we are both fucked." So he said sorry. She thanked the manager, walked away.

"Cunt," said Chainsmoke.

The parking lot was packed to capacity. It was Ramadan. Shoppers filled their vehicles with purchases. The garage echoed with the sound of families, the smell of car exhausts and bread. Big Fella was late. As Chainsmoke lit another one, the balloon hovered like Casper. Time, 11:30 p.m.

When the Mercedes arrived, Chainsmoke, crushed butts at his feet, pursed his lips. He had stayed to vent.

"Waited like a dog," Chainsmoke grumbled as he climbed in.

"Long day?" Abaya asked. Embroidered copper swallows circled Abaya's abaya.

"Some white lady asked me to stop walking, so I did."

"Rest of your day?" she wondered.

"Not good," he replied. "What's it to ya?"

"Poor baby," Abaya crooned. Said without effort. Flat. Without soul.

"Don't patronize me, I ain't your bitch," he snapped.

Abaya opened her eyes wide. "You're not?" She rubbed the fingers on her right hand with her thumb, performed the gesture in front of his nose. "Oh, I think you are. You're my bitch, bitch."

Chainsmoke sulked, staring at the floor mats.

Abaya wouldn't let it go. "Why do this, then?" She pumped her right fist like a piston.

"Tuition," he said firmly.

"Tuition?"

"Yeah, tuition," he confirmed. Abaya peered at him, picking out his eyes through the slit in the mask. "Bullshit," she said. "You born for this."

Chainsmoke glared at her.

Abaya stared back. "I force you?"

"No," Chainsmoke admitted. "But you don't need to. *Coming, walking*, you get what you want."

"Maybe."

"Maybe? If you say so."

Abaya lit a beedi. "Sankar. . . got me. . . addicted to these," she said, taking quick puffs. "Tell me," she said, "in your perfect world. . . if you owned me, what would you do to me?"

Chainsmoke inhaled the second-hand smoke; it felt good. "If I owned you?"

"Yes." Puff.

"I would ask you things."

"Like what?"

Chainsmoke thought for a bit. "Your father's name?"

"Ibrahim," she answered.

"The name of a lover."

"Hamad." Puff.

"The color of your cunt."

Abaya watched him. Inhaled. Beedi smog cirlicued young lungs. Ravaging them like wind weathering stone. Before the smoke left her body. "Tell me your mother's, tell you mine," she whispered. Grinned.

"Fuck you!"

"No dear boy, fuck *you*!"

"On second thought, I wouldn't even ask," Chainsmoke said. "I would just take your cunt and fuck it."

"Really?" Abaya sneered. "Fuck me how, Brown Boy?"

"I would tie you up."

"Where?"

"The front of this van."

"How?"

"Rope."

Abaya pictured it, smiled.

"The engine's still hot. I pin you. Your back burns. My cock opens you—" Chainsmoke dropped his trousers. "—kiss you, bite you, own you..." The rest of it was garbled, muttered in another tongue, as Chainsmoke, eyes shut, jacked off. But his masturbation was violent, as though strangling something shameful, the effort making his body shake, the shaking detaching the mask's nose. And it fell to the floor. Like a big, fat red seed. Hitting Abaya's right foot. Startling her. Making her laugh. Like a witch in a play. Even looking beautiful. As she impulsively reached forward and removed Chainsmoke's mask, smelling cigarette breath. Watching his contorted horny face, seeing it for the first time, smelling his scent. Touching him, laughing at him. Cooing in Arabic. Brushing his prick with her knees. Laughing at him again. Which is how he came. On his chest, on her thighs, on the copper swallows on her dress. Unable to stop, as Abaya crumpled to the floor of the van in hysterics. In no mood to apologize, in no state to see Chainsmoke pull up his pants, pick up his nose, put on his fallen mask, and rush out the van.

Big Fella, habitually tucking into a tiffin dinner of parathas and butter chicken near the front of the van, tensed up as Chainsmoke sprinted from the vehicle. The driver flung his food at the boy, hitting him, and was about to follow in pursuit, grabbing his Glock from the glove compartment, when he heard Abaya's rich laugh. "Your nose, habibi, your nose!" she screamed. Then chuckled hysterically as she kicked out the rest of Chainsmoke's gear. The marmalade sack, the balloon.

The balloon hung in the air. For a moment. Before climbing towards space. Towards the moon.

*

Chainsmoke stopped running. He had darted past cars, startled shoppers. He reached the other end of the parking lot. Swore. Cringed as a woman howled in the distance: "Nose! Nose! My kingdom for a nose!" Then laughter. A woman's. A man's. He needed to return. To grab that sack.

"Kloon?" A little voice.

Chainsmoke turned. Wiped fingers on trousers. "Saarah?"

Saarah grinned, but then she saw Kloon's face, smudged with bright red curry. Blood. Bits of skull, she deduced. Someone had bashed open Kloon's red brain, scooped it out with a teaspoon, and stolen his nose. In an instant, Saarah's face blanched . Her body froze. She shut her eyes.

"La!" she muttered in Arabic. Her scream arrived like bullets, echoing through the parking lot. "BABA! UMMI!"

Her older sister, Grumpy, was dispatched to get her.

Chainsmoke was confused. Thought the girl had gone mad. Then remembered his nose. Removing his mask. Wiping the redness off his clothes, making it worse, spreading it like frosting. "Habibti, don't be afraid, it's me, it's me!" He moved closer.

Saarah felt sick. In Kloon's place stood a strange earth-colored man, a monster who devoured Kloon from the inside out and ate her friend. She tried fleeing but fell, bruising her knees.

As Saarah lay on the ground, waiting to die, Grumpy arrived, bent to pick her up, but almost stumbled herself, giving Chainsmoke a quick peek at Daisy-Duck panties. But she quickly regained her balance and hurried her sniveling sister to the family's Mazda station wagon.

Saarah's amused baba and concerned ummi, after a brief Q&A, a Mars bar, promises to report Kloon's murderer, put her to work with the grocery bags. Grumpy excused herself, claiming she dropped an earring. Returning to face Chainsmoke, as he dragged his marmalade sack to hail a cab.

"Why do that to Saarah?" Grumpy yelled in English.

"Excuse me?"

"You no clown."

"What!"

"Your face, it's white, but those arms, that face—everything's black, Black Man."

"What?" Chainsmoke wrung beach-mud palms. "Black?" he said out loud.

"Bastard," Grumpy muttered loud enough for him to hear.

"Bastard?"

"Yes, bastard. Bastard."

"You know what 'bastard' means?"

"Your mother should know."

"Show respect, little shit," Chainsmoke snarled.

"Most blackies are bastards," she said. "My uncle also told me that you people don't wash. And that your farts smell like curry."

"Listen, you—"

"Bastard, bastard, bastard..." she sang. Then she began to pirouette.

"Wait—"

She wouldn't let him talk. "How many fathers you got? Bastard, bastard, you are a curry-farting bastard."

"Maybe I should tell your baba what a dirty girl he's got," Chainsmoke interrupted, just fed up now.

Grumpy glared at him. "Baba knows I am good."

"Does he? Good girls don't bend over like you did. Good girls don't show their butts to strangers. You knew what you were doing when you showed me your Daisy Duck undies—"

"No—"

Chainsmoke wouldn't let her finish. "Saarah's good, I can tell. You, on the other hand, are a filthy little shit. Dirty mind, dirty heart."

"Stop it," Grumpy said.

"Letting me see your butt like that. Bad girls go to hell for doing shit like that, you know? You know, don't you? Don't you? What do you think your mother's gonna do when I tell her what sort of daughter she's raising? I mean, do you even have hair down there?"

"Shut up!"

"Bad girls make bastards. Know how? I can tell you do. If I bought you a Kit Kat, you'd just let me stick anything I want in there, wouldn't you?"

"SHUT UP!"

"I shouldn't be surprised. Filth like you have no shame—"

"You didn't see my butt, you didn't see anything! I am telling Baba," Grumpy fumed. Cheeks puffed like melons, arms by her side, hands rolled into fists.

"Sure, bring Baba over, I will tell him myself. What his daughter's really like and what she likes to do when he's not looking."

"He won't believe you," she said softly.

"Let's see," Chainsmoke challenged. "Look at your tummy, nice and big like that, you know how many bastards you could fit in there? No one would even know. Why don't you admit it? You've done some sick shit, haven't you? Call your pencil-dicked uncle for me so I can tell him his niece is no fuckin' nun."

Baba, ready to leave, yelled from the car. "Noor! Come, habibti! Leave him alone!" Grumpy turned. "Coming, Baba!"

"You better go, Noor, before I tell him," Chainsmoke chuckled. "Go before the world knows! But you know what I really think. I think it's too late for you. I'm pretty sure your baba knows! That everything's not all right, everything's not OK."

"I hope you die!" Grumpy cried. "You, you curry-farting asshole."

"Noor," said Chainsmoke. "Go. Just go home, you little shit."

As Noor scurried back, holding back tears, moving like she had rocks in her tummy, Chainsmoke raised his arms, mask in one hand, and, as though guided by a slow-moving lever, he began to pirouette, keeping an eye on the Mazda. The man at the wheel, Mr. Ahmad, laughed, as his flushed daughter settled in the back, next to a chocolate-stained Saarah. As Chainsmoke yelled goodbye, he caught sight of a middle-aged man with huge palms, trembling with Parkinson's, being helped towards a parked Volvo by a lady he leaned on, a woman with surly-looking white hair and a patient face, who said, "Almost there, Ed." In her free hand, she held a bit of shopping: produce.

Chainsmoke wasted no time. He grabbed the marmalade sack from where it had been dropped, lugging it behind him like a burglar in a fairy tale. And, measuredly, he began to walk towards the couple, exaggerating his steps, as though his legs were weighted with iron. "Madam, madam!" he shouted. She saw him. "Look," he said. "Look, I'm walking. Bitch, I'm walking!"

CHABTER EIGHT

CUNNINLINGUS

FIRST TIME, IN A Datsun by the beach somewhere in Dubai. It was Ramadan; mid afternoon. No shurtha in sight, few people around. Didn't bite. Licked carefully, quickly. The AC was on, I remember. Unwittingly swallowed pubic hair. Refused feedback. Confident I had failed.

CHABTER NINE

NALINAKSHI

MY NAME IS NALINAKSHI. I am from Nadavaramba, Thrissur. Yesterday, I turned eighty. My husband was fifty-eight when he passed. My sisters are in their sixties. They live with their grandkids and daughters-in-law. I also have a boy, my only son, Haridas Menon, my Hari. Ever since Hari could crawl, I knew he'd be a wanderer, destined to be a pravasi. And you know what, I was right. As soon as he started to walk, he walked his skinny ass all the way to Dubai. I suppose you're too young to understand what pravasi means, young man, what it truly means. Maybe that's why you singled me out for your research. Whatever comes, speak into the recorder, you said. Maybe I've got the look of an old crone with wisdom to spare. And you know what, you're right, I feel like I'm going to be talkative in my eighties. So let me tell you what pravasi means, but when my voice gets played back to your teachers, tell them Nalinakshi was of sound state and mind as she said her piece. Not a trace of bitterness, not an ounce of pity.

Pravasi means foreigner, outsider. Immigrant, worker. Pravasi means you've left your native place. Pravasi means you'll have regrets. You'll want money, then more money. You'll want one house with European shitters. And one car, one scooter. Pravasi means you've left your loved ones because you're young, ambitious, filled with confidence that you'll be back some day, and you probably will. For a few weeks every year, you'll return for vacations, but mind you, you return older. Blacker. News hungry. Before you've had time to adjust to power cuts and pot-holes, like they had in the old days when phones were luxuries or glued to walls, someone's going to tell you so-and-so died. And it'll be a shock, because you didn't know. And when you go to this person's house to pay your respects, you'll discover some-one else has died. And as you continue to see people you know you're required to see, you'll hear about more dead people. Or ailments. Or needs. Then you'll see the new people, fat babies or wives or husbands. And you'll look at what they've got. Inevitably, you'll think about your own life, the choices you made. How far you've come, if paying for those shitters was worth it. And by the time you've done the math in your head, everything you've missed, what's been gained, you'll come to realize what the word pravasi really means: absence. That's what it means, absence. When you write your book, address my Hari person-ally, and tell my beautiful, beautiful boy, tell my son that's what it's always meant: absence.

BOOK

Consider a man with a suitcase for a
face, a man living by the sea on
brown land infected by strife, a man
with an engineering degree. Buy
Suitcase Face a ticket so he is
welcomed at O'Hare as a tourist. Then
change his name. Turn him illegal.
Put him behind the wheel of a Lincoln
Towncar. Make him drive until his
wife forgets her husband,
his son avoids his father. Make him
drive until the immigrant rues the
reasons he fled, until looking at the
green card hurts. Observe.

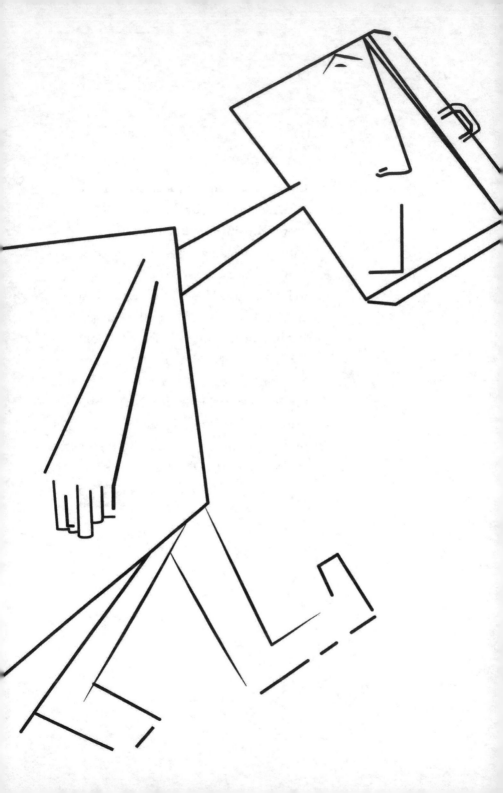

CHABTER ONE
KADA (SHOP). KADHA (STORY).
KADAKARAN (SHOPKEEPER).

BELOW MY BUILDING IS a kada. You know, shop. With a kada-karan. You know, shopkeeper. This kadha. You know, story. Involves him. Kadakaran Moidu is what Amma called him. I called him Karate Moidu because he called himself Karate Moidu because he took lessons for a few months before break-ing his wrist after falling from a chair, ending what would've been a promising Karate Moidu career. So now he had his kada, which became his kadha, that he turned into another kada-karan in Arabee Naadu. You know, Arabee Cundry. All of this, his kada, his kadha, that he became a kadakaran, became his arabeekadha. That was his vidhi. You know, fate.

CHABTER TWO

WATER

MY MOTHER, A TELLER of stories, was born near the coastline, where I was born, too, as well as my brother, on land watched by water, where coconut palms turn lakes and rivers olive. When the monsoons are heavy, the earth here is not only watered, the ground is drowned. The rivers break banks, flooding potholed streets, scaring strays, moving train tracks, leaving homes at the mercy of water, forcing people to wait by dry land, in a cousin's home, wherever, until the water recedes, until the rivers have explored enough and wish to return. By then, fish have nibbled in the kitchens of these houses, slept in the beds of strangers, defecated in their toilets, or died peacefully near makeshift altars, claimed by mollusks, crabs, water birds with wise faces. On decaying fish, bits of flotsam, water bugs leave eggs.

There is a river not far from my mother's home, where my parents made me, near the Hindu temple where they were married, with the head priest who, before he turned to priesthood, used to work in a butcher shop somewhere in Arabia, a frowned-upon but forgiven act. This river, my mother believed, was special, something the jinns may have had a hand in making. When the nights simmered like day, she told us, when weeks went by without rain, the fish in the river would swim up to the bank on certain nights, discarding their scales, fins, tails, becoming people, walking on land like they were testing its hospitality, in case the river beds dried up and they needed a new place to live. But the fish were a bundle of nerves when they ventured out, perplexed by the ways of man: how they walk, drove cars, mined mountains, built machines, bought Gold Spot for the kids. The fish, my mother said, felt vulnerable, and they became tense. In order to keep calm, many openly participated in the vices on offer, comfortably overeating in shaaps selling spicy beef fry, trading stories with alcoholics who didn't want to go home just yet, drinking fresh arrack straight from the toddy tapper's pot, searching for women whose men toiled abroad, searching for men whose women did the same. Near dawn, after a lot of eating or lovemaking or fucking or drinking or wandering, the fish would return to the banks, disappearing into the muddy river, convinced they were river creatures, unsuited for land.

My mother now works on land almost completely bereft of water, where there are no rivers, but instead a salty sea where many years ago, men dove for pearls from wooden Sambuks. She takes care of a girl who is around my age. The girl's name is Ibtisam and she understands our tongue. Only for a short time, my mother promised when she left, but the shortness has grown longer, many years, almost twelve, and I am now grown. Every two years, she would return, laden with gifts. At first, my little brother wouldn't go near her, wouldn't touch the chocolates she brought, or call her Amma, so she seduced him with stories, like she always did, when she used to feed or bathe him or put us to sleep. If she could manage it one day, she promised, she would introduce us to Ibtisam. Then, she promised, she would introduce us to her secret friends, men and women made entirely of liquid, who had little children our age made entirely of liquid. She referenced these families often in her conversations with us when she called, and in her letters. It was our secret, what we were in store for when she finally called for us to live with her, and we would be invited to the homes of her secret friends, where we would play with their children. They hide during the day, she wrote, to escape the heat. At dusk they emerge, exploring a more manageable climate, to partake in its nightlife, to eat at restaurants, to host dinners, to hold hands in the park, to play games, to kiss and not get caught, to teach their children how to ride bicycles. Before dawn, they disappear, only to return the following day.

CHABTER THREE

SARAMA

IT'S QUITE SIMPLE REALLY; my family owes its existence to the forest demon, Surpanakha.

My maternal great-grandmother, Parvathy Amma, was born in a village near Talikulam, Kerala.

The word for great-grandmother in Malayalam is "muthassi." She was the first woman to hold me, to bathe me, my first loved one to die. She decided on my name, Bhagyanathan. She would call me nothing else; she hated nicknames. "Bhagyanathan!" she would yell. When she called my name, she said it like one would address a king. When she said "Bhagyanathan," you would almost expect to hear the rolling of chariots, the neighing of horses, the sound of footmen. I was her king.

Muthassi was a renowned storyteller in my village and in her younger days used to be invited to participate in festivals all over Kerala. Her specialty was telling stories from the *Ramayana*.

Some people have a voice made for stories, their vocal chords fashioned by Brahma himself. Muthassi's voice was like that. Her pitch, unusual for a woman, was very low, a rumble, like the purr of a cat. Age added to its mystique. Her voice grabbed you, didn't let you go; the stories poured into your veins and intoxicated your brain. You listened until she finished; you didn't have a choice.

But she was also a treasure trove of other tales, much darker ones, which she was always happy to share with me. Popping balls of rice into my mouth, she often warned me to beware of the snakes in our garden: "They transform into

197

human form at night, eager to snatch game they slink into the netherworld."

I was around four years old when she started telling me stories from the *Ramayana*. She recited the epic to me out of sequence, concentrating more on the characters than the story itself. "Everybody," she liked to say, "has a past that ought to be heard. The present is paralyzed without a past."

The scriptures I know come from her. I preferred listening to reading. I think she innately understood that.

The night she decided I needed to know the story I am about to share, four crows cawed outside our house at twilight for over an hour. I had just turned ten. It was monsoon season but the rains still hadn't come. I was listening to the radio when the power went out. As usual, she called out to me. She needed someone to talk to in the dark. My parents were to be back the following morning. I had been left in charge, the man of the house.

I was still a small boy and struggling with the kerosene lamp, its heat kissing my thighs, when I walked into her room and asked if she needed anything.

"Close the door, my dear," she said slowly.

"Blow out your lamp."

I did.

The room smelled strongly of smoke and kerosene.

"Give me your right arm," she said.

I did, and she began rubbing my fingers, one by one.

When I was still a child, people noticed quickly that my palms and feet were frog-like, too big for the rest of my body. Some kids in the village hopped like frogs, pretended to be toads, or stuck their tongues out like lizards when they wanted to make it clear I couldn't play with them. It didn't bother me. I was built to be alone.

Muthassi tugged my fingers, at weird angles, bending them in degrees I didn't think possible. When she snapped my index finger off, breaking it like a twig, I stared. There was no pain. I was more alarmed than frightened, worried about Amma's reaction when she noticed. Muthassi smiled kindly.

"Don't worry, little one, I will put it back. I wanted to check, that's all," she said.

And before I knew it, she stuck my index finger back on. I stared at it, wiggling it a little bit to make sure it still did what it used to do.

"Don't be afraid now," is what she told me gently before she calmly unscrewed her head, twisting it off like a bottle cap and placing it on her lap.

"I would like to go outside, Bhagyanathan," she decided all of a sudden. "It's too hot here; let's go by the pond, it's cooler there. Carry Muthassi out."

I held Muthassi's head carefully and walked out of the house towards the pond, a place I was forbidden to venture to by myself, especially at night.

I placed Muthassi's head on the flat stones where Amma did our washing, facing the black and slimy water, which would turn green again at dawn. In the darkness, the pond looked like cobra skin.

"Water is significant to us," she began, eyes drifting towards the pond. "One of our ancestors, The Male, crossed into Lanka over water."

"This creature, a monkey, we are almost certain," Muthassi said, "was a soldier in the monkey king Sugriva's army, first working under the supervision of Nala and Neel, famed builders without whom the construction of the floating bridge would have been impossible. He, our ancestor, along with others, slaved night and day on this massive undertaking until his muscles hurt, until his body refused to cooperate."

At night, he tended to blisters swollen with pus. It was tough work.

A significant number of monkeys and bears from the kingdom of Kishkindha died building the bridge. Many collapsed out of exhaustion, some forgetting to eat or drink, perishing on the job. They were driven hard, not allowed to venture home, forced to sleep near the construction site.

Sugriva was a hard taskmaster. Yet in his eagerness to repay the debt he owed Rama, Sugriva often forgot his soldiers were mortal. Some of them didn't appreciate the treatment and began to bitch and gossip. The situation took a serious turn when rumors started circulating about Sugriva's chicanery in getting rid of Vali, his elder brother. Without Ram, Sugriva would still be on the run from Vali, the grapevine opined; an honorable warrior wouldn't have resorted to treachery in battle, and only an honorable warrior deserved a seat on the throne, deserved to bed Queen Tara. The parties who started the rumor were executed immediately.

I picture this creature often, The Male—marching with other beasts, forced to deal with the drudgeries of war, crossing into an alien land to go to battle for the prince of Ayodhya, a prince he possibly did not even speak to—and I begin to wonder whether the air started to smell of war as soon as he walked over the bridge with other comrades in arms, whether giant vultures circled in the foreground, waiting to feast, and whether my ancestor felt fear.

But the story of my family's lineage does not begin with Rama looking out to sea, imagining the tip of the land that held his young bride captive, as monkeys and bears busied themselves hauling stones to get the bridge built quickly. It doesn't even begin when The Male, a biped like me, marched onwards to Lanka. Our history begins with the humiliation of Surpanakha.

The women in our family, Muthassi shared, could be traced back to a long line of demons. These were women granted numerous boons by the lords of the netherworld and the gods in heaven, rakshashis with power, who were feared, who made mortals realize they were mortal, women who were shape shifters, unafraid of the sound of forests or of being alone with spirits who refused to be born again after their bodies were fire-lit on pyres.

In my great-grandmother's words, "The Female of our race was one-legged, two-legged, three-legged, many-headed, short, fat, squat, tall, alive, hideous, glorious—so alive! We were so swollen with life, with glut, that we frightened those who barely lived."

"The word 'demon' is tainted," Muthassi lamented, "riddled with hyperbole, caked in fear. Demon only implies evil, beings from the netherworld. Rakshashis may only be beasts, may only be beasts. It is a simplification, suggesting that those who navigate the netherworld can only possess organs dark as soot. The truth, my child, is that our ancestors were women who did what they wanted, for whom dharma meant accepting their urges, following them to their very ends, not belittling or suppressing them. Our women tested the gods, made them wish they were half-god, half-demon, down to our level, one foot knee-deep in vice and pleasure, the other foot still tentatively holding on to Mount Meru."

Muthassi's head pivoted to face me, moving like a little clay bowl on the flat stones where Amma beat wet clothes. Her hair, a mop of dirty white curls the color of gnawed bone, danced in the breeze. She stared at me for a long time, as Amma's great-grand-mother may have done when she told this very tale.

"Bhagyanathan," she finally said, "our women folk made mistakes. But sometimes we wanted to make them. We learned by being!"

She calmed down after that outburst, her head rocking a little from side to side from all the fuss.

It was then she spoke her name. When Muthassi said, "The womb of Sarama, 'The Old One,' is where we believe our line begins," it was the first time I had heard of the name. She had never mentioned her before.

Among the rakshashis entrusted to guard Sita at the palace groves, Sarama was as old as the trees themselves, Muthassi said. She was from a time when our women folk were constantly abused by the mortals, hunted like vermin, pinned to trees and sacrificed at will and without warning. It was why they turned to the gods, performing penance, sacrificing. The gods, pleased, granted them many boons. But over time, even the gods grew envious of their power, of their grasp on the underworld, and started scheming and turning against them, wary of the consequences if the rakshashas decided to invade Mt. Meru.

"This war between the netherworld and the heavens lasted eons," Muthassi said. "It has not ended."

Sarama, our ancestor, was old enough to remember Tataka, Surpanakha's grandmother. She remembered Tataka's beauty. And she remembered the monster she mutated into, taller than a mountain, tusks sprouting out of her nose like daggers, wearing the skulls of the ones she killed, a body of pure hate.

"Agastya turned her into the beast she became," Muthassi said. "He killed her husband; in turn, she tried to kill Agastya. Only the forests could home that rage. It was her turf."

In Surpanakha, Tataka's beloved granddaughter, whom Sarama had known since she was a baby, she could clearly see glimpses of her grandmother. A beautiful child, like Tataka, Surpanakha's spirit belonged in the forest, where she was most free, becoming one with the land, living, sleeping, hunting, mating. It was her home as much as it had been her grandmother's.

Many years later, after the war, The Old One still shuddered when she recalled the state of Surpanakha's mutilation. What Lakshmana's blade had done! Oh, what it had done!

"There are texts that write lies about her form," Muthassi seethed. "It is as though the scribes are afraid to be truthful. They write her skin is polluted, calling it foul, bloating her physique, making her out to be a monster so vile she putrefied anything she touched. They lie!" "She was beautiful," Muthassi said,

"a beauty that could drive men and women mad. She knew fully
well every inch of her body; her form evoked desire, possibly
frightening the young god-king and his brother equally. Frightening scribes to have their quills lie so boldly."

"Surpanakha was not Sita," Muthassi admitted. "But Sita
could never have been Surpanakha. They write that she was
brutal," she said, giving me a wry smile. "Her brutality lay only
in the manner she acknowledged and chased her desire. She refused to suppress her wants," Muthassi concluded.

She paid for such audacity, marching through Ravana's palace
doors with sliced breasts, no ears, and a disfigured nose. Ravana's
guards, men used to the bedlam of war, stood by, stunned into silence, letting her pass. She would not crouch, she did not whim-
per, she was defiant; walking bare-bosomed into Ravana's court,
she met everyone's eye. When she spoke, the courtiers and the
ministers turned their faces away, unable to look. She was visibly
in pain. But they heard her; they heard the screams of rage, of
hurt, of vengeance. And when the king himself jumped from his
throne to comfort his mutilated sister, the siblings, reunited for
the first time since the troubling circumstances of her husband
Dushtabuddhi's death, embraced in anguish. And wept.

The ten-headed Ravana, tears of fury in his eyes, caressed
his sister's hair, held her body like she was little again, and ran
after her older brothers in the forests, watched by Tataka, who
doted on her grandchildren. He did this openly, in front of his
courtiers and guards. But she would have none of it, composing
herself quickly. Pity wasn't what Surpanakha had come for. She
refused to let Ravana drape her body with cloth. The pain would
pass; her wounds would remain bare and undressed until she
had her revenge.

Our ancestor, Sarama, awoke from her slumber to the sound
of a ten-headed scream that filled the air with dread, a scream
Muthassi mimicked, her mouth opening as wide as the hole

that swallowed Sita, so wide that her head became all mouth. It was a terrible scream.

In the village, those who heard the guttural cry that night woke and began to pray; animals whimpered; woodland spirits stopped moving. The gloom was exactly as it had been when the leaves of Lanka turned gray: birds falling from the sky, refusing to fly, and the trees beginning to bleed.

Ravana had made up his mind, Muthassi said. He would avenge Surpanakha's humiliation. His prize would be Sita. There would be war. There would be war. There would be war.

Sarama found Sita a silly creature to fight a war over. She was beautiful, certainly, but Sarama had seen different kinds of beauty in her time, beauty that possessed you, turned you inside out, forced you to be impatient. Sita's beauty almost made her untouchable—too pure, too good, too right. Sarama spurned such beauty; it made her uneasy. Maybe that is why Ravana desired Sita, she felt. He wanted to pollute her, to consume her, to make her more real.

Still, as The Old One, our ancestor, helped keep watch over the young princess of Ayodhya, the would-be girl-queen began to intrigue her.

She paid close attention as Sita fought Ravana practically every day, refusing to be intimidated by his advances. Even when the rakshashis tried to scare her into relenting, shaking the earth, turning the sky foul and ominous, threatening to eat her alive, theatrics that made most mortals quiver and piss, she held firm. Sarama smelled fear in the young Sita, but she also admired her audacity, her will. Sarama could tell Sita would never submit to Ravana's lust. If he tried to touch her, Sarama knew, Sita, the daughter of Janaka, would rage against her tormentor, scratch him, maim him, pull out tufts of hair from any of his ten heads, until her body no longer pulsed. Sarama respected that rage, a rage she didn't believe Sita, a would-be girl-queen, possessed at first, the sort of rage that only became evident when

Rama refused to take her back when the war had ended. Because she respected such rage, when Ravana threw Rama's decapitated head near Sita's feet, Sarama told the would-be girl-queen that it was an illusion, that Rama was still safe, and that his forces were crossing into Lanka.

Muthassi pivoted her head towards the pond again, staring at the water, taking some time before moving on to the next phase in the tale. It was important to her that everything was clear.

The evening before the great battle between the two armies—one bestial, the other demonic—Sarama found Surpanakha sitting by the gardens where Ravana held Sita captive. Surpanakha avoided the forlorn-looking Sita, preferring to sit by herself. They would meet later, after the war, after Rama's death. For now, they both stared silently into the open, deep in thought.

The other rakshashis had been afraid to approach Surpanakha. They left her alone to stew in her rage. But Sarama was braver. She was also concerned; inching her way to the mutilated lady, she watched a grieving Surpanakha gently touching what was left of her nose, her ears, her butchered breasts.

Surpanakha felt the rawness of the wounds, imagining the sight she had become. She wouldn't look into a mirror just yet. She couldn't. She had almost caught a glimpse of her new state when she drank water from a stream. She would wait until the war was over, the mortals who did this to her slain. Then she would take the corpse of Rama, fling it at his young widow, and dance pitilessly and mercilessly over the dead man, like Kali. She would delight in watching Sita as she did this. Then, in quiet, she would sneak Rama's remains away, cremating his body, extinguishing it in fire, as Yama, the Lord of Death, would wait patiently on his buffalo, his giant club resting on the ungulate's belly.

Sita's plight would be different. Surpanakha would scheme to keep the princess alive for thousands of years, refusing to let her die, breaking her heart as many times as it could be broken.

Lakhsmana's bones and entrails, she would wear, his flesh carrion fed to scavengers.

When Sarama The Old One, our ancestor, finally reached Surpanakha, she was holding her bloodied breasts, trembling. There were tears. Sarama also realized flies had laid eggs in her open wounds, and the larvae would soon hatch. Sarama reached out to touch her. Gently. Surpanakha seized the gnarled hand, ready to tear it off the person who dared disturb her. When she saw who it was, she calmed down a little, but, still spitting in Sarama's face, screamed, "Not pity, old hag, not pity!"

Sarama, understanding, knelt low, pressed her palms to Surpanakha's feet, and whispered, "It isn't pity, child, your wounds must be tended to. Let me. Let the old one through. I knew Tataka, I knew Tataka."

At the mention of her grandmother's name, Surpanakha relented, allowing herself to be touched and held. And there they sat, the two of them, Sarama tenderly washing Surpanakha's wounds and picking out larvae, as Surpanakha, tired and overwhelmed, fell asleep. The following morning, when the two armies rode out to battle, the beginning of war, Sarama searched for Surpanakha. She had slipped away. The two would never meet again.

When Ravana was finally slain, the war over, our ancestor Sarama stepped out of the palace grounds and walked towards the battlefield, followed by concerned wives and children, family of the missing soldiers in Ravana's army.

The battlefield reeked of the dead, stinking of dried blood, piss, shit, men, demons, monkeys, bears, pachyderms, horses, and giant birds. The wounded lay everywhere, waiting to die or be rescued; rakshashas called out for help, dying monkeys and bears pleaded for water, while other beasts of war¬¬—elephants with no trunks and crushed legs, the horses with broken backs, raptors with torn beaks and burnt wings—squirmed, struggling to breathe. And amidst the wreckage were anxious wives and children, picking through the rubble, calling out and hunting for loved ones, frantic to find bodies to burn or salvage, as the four-eyed dogs of Yama prowled the dead zone with ease.

Into this mayhem walked victorious Rama, followed by his brother Lakshmana, the new king of Lanka, Vibhishana, the monkey king Sugriva, and fellow monkey Hanuman, whose glowing tail lit Lanka for days.

Grateful for their support and relieved with victory, a visibly tired Rama, close to tears, invited the bears and giant vultures who participated in battle to feast on the carrion, their deserved spoils of war.

"As the soldiers celebrated," said Muthassi, "Rama and the others started making their way to the palace gates. For Sita. But all is never as it seems. Behind the scenes lived the uglier underbelly of war, unscrupulous soldiers from Rama's army who scoured the conquered land like parasites, interested in loot and women, the dirtier spoils of war."

But virtuous warriors also fought on Rama's side. Many, although they themselves were injured, offered to help set pyres for the dead, finding sages and priests to perform the last rites quickly. Some opted to sit with the children of dead rakshashas, while their mothers searched for their fathers. Others didn't care; they pillaged, raped.

Even Sarama became prey to such wanton feasting, grabbed by a soldier from Sugriva's camp; bent with rage, The Male, our ancestor, ferociously and brutally violated her on the very battlefield where, moments ago, Ravana's ten heads scanned for Rama, his heart still healthy with life and blood.

Sarama watched the creature forcing himself on her, dirtied from war, raging because of it. She paid attention to his hands, callused from bridge building, tired of killing, tired from killing. She felt pity. And then she was reminded of the war, of Surpanakha's mutilation, of Ravana's insistence on punishing the brothers by punishing the young princess instead, of how after the loss of so much life, one hoped the war was won by a just lord and his virtuous army. And right there, as the creature shuddered inside her, spilling his seed into her old womb, she howled with fury, screaming with such force that she tore a hole in the monkey's chest, exposing his heart. Sarama reached in, taking hold of his beating red organ in the palm of her hand as it continued to pump blood. The monkey—The Male, our ancestor—alarmed, looked at Sarama, his body still trembling.

Meeting his eye, Sarama slowly crushed his heart.

In the celebratory din, no one noticed. Nearby, giant vultures tore through an elephant as it waited to die.

She picked herself up quickly, forgetting in her haste to wipe the mud, spittle, and blood off her body. She would deal with the shock later. For now, she headed for the palace gates. She needed to be there. In the garden. When Rama received Sita. She needed to see the end to all this madness.

Sarama felt a sense of dread when Rama didn't meet Sita immediately. Even Vibhishana seemed embarrassed when he greeted the lady on Rama's behalf, requesting that she bathe and bedecking her in finery. Her lord would see her then.

And when they walked her out, and Rama stood in front of his wife like a guest, a stranger, Sarama sighed. Surpanakha's revenge was complete. Rama had shunned Sita publicly. Neither would fully recover from the hurt. Ayodhya would never let them forget it.

Sarama understood quite well why Rama did what he did. As she waited for Sita to appear in public, even she heard and recoiled from the spite with which soldiers from Rama's own army—men, monkeys, bears, and other half-beasts he had commanded only a few hours ago—discussed the young princess's lost virtue. When a group of them were hushed, the gossiping would stop, only for the cackling to resume soon after. In Ayodhya, too, it would be the same. Yet when Sita stepped into the lit pyre, not a sound was made. You could only hear burning. The crackle of embers. The burning of virtue and the fury it brings.

And as Sarama stared at Sita, she spied tears of rage through the flames—fire that refused to touch the sullied princess of Ayodhya, as though it were afraid. She, Sita, burnt hotter than fire, swallowing fire itself, her anger burning through fire, scorching even Agni, who pleaded with Rama to accept his virtuous queen, whose purity, if questioned further, would burn every living thing into oblivion.

When Rama was appeased, and the test, the public trial, over, the fire extinguished, the young couple faced each other once more, as husband and wife, Crown Prince and Princess of Ayodhya. Sarama did not wait to see Rama walk towards his absolved wife.

Sarama, our ancestor, didn't wait at all. She started to walk. Even as shouts of "Long Live!" burst across Lanka, as garlands rained down from the gods.

She walked, disgusted, away from Lanka, refusing to stop. She could have used her powers to transport herself elsewhere. She could still fly. But she decided against it. She wanted to walk, inhaling the mayhem, recalling the egos that helped mutilate two women and burn Lanka.

She stopped only when she neared the bridge that the creature who raped her helped build—The Male, our ancestor, the father of the child she would conceive. She stared long and hard at the beach.

The water was calm but red, the shore quiet, yet it stank of decomposing flesh. Seagulls circled the shoreline, rats started to surface. Sarama stepped forward, didn't look back. Not even once. The war was over but she believed little that was worthwhile had been salvaged. She began to walk across the bridge. The salty wind would ravage her face but she didn't care. The sound of the sea kept her company until she reached the end.

"And when she reached the other side," Muthassi said, finally, "Sarama, our ancestor, her belly was swollen."

CHABTER FOUR

VEED

THE MONTH I BEGAN masturbating into socks, my maternal grandmother, Amooma, died. Amma was her firstborn and I was her oldest grandchild. This meant Amma and I had to board a plane bound for Kochi in order for Amma to take charge of the household and make arrangements. My little sister would also be traveling with us. At the airport, Acchan hugged Amma, the only time my parents have held each other in public.

Before adolescent impulses possessed me like a demon, I used to be an obedient little boy, interested in doing errands for his mother.

Amma used to regularly send me to the corner store to buy produce. Armed with a list I committed to memory, I would buy vegetables, juice, dairy, and dessert. Everything on credit. I would carry each item piecemeal and place them all in front of Uncle Saleem, the proprietor, when he would note the number of items, write them in his ledger, making up prices at random, and bag the items as he masticated a toothpick. He would, years later, flee the country after defaulting on bank loans, but not before falling out with my father over owed dues.

When I first met Uncle Saleem, he would repeatedly ask me where I was from. At first, I thought he was asking for our flat number so he could make note of it in his ledger. "805," I told him.

"No!" he laughed. "Veed? Veed, *where*? Where aare *you* from?" The English equivalent of "veed" is "home," or "place." In Malayalam, my parents' tongue, "veed" encompasses a family's soul, where ancestors are cremated, where the soil remembers your

211

footprint. But in translation, as "veed" becomes "home," the word's power has ebbed.

"I am from Trichur," I remember telling Uncle Saleem after I checked with Amma.

"*Where* in Trichur?" he asked after that. Mean, I felt, since he was a Trichur man himself.

"Tell him Irinjalakuda," Amma said. So I did.

"And *where* exactly in Irinjalakuda?" Uncle Saleem persisted.

"Near the bus stop, near the little shop near the bus stop, near the temple; near the temple near the little shop near the bus stop. That is where my veed is." It was a lie, in a way. That was where my Amma's veed was. Where her hair grew long and wild, where Muthassi, my great-grandmother, the first living being to hold me, raised her.

In Irinjalakuda is where my Amma's veed used to be, before it was sold, torn down. Yet before ownership changed hands, Amooma needed to die, which she did, wailing from a hospital bed, calling out for her fondest child. My mother, her daughter—Amma.

Four years before Amma and her siblings sold the house, divided its insides like pieces of cake, I helped my uncle, the oldest male, put pieces of my grandmother, lukewarm bones and teeth, into a clay urn. It had rained the previous night, so we sat on our haunches, bare chested, sifting through damp ash the color of chalk and coal, mirroring—I wouldn't know it then—the sea's pallor that morning, water my uncle and I waded into until the swells lapped our necks.

As my uncle balanced the heavy urn on his shoulder, I clasped another, a tiny, clay one, in my palms, as undercurrents pulled us out farther. My uncle carried his mother. I held the remains of her late husband, my grandfather.

When Muthacchan, my maternal grandfather, died, the family elders deemed it appropriate for me to, one day, when older, share him with the sea, so they portioned his ashes, leaving aside some for the only grandchild he knew and looked after until he was three. Then, as the rain fell like fine splinters of wood, my uncle raised what was left of his mother and shattered the urn. On cue, I broke the urn's seal and submerged my powdered grandfather. Water dissolved ash, took teeth and bone. We looked up and prayed, and somewhere out there, Indra, the rain god, understood what was once woman had lived alone in my Amma's veed and what was once man had built it.

CHABTER FIVE

DOG

THE GUARD DOG WAS a mutt. His father, a stray, had been a savvy mongrel, investigating an unlatched gate, pouncing on the drowsing Labrador in heat. The act produced a healthy litter, in particular a large toffee-colored male with cigarette-ash spots, and this creature, given as a present, protected the Gulf gentleman's dead mother's house for over four years.

Six months after the cremation, the house, the first in the neighborhood with a flushable toilet back in the day, with two telephones and an Aiwa color TV, tame parrots in the birdhouse, a boxy Japanese sedan made in an actual Japanese plant parked in the garage at a time when Kerala's roads mainly hosted Fiats, Hindustan Contessas, and Ambassadors, was put on the market. That was a while ago, and the place was now going into disrepair. There was rot in the roof, mold, dust in the rooms, and rumors of termites. The dead woman's children did not live in the house anymore; they had their own houses, their own families. The old woman had died in the company of her live-in maid, a petite woman in her seventies—a lady with no front teeth, sent home for good by the children after they paid her three months' severance for services rendered, with gifts of used wedding saris, a bottle of perfume for her daughter-in-law, some Kit Kats and Mars bars for her grandkids, and the Whirpool fridge. The house was now empty. The windows were shut, the doors were padlocked, but the dog, he watched the house like it was a giant bone, roaming its boundaries like a drone, a visible deterrent for thieves since the house hadn't been emptied of its possessions, a compendium of items from the Gulf gentleman's first tricycle to curios purchased by his mother when she lived with his father in Botswana. In the kitchen storeroom, jars of homemade mango pickle, one of the old woman's final acts, preserved in a pool of chili and coconut oil.

The siblings needed to sell the house because everyone was in debt. No one wanted the house. Well, only one person wanted the house—the Gulf gentleman's middle sister, the one who lived in Dubai—but she couldn't afford the asking price, so it was as good as no one wanting the house.

No one wanted the dog. Even when they had the family meeting, a week after the cremation, where everyone sat around a table with notepads, inventory lists, deciding which table would go to which house, how to divide the jewels, whether the cutlery was actual silver, which grandchild deserved what, the dog was not a topic of conversation, until the very end, when someone mentioned it's a good thing there was a dog to keep an eye on the place.

—Not really, the oldest child, the Gulf gentleman, replied. He wags his tail at beggars. Some guard dog!

—But he's what we've got, the youngest sister snapped. Mother loved him. He might get lonely, she added after a pause.

—So what? the Gulf gentleman fumed. Dogs are dogs! They keep themselves amused somehow. He's not going to be locked in the kennel anymore; he gets the run of the place, gets to do whatever he wants.

But then everyone fought over how much food a dog would want, how much meat would be required to feed an omnivorous beast, how to split the expenses, whether it would be feasible to hire someone to dump some excess food into his kennel every week, hoping the dog knew how to portion out his meals over seven days, but if he couldn't, there was going to be a problem, since finding a person willing to feed a dog watching a house without an owner wasn't going to be easy. There were few takers for this kind of work, especially when the interested parties were told they would be required to spend the night with the dog during weekends, sleeping on the veranda, so that everyone, from the milkman's daughter to the town grocer, knew the house was looked after, that there was a human presence, even though the dog was waited on by the man, as though man's rule over beasts had ended. When the dead woman's kids explained the problem to their uncle, he suggested calling on Mathai, a reasonable man who understood the old ways.

Mathai's family had worked for the Gulf gentleman's household for over three generations. His wife had tended its garden for a few years; his son assisted in planting the pepper and neem trees near the wrought-iron front gates where weaver ants congregated. When the family males paid Mathai a visit, begging for help, requesting he spend his weekends on the veranda, watching over the house, keeping the dog company, Mathai contemplated what he was being asked to do. There would be compensation, of course. His wife urged him to refuse, reminding him of his arthritis, how cold the tiles on the portico would get at night. She also reminded him of their new standing as parents of government employees. He quieted her gently, rubbing her wrist with root-like fingers, the hair on his knuckles as wispy as cotton.

—There is a debt to be paid, he said. I don't owe them this, but their mother was a fair woman.

—But to sleep outside like a sentry is an insult, his wife insisted.

—Indeed, Mathai replied, but they are not forcing me, they are asking.

—These people from Persia are asking you to take care of a dog, his wife seethed. The animal licks its own balls, don't be a fool!

—The animal is good-natured, Mathai assured her. There was no more said as he waved his wife away.

217

—If our sons got wind of this. . ., she murmured.

—If they come seeking quarrel, Mathai said, my house is no longer open to them.

In this manner, the dog had a kind of companionship for almost four years, someone the dog recognized, a man to feed him, to hose him with cold water in the summer, to cuddle with during the rains, to watch over as he slept, to be spoken to as dawn broke.

When prospective buyers arrived to inspect the house, the dog would be led to the kennel—which wouldn't be used otherwise—where he would wag his tail at the visiting strangers who wondered how long the dog would remain, only to be reassured that the dog wasn't part of the sale, but simply a guarantee against burglars, like a gun. And the man? Was he a guarantee, too? Yes, he was. The man was like a man who oiled the gun, kept it in working order. And the man does not sleep in the house? The man never sleeps in the house; he knows his place.

When the dog died, the house was still unsold. The asking price was too much, the agent the children hired to sell the place confided. Then there was the manner of the old woman's death, the loneliness of her last days, which guaranteed the presence of a sad and lonely spirit—a spirit few buyers wanted to inherit. And so the house remained where it was, wasting away, until the dog died, cursing the place even more.

When Mathai found the dead animal, he hadn't been to the house in over ten days. It was the holiday season; his grandchildren were in town for Christmas. To make sure the dog wouldn't starve, he had filled his bowls with extra chow and water, put it all in the kennel, which he left half-closed but unlocked so the birds wouldn't get at it, or shit in it. When the festivities ended, his grandkids fattened on duck stew and warm appams and cold pudding, Mathai remembered his toothy friend; in the morning he made his way to the butcher, where he bought fresh bone, then visited the local shaap for some porrota and beef fry, and

a bottle of toddy for himself. He called out to the dog as he unlocked the gate, swinging the neck bone and the cooked meat in
the air, expecting the usual franticness, the licks, the yelps, the
cold nose on his neck. The dog did not come. Mathai assumed
he had gone to the back of the house to chase squirrels as he normally did, or pester crows, but when a few minutes passed with
no sign of him, Mathai went to look for the guy. He found the
dog curled up near the old cowshed, near the servant's outhouse,
by his favorite playthings—an old branch, a tennis ball the sun
had hardened—a place where he buried his kills, *that* lame cat,
that squirrel, where he went to be a dog without being observed.
He was a little wet from the rain, but the bugs had already arrived. They knew where to find him.

—Good friend, Mathai said.

He then hosed the body down, dried it with rags, before
wrapping the corpse with banyan leaves, tying it with twine, before digging a hole in the earth, near the bedroom window of
the old woman who had died, who spent some nights talking to
this dog as she lay in bed, telling him what she planned to do the
next day, that her grandson was coming to live with her, that it
embarrassed her that her medication made her fart all the time.

The dog's grave was near the pepper tree Mathai's own son
had helped plant, a tree the dog's spirit would now inhabit, still
watching over the house like before, without being able to bark
or sniff or pee, but in two years the house would sell, the siblings
would splinter, and men would show up with machines and
saws, cut everything down, level the ground, destroy the dog,
which became part of a tree, strip it all away, as though there
had been no old lady, no house, no children, no tame parrots,
no crows, no Botswana, no pickle, no Mathai, no dog, no life.

CHABTER SIX

███████

THEY BROUGHT GULF MUKUNDAN home in a rickety taxi from Kochi Airport. Satheesh, his youngest brother, helped him out of the vehicle. The Amby had broken down twice on the highway. Neighbors surrounded the car. The men were expected hours ago. "Make way!" yelled Satheesh. "Nothing to see here."

"█████," a voice cried out.

Satheesh drew his brother closer. "Who said that?"

The taxi man honked. "Forgot to pay, Boss!"

"Welcome home, █████!" someone else yelled.

The taxi man was getting impatient. "Settle your account, Boss!" he shouted. He revved the engine. He honked again.

Mukundan's bedridden mother wondered about the commotion. She hadn't been told of this. The doctor had warned them earlier in the week when he stopped by to check on her. "She may go into shock when she sees him," he said. "Or she may get better. I just don't know."

"What's out there?" the old woman yelled.

Grown men jeered as Mukundan passed. Satheesh shushed them. They didn't care.

Mukundan's wife, advised by Satheesh to stay home to prepare herself, greeted her husband at the door.

Gaunt, the lawyer warned over the phone. Skin like rock. Eyes like lemons.

She touched his face, felt the roughness of his stubble, grabbed an arm and wrapped it around her shoulder. Light, so light. His skin had splotches, as though he were about to molt.

She looked for their son. He was there. Young Saji held his father's pant leg tightly. He was delighted to have his acchan back. He inhaled Mukundan's sweat, patted his thigh, where the muscles had atrophied.

"Acchan, acchan," Saji kept saying. And just kept looking at the man he hadn't seen in three years. Had it been that long? He knew his father had been in prison, that he had been pardoned, that just this morning he breakfasted with fellow inmates somewhere in Abu Dhabi, before he was put in a police van with other pardoned men and driven to a waiting Indian Airlines flight. And here he was now. In the three-bedroom, two-bathroom house he built with Gulf cash. The first person to do so in town, the man to see if a nephew, niece, or distant cousin needed work papers drawn up, who advised Gulf-bound dreamers where to try their luck. Whether it was more profitable working in Das Island or Al Ain. If Dubai held better prospects than Manama. If housing in Khalidiya was cheaper than Tourist Club. Whether knowing all of this was worth the trouble, that money was directly proportional to effort. And that if they chose to go, life was bearable—and their families wouldn't forget them.

Mukundan, a patient man, never lied. "There are so many of us there," he'd share. "You learn to cope. Longing for the homeland is what marks you out to be a Gulf-party man." And the men would listen to Gulf Mukundan, their Gulf-party man with Gulf-party connections, Gulf-party money, and Gulf-party status.

People liked to say Mukundan knew the Gulf so well he must've roamed the sands in an earlier life as a Bedu. There was no other way to explain his assimilation, his ease with the place. The man's contacts were first class. His Arabic was superb. He knew police in the labor department, broke fast with his Arabee bosses during Ramadan. And he felt no shame calling in favors, sending parcels back home through various contacts, bailing out laborers, introducing struggling business owners to loan sharks who promised lower interest rates. He even helped fast track the necessary paperwork if a body in the morgue needed to be sent home for burial. Gulf Mukundan was what everyone in town aspired to be.

And then he shagged a man.

Raped him, the victim claimed. Got caught. And here he was now. Three years later. Standing next to his loyal wife and young son. Back home. The Gulf-party ████████.

Saji stayed by Mukundan's side for hours, guarding the man like only a child could protect his father. He was there when visitors, relatives, and friends of the family arrived. Looking bullish. It didn't matter. They asked Mukundan the questions they came to ask.

Mukundan deflected the barrage well. When pressed to talk about life behind bars, whether AC was provided in desert jails, if there was torture, what *exactly* did he do, Mukundan patted his son. "Not in front of the boy," he'd say. "Later."

"They asked you to convert? Is that why they let you go?"

"Later."

"I don't mind," said Saji. "Talk, talk."

"Yes," they said. "He's old enough."

"Later," Mukundan replied. Curt.

Saji listened as well wishers assured Mukundan they didn't believe in gossip. People talk, everyone kept saying. "Let them," said Mukundan.

"Look," said Mukundan's uncle, "you know what they're calling you? Calling us? Is it true a newspaper published photos after police arrested you?"

"Not with Saji here," repeated Mukundan. "Later."

OK, sure, sure, is what people said, but out of earshot, while they were putting on their shoes, pulling out umbrellas, done saying their goodbyes, back in their cars or scooters, or waiting at the bus stop, as rain bulleted the smoggy town, they bitched about Mukundan's reticence, couldn't understand why he didn't want to clear his name, that it was OK if he busted a hooker's face, simply confirm it was a Filipina or one of those African bitches, not some man, for heaven's sake, not a former friend, both caught in the nude. The confession could only help him, grant that poor lady he married some relief, save that boy of his from a life of shame. Otherwise, the town's young would never let Saji forget his father was better off neutered. The kids in school would draw a mustache on a mango, fuck it with a stick, and force Mukundan's boy to watch. Or they'd call him Little ██████.

Saji didn't care what the family well-wishers thought. Acchan was home and Saji was going to protect him. He was a big boy now. Eight. His mother had told him where his father was two years ago, put in prison for fighting. "We know you are big enough to handle it," she told him. "Don't believe what people tell you," she warned. "Your father needs you. He expects you to take care of me."

Saji intended to watch out for his father, too. He had gotten bigger in his father's absence—tallest among his cousins. When Mukundan needed to use the toilet, Saji refused to let him go alone. "Coming, too," he said. Mukundan took him with him. "Turn around," he said, and Saji obeyed. Finally, at night, after the visitors left, his mother pried her son away. "Let me claim him for a while," she smiled. "Tomorrow, he's yours," she promised. Saji relented. But he grew restless sleeping on the cot laid out next to his grandmother's bed. He made his way back to his parents' room. The door was shut, but a light was on, slinking through the cracks like melted bars of gold. He heard them fucking. His mother was loud. Guttural. It was as though she was being torn apart, and she wanted the whole town to hear; it's possible everyone did.

All night. With Saji curled up by the door, his parents fucked all night. His mother cried a little every time they finished. But his father, Saji barely heard his father. If he knew any better, he would've wondered about that. His father used to be a grunter. Years ago, when Mukundan had been home on leave, he reached for his wife, assuming Saji to be asleep. Mukundan covered his wife completely back then, like shade. Then shadow. Erased her with his body. Their whispering roused Saji. He turned, out of habit, towards his mother. He couldn't spot her silhouette in the dark. He felt his stomach tighten. He squinted. "Amma!" he shouted. "Amma!" And that's when they knew their son was awake. Aware. Mukundan placed one palm over his son's eyes, the other on his tummy, as his wife fixed her nightgown. "Relax, son, Amma's here, we were just talking." Saji didn't remember any of this while he slept outside his parents' bedroom door. It wasn't important. His father had returned home.

The next morning, after a breakfast of steamed plantains and eggs, Gulf Mukundan told his son they were going to go out for the day. Dressed in clothes still warm from the iron, they took the bus to the city. The first thing they did when they arrived was to stop for sweetmeats, buying extra for later. Then they caught a matinee show at Wonderful Theaters. "Super pitcher, son," the man told Saji as he handed him the tickets. "Lots of di-shoom-dishoom. Too good, I tell you, tooo, tooo good!" Lunch was buttered chapatis and chili chicken, all washed down with cola. Mukundan suggested they stop by a bookshop next, where they bought comics, notebooks, and color pencils. They hag-gled with a vendor selling glass bangles after that, before wait-ing in line at the liquor shaap to buy a bottle of Old Monk rum. A tubby man hurried by them as the line inched onward, ig-noring Mukundan's attempt to get his attention. "I know him," said Mukundan to his son. "Got him that warehouse job in Jebel Ali Free Zone." By evening, as the shop and street lights swelled with light, like expanding stars, the air full of crickets and moths, father and son were both fat and giddy.

On the journey back, in a speeding bus with seats the color of pond scum, as the crows, too, were flying home, Saji asked Mukundan if he went to jail because he almost killed someone, as Amma said he had. "Not intentionally," said Mukundan.

"Did you mean to?" Saji asked.

"It's complicated," said his father. "I broke the law." He wanted to say more. "There is a time for things," he explained. "When you are old enough to take the bus on your own, you will understand."

What to tell the boy? That he was in charge of arranging the women that fateful weekend, and that bitch-ass Filipina pimp botched it? That only two showed up to service six, and that he'd been waiting with Dileep, an old schoolmate and one of his roommates, to go next? That they couldn't help themselves when they heard their four friends ferociously humping the woman with the lisp—"Ma num is Europe," she had said, as everyone got introductions out of the way—and her partner, the woman named Brazil? "Welcome to India!" the men had whooped with excitement.

"No kiss," the women warned. "More dirhams kiss kiss, OK?"

The men consented. " 'Kay 'kay! No kiss kiss."

"An' take bath," said Europe. "No bath, no this." She shielded her pussy with her palm.

The women needn't have worried. The men had showered and shaved.

How to tell a boy this, his boy, that as they waited, drawn to the sounds of palms slapping ass, the odor of paid sex, Dileep asked Mukundan if he ever wondered what it was like to be a woman. "To be impaled," he said. "To be opened up, you understand?" Mukundan said no. "I've thought about it," Dileep said. "C'mon, we've all thought about it. You, too, right?"

It was an invitation. It must have been only that. As young boys going on eleven, they had experimented on each other, practicing stuff they saw in films, role-playing. They kissed in private, sucked on each other's tongues after eating fruit-flavored candies. Then as they grew more comfortable with each other, their fingers wandered over to their cocks. They jacked each other off a couple of times. No sucking, that was gay shit. Yet after fooling around for a year, they stopped, amicably ending whatever it was they were doing. It was as though their lust for each other needed to fade in order to accommodate a stronger yearning for pussy. It was also as though nothing had ended because nothing had begun.

They never spoke of what they did, even in jest. Then, as young men in the Gulf, they ended up tag-teaming some nanny from Colombo. None of them moved after they were done—their legs were all touching. It had excited him. But this—what Dileep was suggesting—was different; it was something broke sex-starved laborers did, or men in taxis by Muroor Road. Not them. Sensible forty-something men. Fathers. Men with wives. Respected breadwinners, men with class. But Dileep was looking at him. "Maybe it's nice, you know?" he wondered aloud to Mukundan. "To be someone's bitch, pounded like that." How to tell a boy this, his boy? That he reached for his friend then, kissed him, held him down. Inhaled the man as he sucked his tongue. They were sober, crazily alive. It had been so easy, returning to boyhood. Like blinking.

Someday, he must tell the boy how it felt to ease into a man like that. The comfort it gave him, an unexpected bliss. Dileep's legs locked around his hips. Dileep, smiling. It made Mukundan smile, too. They were both smiling when Brazil walked in on them to grab a drink of water. She laughed. "Sorry," she said. "So, both you homos?" Dileep bucked, throwing Mukundan off him. Kicking him repeatedly in the ribs. Like a madman hitting a tethered goat with a hammer.

"He make me do," Dileep yelled in English, grabbing his pants. "Force me to!" Mukundan steadied himself and punched his friend hard in the ribs. He hit him again. And again. Dileep staggered. Brazil backed away.

"What you doing?" she yelled. "Stop! You kill 'im!" Mukundan turned around and picked up an object from the shelf, an ashtray. He swung. "Please, man! Sir, you stop!" she yelled, clutching her cheek. "STOP, MAN! SIR! SIR!" Within seconds, butt-naked Europe was by Brazil's side, yelling with equal ferocity, as two of Mukundan's roommates tried re-straining him. Brazil cupped her nose. "Boken, boken," she sobbed. Europe screamed louder. One of the men tried to calm her down.

"More money, give more money, OK?"

"What he did to face?" she said.

"We fix face, OK?" the man said. "OK?"

"No OK!" Europe screamed. That's when the man hit Europe.

"Shut up, shut up, shut up!" he said. Then the men, including Dileep, began kicking the women.

"Please, sir, no money, free, everything free!" Mukundan went to the bathroom to wash his dick.

The tenants in the flat next door called the shurtha. The building watchman came, too. He banged on the door. "What-ever you're doing, open up now! Police coming!"

The shurtha arrived within minutes; a patrol car was stopped for dinner nearby. Mukundan refused to talk. He put his trou-sers back on, accepted the charges, the sentencing, the lashes, the mandatory counseling. He asked a friend to call his wife. She wouldn't find out for over a year what the charges were. Or that Brazil lost teeth, got deported to Manila with her buddy Europe. That Dileep drowned in a bucket of water in prison a few weeks into his sentence. He didn't know how to tell his son all this. Perhaps one day. Not now. He wouldn't know where or how to start, or to confess that he didn't regret what he did, and may do it again. He wasn't sorry. But Saji was waiting for a re-sponse; something needed to be said.

"My friend Sunil says Amma's lying," said Saji. "You went to jail because you stuck your tongue down some boy's throat, Sunil says."

"You believe Sunil?"

"No," said Saji.

"Why not?"

"If I tell you, promise you won't tell Amma?"

"Of course, son."

"I stick my tongue down boy throats all the time. They kiss back. They suck back. I'm not in jail."

"Sunil, too?" Mukundan asked.

"Sometimes," said Saji. "But he only lets me suck his tongue if I kiss his neck first... You tell Amma?"

"No," said Mukundan. "Can you keep a secret, too?"

"I am the best secret keeper," said Saji.

"In Abu Dhabi, I had two jobs," whispered Mukundan. "Shop manager most days; weekends, I pretended to be a building."

"No, you lying," said Saji. "You're too short to be a building."

"It took some time to learn how to do it," Mukundan said. "Every night, I stared at construction bricks. I mean, you have to choose your bricks, see what they're like. You've got good bricks, shitty—don't tell Amma I said that—bricks, and so-so quality bricks. But then I'd see one I liked. And I'd take it home. Just to have a look, know what I mean, son?"

"I pretend I'm a fish sometimes when swimming in the pond," said Saji.

"And do the fish come to you?"

"Yes," said Saji. "They swim by my ankles, my ears."

"Are they telling you secrets?" said Mukundan.

"I don't understand what they're saying," admitted Saji.

"Keep listening," said Mukundan.

"What's it like being a building?" said Saji.

"I was a little two-story building," said Mukundan. "My friends didn't recognize me. They'd walk past me. But after a while, I started confiding in people, you know. About my skill, that I could become this building. And you know, I started getting calls. Friends pulling in favors. One friend rented me out to bad women who did dirty things for bad men, charging high rates, making my friend and me a lot of money. But I got greedy, son."

"I pinched Mani Aunty's baby because she wouldn't hug me," said Saji.

"So you know what it's like to want something, right? When you don't have what you want, you get mad."

"Yeah, mad."

"I wanted to make more money, wanted to learn how to turn myself into a mid-sized hotel. But you needed a permit to do that. I didn't care."

"What's a permit?" said Saji.

"It's when you need to have permission from something to do something else," said Mukundan.

"Like getting all my sums right before I can watch TV?"

"Very similar," said Mukundan.

"So you became a hotel?" said Saji.

He began moonlighting as a mid-sized hotel, admitted Mukundan, charging patrons even more, eventually getting caught because these things don't stay secret for long. Angry officials lugged him off to jail, then to court, where he was made to promise he wouldn't turn into a building or a hotel without a permit ever again. "So I did." But he got sentenced, and the judge and the jailers brought their friends and family over to show them the man who could turn into a hotel. So they would take him outside to the yard and threaten to report him when he refused to oblige, taunting him until he simply gave up. Food. Drink. Exercise. Gave it all up till he didn't have the strength to brush his teeth or wash his hair or speak to visitors, and he began to forget the things he used to know. Like where he lived, or that he loved overripe bananas, or that he used to turn into a mid-sized hotel and made good money doing it. He forgot many things, he said. He forgot to cut his nails and wash his armpits. He forgot his counselor's name. He forgot to wear clean underwear or eat. He forgot the voice of his wife and his son. He stopped praying. He couldn't remember when his father died. He lost track of dates. And one day, they decided to let him go, because they could, because they realized they had forgotten him, that he didn't need to be there anyway, because the Indian consulate had made some deal with the government, that he was free to go, but they'd forgotten to process his paperwork. "It was great news." But he was forced to leave a part of himself behind, he told his son. "They made me," he said. "Give," they said. "Give!" And he did. He gave. The jailers turned that part—"what I gave!"—into paste, smeared most of it on the walls of Mukundan's cell. They diluted the rest of it in water and mopped the floors. It was how they would keep him there, leave that part of him there. A memory. Then he left. And here he was now. With his son, Saji, telling him all this, telling him the truth, so Saji didn't have to worry anymore: Mukundan had served his time.

"I don't believe you."

"Look at my skin," Mukundan insisted. "Why do you think it's this way? Look at me! Some of me—elsewhere."

The next day Gulf Mukundan left home. He didn't leave a note, didn't take anything with him, not even clothes. He didn't say goodbye.

The town folk checked the river first, then the pond by the house, the water wells in the area. They spoke to the fishermen returning with their catch from a few miles away. They then checked the trees, the banyans and the palms, empty houses, anywhere a man could hang himself. Jump. They didn't find him. They asked the medical stores if a man fitting his description had bought pills, and they asked the little shops if a man fitting his description had bought rat poison or cleaning detergent. They found nothing. They then checked the temple's rest houses, the rail tracks, and the morgue. They checked the hospitals across six districts, phoned his former friends in the Gulf and relatives in other states. They bribed hospital peons and police constables and roadside vagrants for information. They put his picture on lampposts, in movie halls, showed it to the people in the street, but it was useless. They found nothing. Mukundan had vanished. His uncle wasn't happy. He wanted a corpse, something putrefying in a ditch, a letter in the mail, some sort of closure, but his nephew disappointed him. "His kind, better off dead," he told Mukundan's wife. "You sure he's not out there sucking someone's cock? If only he'd hanged himself in his room like any reasonable man. I mean, couldn't you tell, woman? Don't the women in your family know how to hold onto their husband's dicks? You could've sucked his balls, put a finger in his ass, at least kept him. Or if your cunt couldn't handle him, could've called a friend with tits or something. Or arranged something on the side without him soiling the family name. Think what's been done to our reputation! Pathetic, just pathetic!"

Saji waited by the door every evening for his father. He did this for weeks, and then decided one day on his own that his acchan may take longer to return.

That week he wandered over to a roadside construction site by their house, where sun-blackened barefoot women lugged flesh-colored bricks on their heads. He stole a brick, took it home, and put it in his room.

Every night he stared at the brick for over an hour. What was he supposed to look for, again? He felt his skin. And if this brick didn't work, how was he going to pick the next one? He wondered how long the mutation would take. His father had explained he needed to concentrate very hard to do what he did. But Saji couldn't wait. He began to cheat. He rubbed the brick on his skin till it chafed and began to bleed. He did this until his mother found out and threw the brick away, but he wouldn't explain himself. "Tell me!" she cried. He wouldn't. When he healed, he found another brick and took it to his room and looked at it constantly. He tried closing his eyes, feeling for signs that his skin was turning coarser and he would finally know what it was like to experience what his father did. He even brought the brick to school, taking it out at recess.

He did this even as his great-uncle was making funeral arrangements for his father. They hadn't found Mukundan but it didn't matter. In circumstances where remains couldn't be found, there was another way to insure Mukundan's tortured soul could move on. Mukundan's wife granted consent. Saji would play the part of the grieving son. The neighbors weren't told of the ceremony, but they found out. Mercifully, they left the family alone.

On the decided day, the priest, some nut-job Mukundan's great-uncle found, was given a bag filled with Mukundan's possessions. It had the clothes he arrived back home in, his Indian passport, his canceled Emirati work permit, the letter from the judge pardoning his crime, photographs from the Gulf, his wife's wedding ring and chain, personal letters and bed sheets, a dinner plate and coffee mug, his address book, his birth name written out in Malayalam on a piece of paper, and the date of his death engraved on a piece of bark: June 4, 1991. The items, as well as a carved wooden puppet dressed in a full-sleeved shirt and dark pants, were placed on a wooden pyre, and then covered with a white sheet. A pot of ghee was poured on top. The priest, smelling of camphor and Marlboros, spoke to the gods, explaining that a man had died. He spoke of birth, life, death, and rebirth. He talked about souls. He spoke in a tongue his ancestors probably used over a thousand years ago, but he could have mispronounced anything and no one would have known. When he was done, he called for the dead man's son. The boy was nudged in the priest's direction.

Saji, forced to bathe, wrapped in a white sarong held up by a leather belt, naked above the waist, was given a lit piece of wood longer than his arm. His mother had been asked to remain indoors.

"Go on, son," the priest said. "It was written this way. Give him peace."

Saji refused. "Acchan's coming back. Why you say he's dead?"

Mukundan's uncle slapped Saji hard. "Boy! Stop this foolishness. Light the pyre; you want your father's soul to squirm?"

The sound startled the crows on the telephone lines. They began to caw. "Do it!" he yelled. The boy wouldn't budge. Mukundan's uncle slapped him again. He pinched Saji's left ear and then took his hand in his. Made him put flame to wood. Then he forced him to stay, as Saji struggled. "He's gone, you understand? Finally, dead." Saji watched his father burn.

Everything burned.

That night, Saji took the brick from his room and began to rub it all over himself. Thoroughly, like a bar of soap. Then he went to find his mother. She was sitting by the veranda with the women of her family. She was now. Widow. Widow. Widow. Widow. Gulf Widow.

Saji placed what was left of the brick at her feet, his eyes round and frog-like. He looked at his mother. "I can't do it," he said. "I'm not good enough, Amma." Her son was naked. His arms and legs were bleeding. His body was covered in sores and red dust, flesh raw from the rubbing. He smelled like brick, like dirty earth, like ancient dust. As though he had emerged from the ground after mining it for days, decades even, searching for something, coming out empty.

And his mother looked at her boy and laughed. "Admirable how you could love a man you barely knew," she said. "It's as if you're desperate for the world to know that you miss your father. I miss him, too, you know. But I suppose I'm left with you now. I won't be allowed to miss him because I'll be staring at you as you grow more and more like him. I won't be allowed to forget him because you'll inherit his mannerisms. One look at you and everyone will know that you're your father's child. So tell me, son, be truthful now, children who lie to their mothers rarely fare well in life. Do you think about boys?"

CHABTER SEVEN

BLATTELLA GERMANICA

WHERE I LIVE NOW, where the lake is a masquerading sea, every summer, or at least when it's pouring outside, a water bug the size of a little ship crawls out of the sink in the bathroom and decides to take a stroll. It's always one bug. When I squish it or gas it, a day passes and then another one arrives, as though the bathroom is a port of entry or the moon, only one bug allowed to visit at a time. I kill that one, too. After a week, I call my building manager Laurel and inform her that one fat roach visits my home a day, asking her whether they could send someone over from pest control. You mean water bug, sir, she first responds. No, I mean roaches, I say. Of course, sir, she says, I shall send our exterminator to check on the water-bug problem, sir. Laurel, I should really say, these ain't water bugs. Roaches, woman, them roaches, these roaches. And I know roaches. I grew up with them. Not the obese or indolent kind, critters with limited survival skills, I knew the best in the business, pellet-sized fuckers, *Blattella germanicas*—German cockroaches.

They demolished the building I was raised in years ago. Those who lived in our kitchen, our bathroom, the cracks in the doors, came to feed when we fed ourselves, or when we slept, or when Milo, our irritable canine, pissed or pooped on newspaper in the bathroom, or when there was no one around, the house quiet, when it was opportune and safe to venture out, them sniffing the air with giddy antennae or congregating like mobsters or card players, or scuttling away and fornicating, or defecating or dropping turd-colored egg sacks polished like shoes, or simply roaming for fun, strolling, scratching a back between toothbrush bristles, passing the time, finding a way into the fridge and not leaving because cold grub smelled so good it seduced, seduced so good it killed. If any of those bugs survived the demolition of our building, then let me tell you this: somewhere, in a house, in the kitchen or bathroom or anywhere there's a crack in the wall or the floor, these insects are conspiring to take over the building, to observe its tenants, mimic their habits, learn their language, to subdue them, to eventually become them, take over their roles.

I've seen firsthand the perils of infestation. I've seen ungodly things. What the bugs become. I've seen them practice pretending to be other things. At night, I've seen unmentionable things, heard frightening things. Roaches in little shirts and trousers and skirts, in panties and briefs, roaches who spoke what we speak, roaches who taught themselves to walk upright. Roaches who turned human.

I wasn't young or slow in the head. I didn't take meds. I was seventeen—seventeen—when I knew the bugs could talk.

Our kitchen door back then resembled the color of dried cocoa, riddled with cracks and punctures, like the bark of a rotting tree. That night, as my family slept, I waited on my haunches by the kitchen door, ready to pounce as soon as the clock struck two, when the kitchen turned most humid, pleasing its nocturnal tenants, and I wanted to be there when they ventured out to feed. I had reasons. At dinner earlier that night, as my friends ate at the table covered by Amma's best tablecloth, roaches crawled in plain sight, on the carpet, by the AC, under the sofa, near the lamps, the TV, around the rim of Milo's water bowl, in his food. Amma flicked them away. I then flicked them away. It was disgusting. It was embarrassing. Light no longer deterred the critters. Never again, I vowed, never again, and so there by the kitchen that Amma always closed for the night, I crouched like a primitive man brandishing a wooden club, waiting. To kill.

My left trouser pocket held bug spray; my right hand gripped yesterday's newspaper, rolled fine for murder. That's when I heard a cackling. Voices, from the kitchen.

I understand Malayalam, I speak it. Arabic, I can manage, and a few others, like Urdu and Farsi and Tamil, I can identify by ear, recognizing the cadences from multiple tongues. That night, what I heard combined every language I knew or sorta knew, maybe more, resulting in a lexicon so strange, so distinct, so familiar yet distant, a mysterious patois, words perhaps heard then taken from maybe the Egyptians on the eleventh floor, the Sudanese family on the fifth, the Palestinians across from us, the Mallus, the Bombaywallas, the English woman, the Pathans, the Sri Lankans and the Filipinos, words spoken to sons and daughters, to husbands and wives, between lovers and foes, words collected and taken out, poured into heads, practiced in secret but out loud, words selected then changed, pronounced and mispronounced, combined to form new sounds, to conjure old ones, to produce meaning, to obfuscate secrets or express joy. Very words I heard in our kitchen, spoken, it seemed, by a large congregation. Burglars, I assumed. Burglars in our little kitchen, a family of burglars, a bunch of polyglots that had somehow gotten in, speaking in code, and I needed to do something, or warn my family, or get the dog. But I didn't. I rushed the door in a moment of madness. Rushed in, locked the kitchen door, and switched on the lights. The first live thing I saw was a white roach in a sport coat and shorts made out of dry and putrid vegetable peelings. It stood upright, like a man, and smoked a beedi smaller than a needle's tip. A few feet across were many bugs of his kind, putting on little clothes, wearing little clothes, attempting to walk like men, swaying from side to side, practicing, it seemed, coolly looking at me, talking over me. Still talking in a language that wasn't mine.

I felt for the spray can.

They ran. Scattered. I ran after them, stepped on them, swatted them. I upturned things, beat them until they turned to mush. I sprayed until my finger hurt, until the nozzle discharged only bits of foam. I killed as they hurled instructions at each other, escaped into cracks, abandoning friends, warning others. I killed as they swore, as they pleaded, as they said nothing. What transpired couldn't have lasted longer than ten minutes. I waited then. Twenty more minutes, the time it took to find bugs pretending to be dead. Then I swept them all into a big pointy pile and left them in the center of the kitchen for Amma to find in the morning. But before I left, I crouched low, near enough to smell the gas on the bodies, and I paid attention to the dresses the bugs wore, to the bespoke shoes on their many feet, to the craftsmanship; I also paid attention, in case someone was still barking instructions, in case a critter still lived. Outside, disturbed by the din, Milo had waited patiently for me. He licked my ankle, guiding me to the couch in the hall, where I fell asleep with his bum next to my face. I slept until afternoon, when my headache woke me. When I asked Amma what she thought about the mess in the kitchen, she didn't know what I was talking about. I discovered then that the roaches not only ate their dead, they also returned for them. So a month later I went back to duplicate what I did, and the bugs were there, in their human dresses, speaking their human languages, taking instructions from someone else. I killed them all again, I made an even larger pile, I took pictures with my grandpa's old Nikon, but the film went bad, and in the morning, once again, the pile I made disappeared, which made me mad. I pressured Amma to ask Acchan to have an exterminator come and speculate on what could be done. The exterminator refused the job. Too late, he said. I could take your money, he said, but they're everywhere, as if announcing a victor, and it wasn't me. I think the bugs knew. They began talking to me and taunting me. As I brushed my teeth or took a dump or fell asleep on the couch watching TV, one would run by my ear, shouting Wictory, Wictory! They took notes in the open, listening as my parents talked to me about life, listening as I disappointed my family, when I told my Amma to fuck off, when I shoved my Acchan around. The roaches muttered good-bye in eleven different tongues when I left for college, never to return. So when I tell Laurel I know roaches, I mean it. They took over my house once. It mustn't happen again. These fat imbeciles roaming my bathroom, one at a time, one day at a time, may not have the *germanicas'* chutzpah, but I am not taking any chances. My neighbor, Helen, a crone with bent spine and pink lipstick, mentioned spotting a fat bug in her bathroom the other day, too. Beeg, she mimed, beeg! These may be reconnaissance missions. Maybe someday these averse bugs will emerge from the bathrooms in droves, dressed like professionals or labor or like my dumb super, who doesn't speak a word of English and simply smiles, speaking American with an accent, dragging us from our beds, tying us up, taking us to our own bathrooms, pushing us down those sinks, flushing and kicking us out and moving in because it's time. The exterminator, Laurel, get me the fucking exterminator! Because there is something Laurel should know. After I've killed each fat bug, I leave pieces of their bodies in the bathroom, near the sink, in the tub, the basin, by the window near the exhaust. Every morning, when I wake up to piss, the body parts are all gone, returned to whence they came. Then that evening another averse bug arrives, like an offering. It's a trick, a game, but I'm onto them. Before I whack the bug, I check if it's wearing shoes or a skirt or a jacket or a tie or crotchless undies made of putrid garbage, whether the bug's taking notes, whether it's attempting to walk upright. I watch it before making my move. Then I get as close as I can to this thing, corner it almost, and ask, Do you speak English? Yesterday, Laurel, I got my first response: Yes, Boi, a little.

CHABTER EIGHT
IVDAY (HERE). AVDAY (THERE).

IVDAY, AMMA SAYS, IT'S getting cooler, relentless rains. The dog's taking the move badly, barely eats, sleeps all day, barks all night. The neighbors have complained. Avday?

Ivday, I say into my phone, nippy, snow is expected again. My boots have salt crusts, the radiator in the bathroom is useless, my trousers are tearing at the crotch. It has been busy, life. There is paperwork to procure, $7,565 in cash to buy a cheap American bride (a money-up-front, take-it-or-leave-it deal), and full-time employment to be found. Tell me again how you make your fish, I say.

Avday, is the fish good? Amma wonders. What do you know about fish? Where you find time to cook fish? Come home, my boy. Ivday, Acchan will buy fish. Then eat as much fish as you want. Avday, I know, Americans prefer the bland stuff. Only salt and pepper for them. Or they make fish sticks. Avday, you get only sushi.

Ivday, I'm fine, I say. Amma isn't convinced. I left home eight years ago for the Midwest. A boy bound for college. I haven't returned since, undocumented for the past three. So Amma assumes things. That ivday, I miss avday. Sometimes that's true. I miss Acchan's habit of watching my face for signs of stress. Don't worry, don't you worry, he'd say, everything will be OK. There is a sister somewhere, my baby sister—a young woman now. Ivday, I begin, then stop. Amma waits for me to finish. She senses I have something on my mind. Do I need jaggery for fish or am I confusing it with tamarind? is what I wish to ask, but I've forgotten the word for jaggery. I'm embarrassed. I panic. Ivday, I've been buying spices and tinned food from the Arabs, I say instead, partly in English. I buy cheap produce from the Mexicans, I continue. The shrimp is on sale every Sunday.

Avday, what is the weather now? Acchan wants to know. Amma has put him on the phone. Don't you worry, OK, he says, wear your winter coat, OK? Stay there, OK? Make money, OK? And don't go out in the snow without gloves, son, he says, before putting Amma back on the phone. Avday, Amma begins, is everything OK, son?

All's good ivday, Amma, I say, A-OK. I am near my kitchen window. There is little afternoon light. In a few hours, it will snow. Avday, in a few days, it will rain. A dog will have made peace with his new surroundings. By then, I will remember. Among my people, the word for jaggery is sharkara.

CHABTER NINE

BAITH

"ACCHAN'S ORGANS ARE FAILING," my sister confirmed. "He's loaded up on morphine. Taking him off the ventilator if there's no improvement. Amma hasn't left his side."

What would you do?

At JFK, as I waited for my plane, word got around that immigration had apprehended a human-trafficking kingpin. A Bangladeshi national, I heard someone whisper. At baggage claim, a canine circled him twice, then barked. Suspicious, obese TSA agents held the Bangladeshi by his feet and shook him. Then they stripped him down to his boxer shorts and seated him on a chair. Their leader, wide as a bear, a bit taller than a gnome, walked over, stood on the Bangladeshi's knees, and forced open the man's mouth. He then asked for a Molotov cocktail, which he tossed in. Then they waited. Soon they heard a soft boom. Before frantic knocking was heard from the man's belly. Using a crowbar, they opened him up and out emerged the man's mother wrapped in cellophane and wearing an oxygen tank. "Trafficker," the men radioed.

"Granny porn, methinks," someone said.

"Nay," corrected the startled son. "Don't cuff her! Hands off... MAA!"

This delayed my flight for three hours. But at Frankfurt, in the transit lounge, I am body searched. It is my first time. A German officer smaller than a pony puts his fingers so far up my ass he discovers my wonderland, which he wishes to examine, so helpful colleagues push all of him into me. He seems to like

243

it there, because he refuses to leave. His colleagues don't seem too alarmed, walking away to perform more-pressing airport chores. Other passengers pretend not to have seen a thing, so I am forced to take the little German with me, which puts a dent in my plans. I am trying to get to my father. I am trying to get arrested by passport control at Abu Dhabi International (AUH). I haven't told Amma. Acchan would've understood. I have instructed a lawyer friend to mail a sealed note to my sister if something happens to me. "Like what?" he asked.

"Every day one bird hits one plane," I replied. Before my plane takes off from Frankfurt, my sister calls me.

"It's done," she tells me.

"All right," I say.

"When it's close, I shall call you. Talk to him, OK? Say good-bye."

"OK," I say. I don't inform her where I am. I don't want her to worry.

Normally (until Frankfurt!), immigration, whether it's at JFK or Schiphol, barely engages me in conversation. I look benign, therefore I'm convinced I won't be encountering any trouble at JFK, or in transit at Frankfurt. In fact, at JFK, I fool the lady at the ticket counter into letting me board by showing her a scanned print out of an Emirati tourist visa from a year ago, explaining that the originals are waiting for me at AUH. I gamble she won't check the dates. She doesn't, only asking to see my passport. At AUH, I am hoping for a different reaction. At AUH, I want to draw attention to myself—but only at AUH. Until I get there, I need to bypass security. To tilt the AUH scales in my favor, I take a risk, traveling home—normally a biannual affair—with a plastic screwdriver, pliers, flint, and a biscuit tin full of TNT discretely hidden in my backpack. I also take my prayer beads because counting them relaxes me. Otherwisem I sweat profusely. If everything works out, the rest, I tell myself, should be easy. It is not a sophisticated plan, which is why I am convinced

I might succeed. Over Emirati airspace, when the seatbelt sign pings red to indicate landing in half an hour, I will call a stewardess over and ask her to inform the captain that I am traveling with explosives, which I promise not to use as long as someone important—I wouldn't say who, assuming the right man will be found—meets me on the tarmac. "Then tell them," I tell this stewardess, "that if I die, if the timer goes off, I blow." I expect to be apprehended as soon as we land, not before I insist I be cuffed to the head negotiator, before being escorted by armed guards with spotless shoes to a soundproof interrogation chamber, as laborers waiting near passport control, many with rust-colored hair, some on their haunches, pretend not to stare, as they wait for their sponsors to arrive with work visas—originals, and not the photocopies they brought with them. In that room, the man still cuffed to me, I will ask for hospital-bound transportation. Otherwise, I bluff, I have enough on me to make a mess. The little German was a rude interruption, but perhaps I should be grateful; my capture couldn't have gone any better given the circumstances, but to fail like this! I should explain.

Because I have a little man in my ass, I am a nervy passenger and do not call for the stewardess once we enter Emirati airspace. Even when the plane deploys its landing gear, I stay put. I count my prayer beads, I drink the rest of my apple juice, I curse Frankfurt, I think about brushing my teeth, and I hope, I hope, I hope, Acchan holds on. However, at AUH passport control, an officer with Popeye arms, roaming the premises like a curious stray, takes an interest in me. I have almost sweated through my shirt. As Popeye inspects me, the German man finds it amusing to ask me riddles in English, providing me answers in German. It has unnerved me and my plan has gone off course, my mind empty. Popeye asks me about my flight, then politely requests I spread my legs and arms. The metal detector beeps because the German man has fillings in his teeth as well as a work-issued Mauser. Guns are drawn.

Popeye takes my backpack, orders me to follow him. We do not pass rust-colored hair. We only pass toilet cleaners who smell like hospital floors. Fellow passengers scrutinize me discretely. Many shake their heads. In less than ten minutes, I am sitting naked in a room where there are three ACs, three mustachioed men who do not smile, and a young man everybody in the room calls Rookie. And Popeye. My check-in baggage has arrived before me and lies open like a Nile croc's jaws on a stainless steel table, with little on it except three dog-eared issues of *Top Gear*. The room is otherwise very spare, except for one more item, a humongous glass cookie jar filled to the brim with sesame cookies. "Sesame cookies taste like mud," Acchan liked to complain. Popeye expects an explanation. I have anticipated this moment, but not like this. I do not want the German's story to overshadow mine. All I want is for these men to take me to the hospital so I can sit next to Acchan, waiting with the rest of my family as he passes. Before the German's intrusion, I'd planned to threaten to detonate the homemade explosives if the man at the tarmac didn't hear me out, or didn't submit to being cuffed to me, but sense would prevail and I would be rushed to the hospital. But then Frankfurt happened, Popeye happened, and I now have a man in my body and feel oddly responsible for his safety even though he asks me curious riddles. "Why did the elephant paint his toenails green?" I try to keep calm because I think I know what to do, perhaps even play the situation to my advantage. I recall the TSA's handling of the Bangladeshi incident.

So.

I request matches, a fistful of TNT. I swallow. Nothing happens. The little German is TNT-resistant. I think I hear him humming. I request some more TNT, which I swallow along with two more lit matches. Then, as an afterthought, I light another match, and drop that in along with the whole matchbox. This does the trick. There is an audible boom. There is a man's cry, more heat than I am used to in my tummy. But no knocking. I stay Zen. I ask for access to my screwdriver, and then request help being taken apart. Piecemeal. So I am dismantled. My brain pulled out, my blood poured into buckets, my limbs put in a tub, alongside my organs. My skin is then hung on a coatrack and my bones collected in trash bags.

In the process, they find the bothersome German, but there is bad news. Apparently, I used too much TNT. His last words, a laborious effort, were "Greet. . .ings—from Deutschland!" It was an end as dramatic as a Wagner opera, but he had enough time to scribble a note on the back of a random business card he probably pulled from his wallet. It is in German and a translator is required.

As we wait for the translator, Rookie puts me back together, but there is some blood and three pieces of bone left over, and an organ none of us can identify; these are all put in a chilled plastic bucket I hold. Then the translator arrives, a woman so large I need to look up, and then look up some more. What a head! It could've covered the sky. Rookie gives the large woman the partially singed paper and she pores over it with a magnifying lens and forceps. "Hmm," she says. "Hmm," she says again. Her routine annoys everyone.

"Could you please hurry up and tell us what he wrote, Madam?" Popeye fumes, as the mustachioed men look on. I would like to know, too, and I attempt to nod my head in agreement, but I can't; Rookie screwed it on too tight and I am unable to look left or right.

The large woman makes a sound, and, looking directly at me, says, "He wrote, 'Help! Fire!' "

In an instant, I have become a murderer, and the mustachioed men, I notice, are seething. The German consulate will not be pleased.

"Explain yourself!" I am commanded by the man with a mustache so fat and lively it would be coveted by Rajputs.

This is my moment. I fidget. I ponder hard. I start my confession.

"My name is ദീപക് ഉണ്ണികൃഷ്ണൻ," I begin, "I used to live here." Popeye leans against the table, stroking his chin.

"Go on," he prompts, "about the man you killed—"

"My sister's name is ██ ██████. She was born here."

By now, even the translator has seated her robust bottom in a chair, listening, biting into a cookie. Popeye raises his brow.

"My father's name is ██ ██████. My mother's name is ██████ ██████. When they first arrived in this city, Edward Heath was Britain's prime minister. Heath died in 2005, my father should die before the end of the day."

Someone lights a cigarette. Another dials the German consulate.

"My grandfather's name is ബാലകൃഷ്ണ മനേോൻ," I continue. "He died here, too."

I stop talking. Popeye walks over, hands me a glass of water.

"I visit every two years," I tell the room. "I am studying pathology."

Popeye watches me for a while, adjusts the knob on his walkie-talkie, motions his subordinate to hand him another cookie. "And the purpose of your visit?"

"Family," I say, "family."

"Family expecting you?" Popeye asks. "Father expecting you?"

"My father is on life support, or he was—I am not sure anymore," I explain.

"What happened?" he asks, munching his cookie.

"Someone beat him with a pipe three days ago, put him in a coma," I share.

Popeye and the others process this information. Someone's checking if the recorder is working. Men have come with a stretcher and a body bag. Popeye is told something. He looks at me, looks at the messenger, nods.

"I phoned the consulate in D.C.," I continue. "I live in Okla-
homa, and I told the consulate man, 'Father's on a ventilator, possibly brain-dead, organ failure, life support could be
switched off any time—' "

"Sir—" Popeye interrupts.

I don't stop. "The consulate man asks about my nationality.
I tell him. He says, 'Tourist Visa, three to four days.' 'I don't understand,' I tell him. 'I was raised in Abu Dhabi, it's home, my
father's on his deathbed.' 'Sorry,' the man tells me. 'Three to four
days—' "

Popeye tries to get a word in. "The dead—"

I ignore him once more. "I beg him, 'Make an exception,
please! There must be loopholes. My—' "

"SIR!" Popeye interjects with authority. "Explain the dead
man, please."

I am livid. I don't care what Popeye wants. "If he dies before I
get to him, his body won't be immediately released to my family.
Mandatory postmortem. Murder case. Let me see him before
that. Before they tear him up, it's important I see him. Please,
please!"

"The dead German, sir," Popeye tries again. "Why kill the
man in our presence?"

I hear nothing. "I used to live here," I cry. "I used to live here!
My father is not breathing by himself, you understand?"

Popeye's colleagues restrain me, but I fight. I bite, I claw, I
spit. Popeye repeats himself, "The dead man. The dead man?"

"Is your father alive?" I ask. "Do you people have fathers?
Does anyone understand?"

I finally eat away at Popeye's patience, as he orders his men to
dismantle me once more, which they do, and after the cookies are
emptied, my head is placed inside the cookie jar. The rest of me
is haphazardly arranged on the table or placed in buckets again.

"I am sorry about your father," Popeye tells me before he
leaves the room. "But you've killed a man in our presence. I

cannot let you go. I will, however, inform your sister of your arrival; she may visit."

Tamely, I plead. "A son has rights!"

"I'm sorry," says Popeye, before sealing the jar, muffling my screams, ordering the mustachioed trio, the lady with the sky-wide head, and Rookie to follow him out. I wait there in that state for what feels like hours. I fall asleep, my forehead resting against cold glass.

I am awakened by a ringing mobile, its volume set to high, placed on the table next to my suitcase, next to my limbs. There are cookies on the floor. I recognize the ring tone. It is my sister. I am expected to say goodbye.

CHABTER TEN

PRAVASIS-

THE NAMES

Stranger/friend/reader, you may not know some/most of these names. Almost all of them have read/heard my work. I have trusted three or four with my mind, and my life. All of them have seen me fail. A handful took time to read the galleys. These names include those who've known me through crappy drafts, or before I wrote a bloody thing. These names include English teachers from Abu Dhabi Indian School who permitted me to take my time with English in order to tame it. These names include professors from Fairleigh Dickinson who took me grocery shopping when I was hungry, put money in my wallet, fought for more money on my behalf, and apologized when they couldn't do more. These names include teachers and peers from the Art Institute of Chicago whose work deserves to be read, seen, or heard, who've shared their stories with me, and influenced my own writing in ways impossible to articulate. And these names include those I find tough to categorize, people who've stumbled into my life for short but important periods, people I've lost or left, fought and loved, conversed and walked with, folks who've reappeared only to disappear, men and women who've gone to bat for me, guided me through quagmires, and asked for nothing in return for what they've done. I'll always be grateful, especially to those I've hurt. Then there are those who've remained, who continue to share my life. Take away these names, remove their impact, there is no book. And if your name ought to be here, and I've forgotten, forgive me. Swing by to yell, then let me make you something to eat.

Ted (& Yoshimi) Chesler. C. Sharat Chandran. Gayathri Attiken. Grace & Neeta Natrajan. Joxily K. John. Carl Muller.

Mahender Reddy. Anirudh Manian. Milena Jankovic. Roberto Palma. Ceridwynne Lake. Patrick Mevs. Elenor Collings. Despina Lamprou. Steven Lawrence. Michal Shapiro. Lorelei Stevens. Halley Margon. Angad Dhawan. Ahmad Makia. Lantian Xie. Raja'a Khalid. Rahel Aima. Vijitha Yapa. Jim Savio. Andrew Bush. Sakar Mohammed. Mohit Mandal. Diana Gluck. Josephine D'Souza. Anita Alex. Rajani Varghese. Jyoti Seshan. Jane "Tinker" Foderaro. Duane Edwards. Bernard F. Dick. Adele Falken. Sara Levine. Janet Desaulniers. Beth Nugent. Todd Hasak-Lowy. Jesse Ball. James McManus. Adam Levin. Beau O'Reilly. Amy England. Mary Cross. Ruth Margraff. Judd Morrissey. Daniel Eisenberg. Leila Wilson. Calvin Forbes. Barbara DeGenevieve. Deb Olin Unferth. Ken Krimstein. Alec Vierbuchen. Heather Lynn Shorey. Cory O'Brien. Doro Boehme. Rachel Wilson. Ryan Wright. Carly Gomez. Suzanne Gold. Bert Marckwardt. Nick Pavlovich. George Tully. Chelsea Fiddyment. Brothers Grimm Revisionists (Spring 2013). DeGenevieve's Sophomore Seminar Class (Spring 2013). Buskers of New York & Chicago. Music by the Roma, sustenance for anything relevant I've done.

p.s.: A special shout-out to my tenacious agent Anna Ghosh, the dreamers at Restless Books—Ilan Stavans, Joshua Ellison, Nathan Rostron, Brinda Ayer, Jack Saul, Julia Berick—colleagues in the Writing Program at NYU Abu Dhabi, the poet/artist Jill Magi, the artist Michaela Lakova, the photographers Silvia Razgova and Philip Cheung, and Sangam House. And to Raya, my confidante and reader of every draft, who found me broken, but doesn't mind me broken, to you I say: Blagodarya.

ABOUT THE AUTHOR

DEEPAK UNNIKRISHNAN is a writer from Abu Dhabi and a resident of the States, who has lived in Teaneck, New Jersey, Brooklyn, New York, and Chicago, Illinois. He has studied and taught at the School of the Art Institute of Chicago and presently teaches at New York University Abu Dhabi. *Temporary People*, his first book, was the inaugural winner of the Restless Books Prize for New Immigrant Writing.